THE
LEGEND
OF THE
PHANTOM
EFFECT

THE
LEGEND
OF THE
PHANTOM
EFFECT

John Henry Hardy

ARCHWAY
PUBLISHING

Scripture taken from the King James Version of the Bible.

Archway Publishing books may be ordered through booksellers or by contacting:

Archway Publishing
1663 Liberty Drive
Bloomington, IN 47403
www.archwaypublishing.com
1 (888) 242-5904

ISBN: 978-1-4808-7061-1 (sc)
ISBN: 978-1-4808-7062-8 (e)

Library of Congress Control Number: 2018962566

Print information available on the last page.

Archway Publishing rev. date: 11/16/2018

FOREWORD

There are an estimated 200 billion stars in the Galaxy of the Milky Way and 40 billion of them are Earth-like suns. By the Law of Probability, there are possibly 8.8 billion planets that are similar to Earth, and millions of them may also revolve around a sun.

The Legend of the Phantom Effect is a tale of one of those billions of planets that lie hidden amongst the stars, and yet the mere possibility of a humanoid race living on another planet may be beyond the scope of our imagination in light of our belief in Genesis. Their sun is dying, but these extraterrestrials have created an advanced civilization and are secretly migrating to a troubled Earth. They come in peace and good will and have much to offer mankind, but Earthlings continue to deny their existence and see their covert arrivals as UFOs.

Will the world one day accept the existence of these ETs and learn from them, or will Earth's power hungry dictators and the free world leaders become alarmed at the frequency of those bizarre sightings and accuse each other of treachery? If a nuclear Armageddon were to ensue, would the ETs help the human race survive, and if so can or will a new and peaceful world order rise from the ashes of planet Earth?

John H. Weisneck

CHAPTER

1

It was Christmas Eve, and Harpie Colcek was really pissed off. Instead of spending the holiday at home with his wife, two children, and four grandchildren, he had been tasked by his editor with keeping a 10:00 p.m. appointment with Paul McCusker, the four-star general commanding the North American Aerospace Defense Command at Peterson Air Force Base in Colorado Springs, Colorado. To make matters worse, he had to drive through a blinding snowstorm to attend the meeting.

Every time his car slid on an icy hairpin turn, Harpie let out a string of curses as he steered in the direction of the skid. He didn't want to be here, but he was a reporter for the *Rocky Mountain Times,* and his assignment couldn't be canceled.

"While that asshole Claude Hoskins is home partying and boozing it up," Harpie mumbled, "I'm out here driving in this white crap, and all because some politician told him something strange happens at exactly 11:55 p.m. every Christmas Eve. As if I give a damn."

As he neared the base, he saw signs warning him that he was driving into a restricted area and that the guards were armed and authorized to use deadly force if necessary. He looked in his rearview mirror and spotted a jeep with several occupants following him.

When he arrived at Peterson Air Force Base proper and showed his correspondent's ID card, the guard said, "Yes, sir, Mr. Colcek, the general's waiting for you." The guard raised the barrier.

Harpie drove into the compound, where another armed guard, with the name Kolbe sewn above the right pocket of his jacket, directed him to a snow-blanketed area marked "Visitors Parking Only." A slew of security personnel, with snow accumulating on their helmets, were securing the compound.

Harpie thought, *I guess I'm not the only one working on Christmas Eve!* He got out of the car and anxiously glanced at the automatic rifle the guard carried.

Airman Kolbe said, "Follow me, sir," and escorted him toward a tunnel marked "Cheyenne Mountain Complex."

Harpie's exhalations were miniature clouds that soon disappeared into the frigid air from the exertion of walking at the 9,500-foot elevation. The cold stung his nose, cheeks, and ears and felt as though his head had been thrust inside a freezer. At this altitude the snow was relentless and almost blinding, yet he could still make out the distant monolith that he recognized as Pike's Peak.

Moments later they approached the north entrance to the complex. The warmth inside felt wonderful.

The moment they entered, an air force captain sternly warned the reporter, "You can't bring any arms or explosives inside, Mr. Colcek, and you *will* be arrested if any are found on you. Your escort is authorized to use deadly force if necessary if you try to escape."

Harpie nodded and swallowed hard.

The captain patted him down and then pinned a badge on his coat to indicate he was an authorized visitor.

Harpie and Airman Kolbe walked through a massive metal door and down an asphalt road laden with concrete barriers and semicircular walls carved from solid granite.

"What are these obstacles for?" Harpie asked.

"If there's a surprise air attack and that metal door is open, the atomic blast wave and the resulting debris will get blown into this tunnel. The shapes of these obstacles will shield everyone and everything inside by steering the blast wave and the debris toward the south tunnel and back outside."

Harpie glanced around and realized how enormous the complex was. The granite obstacles made him feel like a lost soul being escorted into the subterranean world of the damned.

"This place is humongous."

"Yeah," the airman replied. "The contractors cut out seven hundred thousand tons of granite to make this command center. The complex is so big that the buildings in here are painted in different trim colors so people won't get lost."

"There are buildings in here?"

"Yes, and they're all located in a series of protective granite tunnels. The complex has six million gallons of water stowed in granite-lined wells located farther inside, and more than half a million gallons of diesel are stored in metal tanks buried underground. Even the generators are protected by stone walls and those shops over there?" He pointed. "Those are storage facilities with thousands of spare parts; we call them Walmarts."

They walked deeper into the mountain, passing a Subway sandwich shop, and soon arrived at a series of metal buildings.

Airman Kolbe said, "All the edifices in the complex are built on springs to absorb shocks, and the pipes that carry liquids and gases bend under pressure. Even the walkways are constructed in such a way that they'll sway back and forth to survive nuclear shocks or earthquakes."

They entered a building with a rather large room. The guard said, "This is a gym, but it readily converts into a hospital. The beds and other medical equipment are hidden in the walls. If anyone is injured, they're treated here and then immediately sent back to the command center if they can function; there is no one to take their place."

Kolbe led him to the general's office.

General McCusker was a burly man with a chest full of ribbons and a tight-lipped, no-nonsense smile. His white buzz cut and intense blue eyes lent an air of authority to his stalwart presence, and his demeanor suggested a man who was not to be trifled with.

He smiled and extended his hand. "I'm surprised Intel declassified the information I'm about to disclose to you," the general said in a rather stern voice. "I wondered why the president gave a release priority to the *Rocky Mountain Times* as opposed to the larger news media in the major metropolitan areas."

Harpie just shrugged at the slight.

"Then the FBI disclosed that your editor, Claude Hoskins, is the president's cousin. Even so, you will not release any information concerning this complex to anyone until I have scrutinized it and the secretary of defense gives his stamp of approval. Got it, Harpie?"

"Yes, sir."

They walked farther into the complex, passing through another massive metal doorway. "The doors weigh twenty-five tons and are made to withstand a nuclear blast. This entire complex is protected on all sides by at least twenty-five hundred feet of granite that not only shields the complex from an atomic blast but protects it from the effects of an electromagnetic pulse that could knock out our power grid.

"The combination of the granite walls and metal doors safeguards the equipment from solar eruptions, which would cripple our radar and voice communications. Except for periodic tests, the last time these heavy doors were closed was during the threat situation on nine-eleven, and that's when we discovered the enclosure made a few people ill."

"It made people ill?"

"Yes Harpie, but it wasn't because of the isolation. The thought of their loved ones being exposed to a nuclear holocaust while they were safe in here sickened them."

"I never thought of that."

The general continued. "Living in here and not knowing what the weather is like for months at a time can get to you. We have monitors everywhere so our people can see the sun and the sky and hear the news about the outside world."

"Interesting." Harpie jotted in his notebook.

"Can you feel that slight breeze?"

"Yes, sir."

"This whole complex is pressurized to keep out radiation and biological particles. If a contaminant seeped in through any minute crack in the granite or gaps around the metal doors, it would pollute the complex. But those particles can't move against the air pressure inside. If for some farfetched reason the air pressure system failed, we would evacuate through that tunnel you see over there." He motioned his head to his left. "It's a duplicate of this command center and is under the direction of a Canadian four-star general."

"A Canadian general?"

"Yes. We're partners with Canada in this endeavor. Remember—we're the North American Aerospace Defense Command, and Canada is certainly a part of North America, as are Mexico, Bermuda, Greenland, Central America, all the Caribbean countries, and any territories or possessions that lie therein.

"What I'm going to show you now has been occurring since NORAD became operational back in the fifties, and over the years, our radar operators have dubbed the phenomena Santa's Ghost or Santa's Sleigh. However, the official US government designation is the Phantom Effect. We use the word *phantom* because we're still not sure what the hell it really is."

They came to an area known as the Global Strategic Warning and Space Surveillance System Center. Harpie learned it was manned by members of the 721st Communications Squadron of the US Air Force. He saw dozens of radar screens, computers, and other equipment that was top secret and whose purpose was to detect missiles, suspicious space behavior, and rocket launches and to monitor the tests of nuclear devices anywhere in the world.

"Other than the radar screens," the general told him, "all the equipment has been temporarily covered up with sheets of canvas so that not even legitimate visitors like you can see them. Remember—if anyone ever tried to smuggle any kind of a camera in here, they would be prosecuted under federal law."

"I know," Harpie replied.

"The operators who man this equipment must determine what's good, what's bad, what's neutral, and what must be passed up the chain of command to those who are authorized to make decisions. They must also determine when the twenty-five ton metal doors must be closed."

Harpie noted that the staff sergeants manning the radars were being supervised by a civilian.

The hours passed quickly, and Harpie wrote dozens of pages of notes, but the brightly lit complex was deceiving. Harpie was caught off guard when the general said, "We still have a few minutes left. Sergeant, bring me my usual black coffee. How do you like yours, Harpie?"

He glanced up at one of the monitors. The eastern side of Cheyenne Mountain was aglow with the security lighting near the entrance tunnel, but the western side was darker. He could barely make out the falling snow.

No wonder they have TV monitors in here, he mused. "Cream and two lumps of sugar," he finally answered, and the sergeant immediately hurried off to get the brew.

"Where did your parents come up with a name like Harpie?" General McCusker asked.

"My parents were bird watchers, General," the reporter replied. "They traveled through Central and South America in pursuit of their hobby. They liked the name and ferocity of the harpy eagle—I'm its namesake, although my name ends with *ie* and not a *y*."

The general chuckled and Harpie smiled. The general continued updating him on how the center functioned while they sipped their coffee.

The civilian supervisor approached and said, "Thirty seconds, General."

At a radar set manned by Staff Sergeant Dale Ribose, whose name was printed on a placard above the cubicle, the two men anxiously waited.

"There it is, sir—right on time," the radar operator said as he looked at the twenty-four-hour clock on the monitor. "It's exactly 23:55."

"I don't see anything," Harpie said.

"See that faint blip?" The general pointed at the screen.

"Yeah. You mean to tell me that little speck is what this hullabaloo is all about?"

"Do you know what that is, Harpie?"

"No, sir."

"It's some sort of aircraft."

"How do you know that? I mean, it's just a speck—a mere shadow."

"You probably know that on Christmas Eve 1955, we began a program NORAD called Santa's Sleigh, so we could allegedly track his progress while he's out delivering presents to children around the world."

"Yes, General. I'm well aware of that annual fantasy trip."

"Of course, on every major holiday we're on full alert," the general continued. "Terrorists would love to catch us napping while the nation is celebrating the holidays. Since we couldn't be home with our families to enjoy Christmas, that's when we injected a little humor into the situation and dubbed that harmless little blip Santa's Sleigh. We thought it was some sort of minor space phenomenon like a small meteor impacting the earth, until we realized this happens at the exact same date and time every year.

"We didn't know what it was until we invented our own stealth bombers and fighters and saw what they looked like on radar. It was on a day in spring when one of our techs first saw one of the stealth bombers on radar, and he remarked that it looked just like that faint blip we call Santa's Sleigh.

"It has appeared every December twenty-fourth at exactly 23:55, just as you're seeing it right now. We've had thousands of military personnel and volunteers out day and night in every state from Colorado to the Canadian border on Christmas Eve for the past fifteen years. However, no one has ever seen it or heard it or has any idea where or if it lands on the North American continent, and that's when we decided it was really Santa's Ghost. The Canadians haven't had any luck finding it either."

"It must be a natural phenomenon then," Harpie replied.

The general said, "No, Mr. Colcek, radar doesn't lie. We can see it's some kind of aircraft because it doesn't impact the earth but levels off just before it drops below our radar net as if it's landing."

"You mean it could be a flying saucer?"

"No, we never ever use that term in NORAD!" the general tartly replied. "And don't ever use UFO in any of your reports."

"Okay, sir," Harpie answered.

"What concerns us the most is that we don't know whether another country is planting agents here or perhaps smuggling nuclear weapons or parts of those weapons into the United States and then assembling them here; that info is not to be divulged in any of your reports either, Harpie."

"Yes, sir." Harpie continued taking notes. He glanced up. "If the flight originates in another country, surely your equipment can pick up the craft's vibrations and identify the launch site."

"There is a possibility they may have found a way to disguise a launch."

"But there's never been a nuclear attack on American soil in all the years since NORAD discovered Santa's Ghost. Maybe the flight doesn't originate on this planet."

"I just told you not to even allude to flying saucers, Harpie. Now you know why I have to scrutinize everything your write about the Phantom Effect in your press releases," General McCusker replied. "If your paper printed a remark like that, the world would be in a panic, because those sci-fi nuts out there would swear we're being invaded by alien forces and that they were secretly planting ETs here disguised as humans."

Harpie didn't reply. He noted the concern in the general's eyes and his stern expression. *Now I'm sure that aircraft might be some kind of a space ship—or at least the general suspects it is.*

They turned their attention back to the radar screen. "It's dropping down below the radar nets," Staff Sergeant Rebose said as he pointed at the barely visible blip. "Judging by its angle of approach, it's probably landing somewhere in Colorado or Wyoming."

"Get ground recon on the hook pronto, Major," General McCusker bellowed, "and ask them if they saw or heard anything. Find out what the airborne warning and control system aircraft may have picked up."

"Yes, sir," the major answered and double-timed out.

They waited five minutes while the ground and air commanders called in their reports.

"Sir," the major reported, "American and Canadian ground units said they didn't see a thing or hear a sound, but the AWCS commander says they picked up the faint blip as it was descending at supersonic speed and at an extreme angle of approach. Near as they can tell, it probably ducked into one of those valleys formed by the Rocky Mountains and was traveling in a northern direction before they lost it on radar."

"Same damned thing as last year," the general said to no one in particular, and at that moment a female lieutenant colonel entered the control room. "General, please pick up red phone; it's the president."

The general picked up the secure phone that was directly connected to the oval office. A few minutes later he announced, "Someone hacked into the Intelligence network and declassified the *Phantom Effect* files," he said. "At this point, neither the president nor any other US government Intelligence agency has any idea how that happened. Harpie Colcek, you have been privy to top secret information, and the FBI has ordered that you be held in protective custody until they can interrogate you."

Harpie dropped the pad he was writing on and jumped to his feet. "Protective custody?" he almost shouted. "Protect me from what?"

"To prevent enemy agents from possibly kidnapping you to obtain information about how much info the US government knows or suspects about the Phantom Effect. Besides, you don't have top secret security clearance. At this point, the president and the FBI have to assume they don't know who you really are. You could be an agent of a foreign power that may have been planting spies or saboteurs in the United States for years by the very aircraft we are trying to track and to apprehend those on board."

"You don't know who I am?" Harpie shrieked. "I'm Harpie Colcek! Remember, General? A reporter for the *Rocky Mountain*

Times, and I've been for the last nineteen years. The editor confirmed our appointment with you yesterday from his office. Remember?"

"The enemy plants sleeper agents in our country all the time," the general retorted. "Sometimes for decades before they become active. The FBI will determine if you are who you say you are, Mr. Colcek. Until then, you'll be held in protective custody. The guards will take you to your designated quarters."

"My wife—I have to call my wife," Harpie said.

"Agents from the Denver FBI office are already heading to your house with a search warrant, Mr. Colcek. Your wife will soon know you've been detained."

"You're gonna search my house and frighten my wife and family on Christmas Eve?" Harpie shouted.

The general didn't answer. Harpie couldn't believe this was happening. He glanced at the group surrounding him, but nary a friendly face was in sight.

As he walked away, with guards to his front and rear, the general reminded him, "Don't try to run, Harpie Colcek, or whoever you might be. The guards have the authority of POTUS to use deadly force if necessary."

CHAPTER
2

FBI agents Ron Halifax and Albert Dubkowski looked down at the sleeping figure with keen interest. "He could be legit," Agent Dubkowski nearly whispered to his partner, "but we gotta make sure."

Harpie Colcek awoke with a start. Someone was straddling his body, and a strong hand grasped his throat, pinning him to the mattress. He seized the wrist to try to break the hold, but his attacker was too strong. Harpie knew he was going to die! With his heart pounding and his breaths coming in short and jerky gasps, it sounded as if he were sobbing.

"What's your name?" a stern voice asked.

"Ha-ha … Harpie Colcek," he wheezed out.

"Where were you born?"

"Boston."

"When?"

"June 1, 1978."

"High school?"

"Boston Prep." Harpie calmed down a little, and his breathing became easier.

"What is your mother's maiden name?"

"Colbert."

"Born?"

"August 24, 1942, in Kansas City, Missouri."

"Father's name?"

"John Colcek."

"Born?"

"January 31, 1940, in Prague, Czechoslovakia."

They asked him a lot of other questions about his mother and father's siblings; his shoe size; his height and weight; who his best friend was; and when and where he got the tattoo of the cross on his upper left arm.

Everything about his past checked out, and Agent Dubkowski finally released his grip from Harpie's throat. They believed him, but procedures had to be followed.

Harpie sat on the edge of the cot and rubbed his throat.

"We're with the FBI. I'm Agent Halifax, and this is Agent Dubkowski."

"I sure as hell didn't appreciate the way you woke me up," Harpie curtly remarked as he looked up at the two agents.

"We're sorry about that, Mr. Colcek," Agent Dubkowski said. "But we're still not certain about your true identity. The FBI is charged with the safety of 321 million Americans, so we can't afford to take any chances! Certain foreign governments are always desperately trying to find out more about this complex and what we know about the Phantom Effect!"

"You have to understand," Agent Halifax explained, "you erroneously had access to top secret government information. Someone hacked into our computer net and declassified the Phantom Effect.

Many would interpret that as an alien invasion, and it could raise fear and cause havoc here and in every country around the world. Terrorist organizations would love to see that kind of global chaos crop up, especially here in the states."

Agent Dubkowski said, "People in every country on earth might end up killing each other, if they believed their neighbor was an alien monster from another planet. When it becomes known who leaked that information, many will believe that you and your family are aliens too. Consequently, fruitcakes like those innate militia groups would be gunning for you, your wife, Gloria, your daughter, Carrie, and son, Jack."

Harpie stared at the agents in horror. "The president authorized my editor, Claude Hoskins, to do a routine news story on a strange incident that occurs each Christmas Eve. That's all I know, and General McCusker confirmed my invitation."

"The president had no idea the system had been hacked and the information had thus been criminally declassified at that time, Mr. Colcek," Agent Halifax replied. "Otherwise, she would not have authorized your editor or anyone else to write a story about the Phantom Effect."

"What about General McCusker?" Harpie asked. "He knows Claude is the president's cousin. Surely the president doesn't suspect her own cousin?"

"General McCusker receives a typed statement that is automatically generated by the computer when any info pertinent to his command is declassified," Agent Dubkowski replied. "It doesn't matter anyhow. You've been exposed to top secret government information, and you don't have top secret security clearance—end of story."

"I don't want anything to do with this whole fiasco," Harpie snapped. "I demand to be taken before the proper authorities to secure my immediate release. That is my constitutional right!"

Agent Dubkowski said, "Unfortunately, Mr. Colcek, at the moment you are at the center of this fiasco, and since this is a matter of national security, no writ of habeas corpus is required."

"So you're telling me I'm fucked?" Harpie shouted.

"Yes, Mr. Colcek, you're fucked," Agent Halifax retorted. "If you know anything about who declassified this top secret program, you'd better come clean—now!"

Harpie shook his head. "I don't have a clue."

There was a long moment of silence as the two angrily stared each other down, until they heard the distinct sound of the cell door being unlocked. They focused their attention on General McCusker as he came strolling into the room and sat in the only chair in the disciplinary quarters.

"I just got off the phone with the president, Mr. Colcek," the general said, "and she has given you two options. Number one: you remain in federal custody at an undisclosed location until the issue of how, why, and by whom the Phantom Effect was criminally declassified."

Harpie cringed, but the general and the two agents ignored him.

The general continued. "Number two: you can be sworn in to the US Air Force as an airman basic, without pay or retirement accretion. Your permanent duty station will be your home in Denver. In essence, Mr. Colcek, you will be subject to the uniform code of military justice and will remain so until this whole issue has been resolved to the government's satisfaction."

Harpie was too horrified to say anything for a long moment and then asked, "Why do I have to be in sworn into the military?"

"So you will remain under my absolute control," the general answered. "Being in the military makes you subject to the UCMJ twenty-four/seven, and you can be arrested for any reason, including being AWOL if I and the FBI don't know where you are, where you've been, or where you're going.

"If you accept option number two, you can never divulge to anyone—not even your wife—what you witnessed on the radar screen several weeks ago or what you saw inside this complex and how it's constructed. You'll never write any news article about what you saw here, or spread rumors about flying saucers, aliens, or anything else that may cause national or international pandemonium or insurrection. If you do, you will be charged with treason and sedition and will be confined in the military prison at Fort Leavenworth, Kansas, for the rest of your natural life. Got it, Mr. Colcek?"

"Yeah," Harpie replied as he massaged his throat.

"Unfortunately," Agent Halifax said, "you'll be surveilled and scrutinized for the rest of your life unless the matter of the Phantom Effect is resolved. You will wear a monitoring device. The government seized your passport and nullified it when your home was being searched on Christmas Eve. You can never leave Colorado without the permission of the government.

"Also, you can't visit a foreign dignitary, consulate, or embassy *ever*, and since you'll be on a probationary release status, you must report to a federal probation officer in Denver once a month, and he or she in turn will report your status to General McCusker. Most importantly, do not pursue any aspect of the Phantom Effect on your own; only government agents and scientists are allowed to do that."

Harpie was stunned, but he nodded. They had piqued his reporter's curiosity, and he was now certain government officials suspected the Phantom Effect might be a UFO, and they were trying to avert a chaos of pandemic proportions.

Then he got an idea. "Why can't I just get a top secret security clearance?"

"Because you wouldn't qualify," Agent Halifax replied. "We already looked into it. Your father kept in touch with his German relatives in the Sudetenland, which was a part of Czechoslovakia, and they had ties to the Third Reich. Others fled to Russia before the

Nazi invasion and subsequently became members of the Communist Party."

"I didn't know that," Harpie answered.

It wasn't much of a choice. After Harpie was sworn in as an airman basic, they attached a monitor to his ankle. Then the guard escorted him to his car, which, unbeknownst to him, had a GPS device mounted underneath it. The snowstorm had ceased days ago, and the crisp mountain air felt wonderful. He felt a sense of freedom after spending two weeks confined in a disciplinary cell inside the Cheyenne Mountain Complex.

He breathed a sigh of relief when he left Peterson AFB proper, and the guard vehicle that was following him disappeared from sight. But he didn't notice the civilian vehicle that tailed him the moment the wheels of his car touched the asphalt as he drove toward Interstate 25 north, heading for Denver and home.

When Harpie arrived home, his wife, Gloria, tearfully greeted him at the door. "Oh, Harpie," she wailed as she hugged him. "The FBI was here two weeks ago and said you were in protective custody. What did you do?"

"I didn't do anything. They made a mistake, and I was accidentally exposed to a government classified program at Peterson Air Force Base, and I don't have top secret security clearance. Now they think I could be a mole—you know, a spy who was planted in the country years ago."

"They suspect you of being a spy? That's ridiculous, Harpie. What kind of information did you have access to?"

"I can't ever tell you or anyone else anything about it, dear; otherwise, I could be in real trouble."

"Oh! I thought you would be home on Christmas Eve like you promised, but the FBI showed up instead, and they tore our house apart. They even opened our Christmas gifts, and their gruff behavior frightened Carrie and Jack and our grandchildren.

"Then Jon and Sue called from Texas to wish us a Merry Christmas—you know how sentimental your brother can be—and they were flabbergasted when I told them you were being held in FBI custody. Carrie and Jack already had plans for New Year's Eve, so I welcomed the new year alone. The FBI ruined our entire holiday season."

"I'm sorry, dear," Harpie replied, "but I spent both holidays alone too—in a disciplinary cell."

"I know. It was our worse holiday season ever." Then she looked at him wistfully and said, "To make matters worse, someone broke into our house about a week ago. I was in bed but couldn't sleep because I was so worried about you, and suddenly I saw these shadows—there were two of them! I was scared to death, Harpie. I pretended to be asleep while they went through the entire house. After they left, I looked everywhere, but nothing seemed to be missing and all the doors and windows were still closed and locked. I don't know how they got in, so I knew there was no point in calling the police."

"It was probably just your imagination," he said as he let her go and brought his finger to his lips to keep her from saying anything else. "Remember—you were very upset at the time." She looked puzzled, but he tapped his lips several more times in rapid secession to warn her not to say anything more.

She took the cue and said, "I guess you're right. I was just so tired and upset."

He winked at her, and she knew she said the right thing. He hugged her again and whispered, "It was the FBI. The whole damned house and the phones are bugged."

She withdrew from him in horror and remarked, "I'm gonna call Carrie and Jack to let them know you finally got home, okay?"

"Yes, dear," he replied. Then he put his arms around her again and whispered in her ear, "Be careful what you tell them; remember—the phones are tapped."

🚀

The next morning Harpie reported to work at the *Rocky Mountain Times* in downtown Denver, and Claude Hoskins immediately called him into his office.

"We didn't get an exclusive story from you, Harpie, and General McCusker hasn't returned any of my calls. I called Gloria, and she said you were being detained by the FBI. What the hell happened up there?" the blue-eyed, six foot, redheaded editor asked.

"I'll tell you what the hell happened, Claude," he almost shouted as he sat down. "The FBI threw my ass in the slammer because that story you sent me to cover at Cheyenne Mountain was highly classified."

Claude's jaw dropped. "I'm sorry," he said, "but my source assured me it had been declassified. In fact, General McCusker said so himself when I confirmed your appointment."

"You're sorry, Claude?" Harpie tersely replied. "You and your shenanigans ruined our entire holiday season, got my wife and family upset, and now I've got to wear this goddamned monitor on my leg for the rest of my life." Harpie pulled up his pant leg to show him the monitoring device. Claude's mouth dropped open again, and he plopped down in the chair behind his desk.

"You mean to tell me that the FBI hasn't been here to interrogate you yet?"

"No," Claude whispered.

"No?" Harpie shrieked. "Well, they're gonna want to know who the hell your source is! Do you know why they haven't been here yet?"

"No!"

"It's because you're the president's cousin, and she's probably protecting your butt! She made me the patsy in this deal to protect you, but sooner or later the FBI is gonna be all over you like stink on shit."

"All I know is that my source goes by the name of Randy, and he works in the DC area," Claude said as he nervously lit a cigarette. "I paid him five thousand bucks to get that interview a day ahead of every other paper in the country, which makes it an exclusive."

"Well, Claude," Harpie replied, "you just lost five thousand bucks."

"Maybe, maybe not." Claude suddenly sounded more confident as the nicotine took effect. "Start from the beginning, and tell me everything you found out about that mysterious little blip."

"I can't. The feds told me if I so much as utter a single word to anyone about what I saw or heard, they would charge me with sedition and treason, and I would end up in a federal pen for life. In the end, they could also charge you with being a coconspirator."

"Well, I'm not worried about the FBI; the president has my back."

"Good luck on that one," Harpie said with a smirk.

"Tell me, since you don't want to disclose anything, just where does your loyalty lie? With this newspaper or with the federal government?"

"My loyalty lies with me keeping my ass out of prison—that's where my loyalty lies!"

"My loyalty lies with this newspaper and the bottom line," Claude replied. "Exclusive stories sell newspapers and increase circulation, which means more advertising money; you know that. If you give me the details, I'll run it on the front page with your name in the byline. When and if the FBI arrests you, there'll be such a public outcry the president will force the FBI to release you. The newspaper business is like any other business—the bottom line is what counts."

Harpie knew he was right but didn't say anything else.

"Take a few days off and think it over," Claude said as he smiled derisively. "You know, take your beautiful wife out to dinner, go to a movie, and think about your future in the newspaper business and so forth."

Claude was blunt, and Harpie was too stunned to reply, because while Claude was talking, it occurred to him that the editor's phone and office were likely tapped as well.

In an unmarked government van parked less than a block from the Times building, agents Halifax and Dubkowski were monitoring Harpie's conversation with the editor.

Agent Halifax laughed. "His source goes by the name Randy, and Claude thinks the president is going to cover his ass. He doesn't realize the president is busy protecting her own ass at the moment—the media and the public are gonna want a lot of answers about how our Intel was compromised. I think it's about time we had a long talk with Mr. Hoskins."

Tammy Mullins, Hoskins's private secretary, entered his office. "Mr. Hoskins, there are two gentlemen here to see you. They're from the FBI."

Without waiting to be invited in, the two agents strolled into Claude's office and nodded to Harpie, who immediately stood up when he recognized the agents.

Agent Dubkowski said, "Mr. Hoskins, we need to have a word with you."

"Okay, gentlemen," he smugly replied, "please have a seat. Harpie, I'll see you a little later today, and we'll continue our discussion."

Harpie started for the door, but Agent Halifax seized his arm. "Wait a moment, Mr. Colcek. We want you to be privy to this." The agents heard Mr. Hoskins's cocky and threatening remarks to

Harpie, and they wanted to take him down a peg or two in front of his subordinate.

"Grab you coat and hat, Mr. Hoskins," Agent Halifax said. "It's cold outside."

"Where are we going?" Claude asked.

"Downtown," Agent Halifax answered. "We have lots of questions to ask you."

"What do you want to question me about?" Claude asked.

"Don't play dumb with us, Mr. Hoskins," Agent Halifax replied. "You know damned well what the hell we're talking about—the unauthorized declassification of top secret information. Who told you that info was declassified?"

Claude smirked and merely shrugged. "You can't force a reporter to reveal his sources—that is my constitutional right."

"Is that so?" Agent Halifax replied. "You remember your source, don't you? You paid him five thousand dollars and probably knew the Intel network had been hacked before we did."

The editor paled, and at that instant Harpie knew Claude's phones and office were bugged.

"Your source could be an enemy agent, and since this concerns national security, we don't need a writ," Agent Halifax said. "We can do this one of two ways, Mr. Hoskins. Either you put on your coat and hat, and we'll casually walk out of here, or you can leave here in handcuffs."

"Why the hell can't we talk right here?" Claude asked.

Agent Halifax said, "We can't talk here, Mr. Hoskins, and if you continue to insist that we do, you'll be placed under arrest. That is the end of this conversation—period."

Claude brashly added, "Don't you know who I am? I'm the president's cousin!"

"We know who you are," the agent replied.

"I want a lawyer," Claude said, but then his blood pressure peaked and his face flushed when Agent Dubkowski reached behind his back and pulled out a pair of handcuffs.

Claude immediately stood up, grabbed his coat and hat, and turned toward Harpie with a mortified expression on his face and meekly said, "You're in charge until I return."

Agent Dubkowski turned to Harpie and said, "You said exactly what we wanted you to say, Mr. Colcek, but unfortunately, Mr. Hoskins wasn't listening. Either way, he's in trouble up to his ass."

Harpie just stood there dumbfounded as he watched the editor leave the room with an FBI agent on either side. *So much for being the president's cousin*, he thought.

Months passed, and Harpie reported to his federal probation officer once a month as agreed. He kept in close contact with his brother, Jon, an air traffic controller at Lubbock Preston Smith International Airport in Lubbock, Texas, and his best friend, Monty Galbreth, who lived in Denver just a few blocks from the Colcek home. The three of them had always been close, and sometimes they chatted in a three-way conversation over the phone for an hour or more.

It was New Year's Eve, almost a full year since Harpie had been released from his two-week detainment at Peterson AFB, and Claude Hoskins had been released from FBI custody after lending his full cooperation.

Harpie was on the phone with Jon and Monty.

"Yeah," Jon said, "we're having a New Year's Eve party at my house with a few other ATCs and their wives, and we were discussing the updated radar that Raytheon installed just before Christmas last year."

We were astounded at the radar's extended range and were amazed when a strange thing happened two years in a row."

"What amazing thing happened?" Harpie asked.

"Well," he said, "on Christmas Eve, air traffic is always light, and it gets rather boring, so the slightest bit of activity catches your attention. Around midnight last year the new radar picked up a faint blip traveling at a great rate of speed. It didn't try to contact an ATC, and a few seconds later it dropped below the radar and we lost contact.

"We contacted the FAA, but there were no reports of an aircraft going down anywhere. They figured it was drug smugglers coming across the border from Mexico, and the plane was flying low to avoid any radar nets. The incident was eventually referred to Homeland Security, but nothing came of it. Then lo and behold, Joe Lockhart, who on duty last Christmas Eve and again this year saw a similar blip at exactly the same time and place as last year."

"What time exactly?" Harpie asked as he held his breath.

"Exactly at 23:55 p.m.," Jon replied.

Harpie was stunned. He realized the powerful new radar at Lubbock International had detected the Phantom Effect. *Now I know why ground and air recon could never intercept or find the bogy while searching from Colorado all the way up to Canada,* he thought. *They were searching in the wrong places! Santa's Ghost doesn't land in Colorado or anyplace north of the Cheyenne Mountain complex. It probably lands somewhere in west Texas, and at the speed it was traveling when it dropped off NORAD's radar, it could turn and land hundreds of miles away in a matter of moments.*

The thought was rather frightening. Harpie now knew what the federal government didn't know, but if the FBI was recording their phone conversation, they would come after him again and the Lubbock ATCs to get this new information on the Phantom effect and to be certain they maintained their silence.

However, after two weeks no one from the FBI office contacted him concerning that mysterious bogy that was now appearing on

Lubbock's radar screens. He suspected the FBI agents weren't on duty New Year's Eve and therefore hadn't heard his conversation—or they were testing his fidelity to the oath he swore when in FBI custody last year.

But Harpie had another problem. For months he'd been wrestling with his reporter's intense curiosity, and now it seemed he might be off the FBI's radar at the moment. He learned from Claude Hoskins that they had tracked down his source in Washington, DC. Randy, it turned out, was a White House staffer and knew the Phantom Effect had been declassified, although he didn't know it was because the system had been hacked.

But he sold that information to Claude Hoskins before the president authorized its release to the public, and the staffer was charged with and convicted of espionage. He was sentenced to three years in federal prison and ten years' probation. The only thing the public knew about the charges against him was that he'd compromised a top secret program and had endangered the security of the United States.

The editor didn't get the paper's $5,000 dollars back but there was no prison time—thanks to the president. Instead, he got five years' probation because he lent his full cooperation to the FBI's investigation. The hacker, who actually declassified the Phantom Effect, was traced on circuitous route through Europe, China, Russia, and southern Europe, but neither the country of origin nor the individuals involved were ever identified.

Harpie couldn't sleep well, knowing he was the only man on the planet who knew where Santa's Ghost might be landing each Christmas Eve. The knowledge haunted his dreams, and he woke up several times each night. His daytime reverie kept him from fully focusing on his job at the *Times*. He had to know, and he began devising a plan to spend the next holiday season at his brother's house in Lubbock. He appealed to his federal probation officer, who surprisingly approved a month's leave of absence so he could spend the holiday season with his relatives in Texas.

As soon as their wives were asleep, Harpie and his brother tiptoed downstairs to the dining room. Jon spread out a map on the large table.

"Near as I can figure," Jon whispered, "the blip disappeared both times at about the same place, a bearing of seventy five degrees northeast of Lubbock." He used a protractor to mark off seventy-five degrees on the map, and using a ruler and a pencil, he drew a straight line on an axis of seventy-five degrees.

He continued. "And a bearing of 160 degrees southeast of Amarillo." After marking off 160 degrees with the protractor, he took the ruler and the pencil and drew a line on the map from Amarillo on the axis of 160 degrees. "The two lines intersect near this little burg called Quitaque."

"What's at Quitaque?"

"Nothing really. It's a jerkwater town. To the north lies the Prairie Dog Town Fork of the Red River and to the east is the town of Turkey. If you move west, you'll run into another little burg called Silverton. There's nothing but open land to the south."

"Jon, are you sure you got the bearings right?"

"Yup, I'm very sure. Tracking aircraft is what I do for a living, remember?"

"I mean, why would anyone want to land there?" Harpie asked. "It's a remote area."

"I haven't a clue. Unless they're smugglers?" he guessed.

"Wait—what's that green spot there?"

"That's the image of a pine tree that marks the location of Caprock Canyons State Park & Trailway," Jon said. "It's near the town of

Quitaque. They've got a herd of buffalo there, coyotes, lots of cacti, some water, escarpments, and rattlers."

"So you might be one or two degrees off?"

"Possibly."

"I need to take a look at that place. Can we take a ride up there tomorrow?"

"I'm scheduled to work tomorrow and can't get someone to take my shift on such short notice, but Sue is familiar with the route," Jon answered. "It's a big park, and you'll need a guide. Stop in at the general store in Quitaque and ask for Nathan. He's an old Tiguan Indian, who drinks too much, but he's tough as nails, and he knows the land in the park like the back of his hand. It once belonged to his tribe and then the Comanche. Tell him where you want to go and he'll take you there—for a fee, of course."

In the midmorning hours, Harpie and his wife, Gloria, and his sister-in-law, Sue, merged onto Interstate Loop 289 north, and then on to Interstate 27, heading toward Caprock Canyons State Park & Trailway. They passed the city of Plainview and took the Tulia exit to the snow-covered Route 86 East. Just beyond Silverton they passed the entrance to the state park but didn't stop until they spotted the general store in Quitaque.

"Can you tell me where I can find Nathan?" Harpie asked the clerk.

He pointed his thumb toward a door and mumbled, "Back room."

Harpie thanked the clerk and knocked before he opened the door. An old man with long white locks sat next to a potbellied stove that glowed red from the heat of the burning coals. When he turned to face the visitor, Harpie noticed a pair of piercing brown eyes and a deeply furrowed and leathery face.

"Are you Nathan?" Harpie asked.

The Indian grunted and nodded.

"We're headed for Caprock Canyons State Park and we need a guide, sir," Harpie said.

"Fifty dollars for whole day," the old man said and held out his hand.

Harpie plunked two twenties and a ten in his palm, and the old Tiguan Indian bolted to his feet and headed for the door. He threw the ten on the counter without saying anything, and the clerk reached down and produced a bottle of cheap whiskey and some change. The old Indian opened the bottle and took a swig before placing it and the change in his coat pocket. Without saying a word, he headed for the door.

The whiskey and cold biting wind seemed to invigorate the old man, and when he saw the two women in the solitary car in the parking lot, he turned and asked Harpie, "Why white man go to park in winter? Only buffalo and coyote there now."

Harpie looked at the two women to make sure they couldn't hear him and then faced Nathan. "I'm looking for a place in Caprock that's flat but not down in a valley; someplace higher."

Nathan looked at him in horror and disbelief. "It is bad medicine; not good place. I not go there."

"But you already took my money!"

Nathan nudged the whiskey bottle in his pocket with his elbow, and he obviously didn't want to give the money back either. The old Tiguan thought for a moment and then said, "I take you there but not stay. Your squaws cannot go. Only a warrior can climb the trail."

They approached Harpie's rental car, and he introduced Nathan to the women, who pleasantly greeted him.

The taciturn old Tiguan merely acknowledged their welcome with a nod. Nathan insisted a warrior must always ride up front, so Gloria plopped onto the backseat next to Sue.

When they arrived at the park, Harpie dropped three bucks into the out-of-hours fee box and told the women, "We're hiking up a trail."

"We'll wait in the car," Sue said.

Harpie parked near the rest rooms and made certain the ladies room was unlocked for their convenience. He left the car keys so the ladies could stay warm.

The entire park was covered in snow. The men donned their snowshoes, and Harpie followed the guide as he headed deeper into the park.

Sharp wind gusts made the temperature feel like it was in the teens. Drifting ice crystals stung their faces. In the distance Harpie spied a buffalo herd pawing the snowfall to uncover the grass below. Minutes later the men passed a sign labeled Fern Cave, but the guide kept walking.

At a trailhead hidden by a copse of trees and brush, they began the upward trek. The trail was slippery, and Harpie stumbled several times and had trouble keeping up with the old Tiguan.

The old fool is practically running up the trail, Harpie mused and cursed him under his breath. He recalled his brother's words: "He's tough as nails." *And to think I paid him fifty bucks so he could give me a freaking heart attack,* the reporter seethed.

They continued climbing and the air grew thinner. Harpie slowed down even more and gulped the frigid air; he lost his footing several times, since this was the first time he'd ever walked with snowshoes.

The old Tiguan was forced to wait several times until Harpie caught up, and each time he stopped, Nathan gulped whisky. After an arduous hour and a half climb, they finally reached the summit of the plateau, and it proved to be a rather vast expanse of flatland.

"It's a mesa," Harpie breathlessly exclaimed. "I wanna go out toward the edge." He wanted to see if there were any obstructions that could thwart a safe landing if a pilot chose to set an aircraft down there.

"No, Nathan, not go farther," the guide said.

"Why not?"

Nathan was strangely silent as he gazed out at the flatland. He slowly turned his head toward Harpie and raised his voice above the howling wind. "Tiguan and Comanche legend say when sunlight grow short the ghosts of the silver men appear out of darkness."

When sunlight is very short? Harpie thought. *That would be during the winter solstice on the twenty second of December …*

"My people and the Comanche fight to defend land," Nathan continued, "but arrows splinter when they hit ghost-men. Warriors and their horses die from guns that make no noise. Only red lines shine from guns and burn through the warriors and their horses!"

Harpie felt a sudden chill beneath his fleece-lined jacket. *How can laser guns possibly be portrayed in a legend that might be centuries old? And arrows wouldn't splinter when they hit ghosts; they would go right through. The silver color probably means the men were wearing some kind of armor, like the knights during the middle Ages.*

"Even Comanche not return to fight ghost men," Nathan said. "The day grows short, and soon sunlight will be gone. We go now." His expression seemed to foretell the essence of evil, and he started back down the slippery trail without saying another word.

Harpie lingered for a few moments, gazing at the snow-covered plateau. He thought, *it's a perfect landing field, but the legend doesn't allude to any kind of an aircraft, and why did Nathan's ancestors call them ghost-men?*

Nathan confirmed Harpie's suspicions, and his stomach knotted. "This has got to be the landing site for the so-called Santa's Ghost," Harpie shouted into the wind, and suddenly he felt breathless again. *It's less than two weeks until Christmas Eve. I'll come back here before the sun sets on December twenty-fourth.* But his excitement quickly reverted to fear when he thought, *If the government ever discovers what I'm doing, I'll surely end up in prison for life.*

CHAPTER
3

Gloria Colcek wasn't happy about spending another Christmas Eve without Harpie, even though she would have her brother-in-law and his wife to keep her company. *But this is something Harpie has to do to satisfy his intense curiosity. It's what makes him an ace reporter.*

Carrie and Jack and their grandchildren called and wished them a Merry Christmas. Harpie kissed Gloria goodbye, gave Sue a hug, and shook Jon's hand.

"I wish I could go with you, Harpie," Jon said, "but I'm scheduled to work."

After Jon cautioned him to be very careful, Harpie loaded his backpack and snowshoes in the trunk of the rental car and set off.

Harpie's saw the sign for Caprock Canyons State Park and turned on to the asphalt drive leading to the parking lot. His rental was the only car there, and he suddenly felt alone and anxious. Even the distant buffalo were wary as they eyed a lone coyote circling the perimeter of the herd.

From its perch high atop a dead juniper tree, a golden eagle seemed to be watching his every move as it cocked its head from side to side. Its stance reminded Harpie of a buzzard, as its feathers were being ruffled by the cold wind, making the predator seem larger than it really was. As Harpie turned away, he was startled by the flapping of mighty wings, and he turned in time to see the eagle plunge and seize an unfortunate desert hare that had been hopping across the snow-covered plain. *Death can come swiftly on the Llano Estacado—the edge of the high plains,* he thought. A cold chill rippled down his back, and he hurriedly donned his snowshoes and slung the backpack over his shoulders before heading toward the trail.

Harpie passed the sign marked Fern Cave, and it took twenty minutes to find the trail leading to the top of the mesa. It was a harder climb with a pack strapped to his back, and he breathed harder than on his first climb. He rested a dozen or more times during his two-hour climb and felt relieved when he reached the flat expanse of land that marked the high plateau.

He dropped his pack and pulled out the small cushion his brother loaned him. The reporter then plopped down on a flat ledge protruding from an escarpment to rest, still breathing rather heavily. The coffee in the thermos was still hot, and he treasured its heat as he sipped it while studying the expanse of ground.

It seemed as though only a few minutes had passed since he arrived, but already the shadows seemed to be fanning out from amongst the boulders and the other ridges that he could still make out in the distance. The climb had tired him out. He recapped the thermos bottle and leaned back against the abutment and closed his eyes for a moment.

Harpie was startled by the howling of a wolf pack, and he bolted to his feet. It was now dark, and he had no weapons. Wolves were known to attack bison, cattle, horses, sheep, and even humans if they were hungry enough. But then he remembered he was on a high plateau, and he felt a little safer. The wolves would be stalking the buffalo below, hoping to catch an old adult off guard or isolate a yearling from the protection of the herd.

The wind had ceased its intensity and the air was crystal clear, and when he gazed into the heavens, he saw the crescent moon and a gazillion stars stretching from horizon to horizon. As he scanned the sky, he spied a tiny spark of light. *It is night time in this hemisphere,* he mused, *but the rays of the sun would still reflect off a spacecraft thousands of miles away in outer space. As it nears this side of the darkened earth, there wouldn't be any sunlight to reflect.*

The object appeared to move from one cluster of stars to another at a tremendous rate of speed and then seemed to be looming closer and closer; his heart beat faster. He studied the object for a moment longer, and when he looked at his watch, he realized the time. *I must have fallen asleep; it's 11:50!*

The slight breeze suddenly felt colder, and his mouth gaped in astonishment at the revelation, *"It must be them!"*

Harpie breathed even harder than he did when climbing the escarpment. The possible existence of extraterrestrials shot through his mind with the intensity of a hot poker. If what he though was true, in a few minutes he might be the first human in history to ever video aliens on his iPhone—the undeniable proof of the existence of ETs! He felt for his iPhone on his belt and cursed when he realized he left it in the side pocket of the rental car!

Harpie pulled back the edge of his glove and nervously looked at his watch again; it was exactly 11:53. The only thing he could do now was to wait, and he kept gazing at the tiny speck of light as the glimmer grew dimmer and dimmer as it plunged downward, and then there was only the darkness.

"It must have crashed!" Harpie shouted—yet there was no sound of an impact and no explosion or a fire burning on the plateau.

A moment later, a slight breeze stirred the air, but it was not the winter wind. It was a warm gust, yet he still couldn't see anything or hear a sound. Harpie knew something was here; he could feel it, yet he couldn't see it in spite of the crescent moon light and crested snow. His fearful heart was still pounding, and fear bid him to hide behind the rock ledge he had been sleeping on a just a few minutes ago.

Harpie stared out at a spot not far out on the plateau where he could see a perimeter of melting snow encompassing an area about the length of a football field. He knew something had landed barely ten yards from where he lay hidden, and whatever it was, it was huge and invisible to the naked eye.

Harpie was too scared to move when a figure, in the shape of a man, walked toward him. *No wonder the Tiguan Indians called them ghost-men. He literally appeared out of nowhere!*

The man's steps were herky-jerky and not the smooth, rhythmic gait peculiar to a human. The creature was frightening, with glowing red eyes that seemed to jut in and out of its silver skull, and the reporter held his breath as the creature scanned the area.

The eyes of the seven-foot tall monster looked like a pair of red binoculars as they focused in on something near where Harpie was hiding. The figure raised one of its arms, and Harpie fearfully ducked his head down. Several streaks of bright rubicund light streaks instantly reflected off the snow-covered mesa, and although Harpie couldn't see what happened, he heard a minor explosion when the laser hit something and sent debris flying in all directions.

Harpie feared the monster might hear the thumping of his terror-ridden heart, and he cringed. But when his vision recovered, he carefully peeked above the abutment and froze.

The creature stood about ten feet away now, and its jutting red eyes had retracted all the way back into its skull as it focused on the remnant it was holding in its hand. A strange type of snow fell on

Harpie's cheeks and exposed neck, but he dared not move to wipe it off. The strange snowfall ceased as quickly as it started.

He's holding my thermos, Harpie thought. *He must have detected the heat from the coffee and blew the bottle to bits.* Harpie paled. *If he detects the heat from my head, he'll blow it off!*

The arms, torso, and legs of the creature appeared to be covered with some kind of metal, as was its skull. *The Tiguan and Comanche were accurate in their descriptions of the ghost's weapons and armor.*

Then he heard a strange whirring sound, and Harpie was flabbergasted when he saw the creature scan the rest of the plateau by rotating its head 360 degrees, while the rest of its body remained motionless.

A moment later the creature spun its torso around and walked away, twisting its head from side to side as though scanning the rest of the mesa.

Harpie again heard the low whirling sounds the creature made each time it moved its head, and it suddenly dawned on him, *it's not a man or any kind of a living creature at all; it's a Robot!*

Harpie felt relieved after the Robot disappeared from view but was too scared to move. He shivered as he alternately lay down or sat in the snow for hours, drifting in and out of sleep, yearning for a drink of his hot coffee. But his inquisitive mind became active again, and he crawled over to where his backpack lay in shreds on the ground.

The box of crackers had burst into thousands of burnt crumbs that lay scattered about on the snow, and his clean socks were now useless remnants of burned white threads. The two sandwiches Gloria had made and carefully wrapped in aluminum foil were now tiny bits of scalded mush, and the melted cheese and tinfoil stuck to the inside of what was left of the backpack.

He turned to retrieve the cushion Jon had loaned him, only to discover it was now a useless rag, and Harpie recalled the brief but strange snow that had fallen on his neck and cheeks. *The Robot's laser sent the white polyethylene stuffing from my cushion airborne, and bits landed on my head and neck like snowflakes.* He rubbed the back of his neck and removed the tiny remnants. *But why didn't the Robot detect the heat from my head when I peeked over the ledge? I'm lucky to be alive!*

The hours passed, and soon the sun's rays streaked across the sky from the east, lighting up the plateau. Harpie could now faintly see several white steps elevated above the snowy crest, but not the spacecraft itself, and it all proved to be rather fearful. Instead, what he could see was a vivid picture of a beautiful plateau in the distance and the small escarpments on both sides of it, as well as the rising sun.

Then Harpie thought, *The Llano Estacado is northwest of the plateau I'm lying on … yet I'm looking at a rising sun.* It was even more startling when he thought, *But if I'm facing northwest, it means east would be to my right.*

He abruptly stood and turned eastward and was relieved to see the sun. *How can that be?* he wondered.

He pivoted another ninety degrees and faced south and saw a beautiful plateau. It looked familiar. Then he turned toward the northwest again; it was the same beautiful plateau he saw when he faced south! He turned again to make sure his mind wasn't playing tricks on him.

Fearfully but courageously he moved forward until he spotted the figure of a man coming toward him, and he abruptly stopped, fearing it might be the Robot. The figure stopped too, and it took him a few moments to realize it was his own reflection. He moved forward several paces and reached out his hands until they touched the rough sides of something. Whatever it was, it was composed of millions of pieces of glass-like beads that faced different directions. Its reflections were so clear he could even see the wrinkles around his eyes and mouth and the pores of his skin.

No searcher can ever see this thing when it's on the ground, especially if it's dark—even if they were rather close to it. I had to be extremely close to see my own reflection. At a distance of ten or twenty feet you could walk right by and not see it, even in the daylight.

His fingers explored the smooth, glass-like beads. *This material must also serve as a heat shield and is able to withstand the ultra-high temperature of a rapid entry into earth's atmosphere.*

His curiosity grew stronger than ever, and he gazed down the side of the spacecraft and focused on the steps protruding beyond the glazed side. Then he removed his snowshoes.

Harpie walked cautiously forward, and as he started up the steps, the door slid open. He peered inside, fearing and wondering where the Robot went and whether he would be alive a few seconds from now. But he knew he was likely the first human to ever board a real spacecraft, and the thoughts of the fame and glory this venture might invoke spurred him onward.

The craft was brightly lit by a string of light-emitting diodes that cast a blue-colored ambiance throughout a long passageway. The walls were festooned with a variety of TV-like touchscreens that displayed numerous arcane icons, and strange-looking gauges with small keyboards emblazoned with cryptic symbols. Harpie looked both ways down the long, narrow passageway to make sure the Robot was not in sight.

With a pounding heart he stepped inside. The door slid shut, and a lump the size of a golf ball formed in his throat.

Harpie felt the heat being emitted by the LEDs in the ceiling. They provided warmth as well as light. *But why couldn't I feel heat pouring out when I stood in the doorway?*

Judging by the length of the passageway, he figured the craft was about as long as a football field and perhaps half as wide. *It's bigger than some ships,* he thought. He heard a low humming sound and surmised it was some kind of power plant used for the heating and lighting and perhaps also propelling the spaceship.

Metallic doors with strange markings lined either side of the hallway. There were no handles on them, and he tried to push the first one open, but it wouldn't budge. Then he felt a strange tickling sensation on the back of his head and neck, and suddenly Harpie Colcek was totally paralyzed; his fear intensified. Try as he would, he couldn't move a muscle. It grew more frightening with each passing moment; he tried to run, but his legs wouldn't budge.

For the first time in his life, Harpie Colcek was totally helpless. His heart pounded mercilessly in his chest and he began to sweat. A sudden powerful force abruptly spun him around and seized him beneath his armpits. His feet left the floor. The helpless, panic-stricken reporter gasped as he stared into the fear-inducing and hypnotic red eyes of the Robot!

Harpie couldn't move, but he was shaking with terror as the Robot's eyes moved in and out of their sockets, focusing on his retinas. It kept him suspended in air while it feverishly searched for an answer. But there were billions of scanned retinas in the database, and it would take a few moments to verify him. The Robot didn't find this man's ID. His retinas had never been scanned, and a guard Robot wasn't programmed to deal with a creature inside the spacecraft that it didn't recognize. Other types of Robots could deal with this situation, but a guard Robot couldn't, and if this intruder had been outside the spacecraft, it would have immediately annihilated him.

The Robot's electromagnetic field subsided and released the stunned man, and as soon as Harpie's feet touched the floor, he bolted toward the exit. He hammered his fists on the door, but it wouldn't open. Turning to face the Robot, he saw it pointing a metallic finger at the door, and Harpie realized whatever it was doing it was keeping the door from opening.

Harpie was more terrified than ever. He was now trapped inside the spacecraft with a killer Robot, and the craft could take off at any time. How he wished to God he'd never heard of the Phantom Effect! He swore, *If I survive, I will never return to Caprock Canyons State Park for as long as I live!*

The Robot started down the hallway. It was programmed with only one option when dealing with a misfit discovered on board; take him to the commander. When it realized Harpie wasn't following, the Robot turned and beckoned with one of its metallic fingers.

The panic-stricken reporter had no choice; he was caged. When he obeyed the Robot's gesture and stepped forward, the Robot resumed its walk.

They came to a door and it emitted a coded radio wave, and the door slid open. The pair entered and the door slid shut, and Harpie stared in mortal terror!

The room was full of thousands of coffins. It was an omen of evil, and he recalled the stories of people who swore they were kidnapped by aliens and were intimately examined by them. They'd said instruments had penetrated their orifices, and strange machines had recorded images of their internal organs!

It was all true, Harpie agonized. *Dear God, what are they going to do to me?*

Each coffin had a glass cover, and Harpie could see a piano-style hinge with one side embedded in the glass. The other side was fused to the metal side by welded steel. He panicked again and considered running, but to where? There was no escape. The Robot bid him to take a seat in one of several chairs, and watched his every move. Then another Robot seemed to appear out of nowhere and glanced at the symbol on a coffin. Harpie heard a familiar tapping sound as it typed a code into the computer sitting on a nearby desk. A moment later, the lid of the nearest coffin slowly opened, and Harpie whispered another prayer, hoping the coffin wasn't opening to receive him.

"Dear Lord," he prayed, "please help me. *I'm a dead man!*"

But the second Robot approached the open coffin, fidgeted with something, and forced a body lying inside to sit up. A few moments later the Robot effortlessly lifted a naked man out of the coffin and sat him on the chair next to Harpie, who faced another terrifying ordeal when the corpse seemed to be coming alive!

The resurrected man yawned, rubbed his eyes, and looked around the room. Both Robots bowed as he awakened, and then the man-like creature noticed Harpie.

The second Robot again bowed and said, "Who are you?"

Harpie was stunned. The Robot had no lips or mouth but an orifice covered with a fine metal screen. The man-like creature's mouth never moved, and Harpie realized he was transmitting the thoughts from his brain to the Robot. The mechanical man was somehow converting them to English—not faultless English, but it was good enough so Harpie could understand it.

"I'm Ha … Ha … Harpie Colcek, a reporter from the *Rocky Mountain Times,*" he stuttered.

"What do you want here?" the Robot asked. "And how did you find us?"

The man sensed Harpie's fear, and the mechanical man said, "Do not fear this Robot. It is a maintenance Robot and has no weapons. Only the guard Robots are armed, and they are programmed to never fire them inside the spaceship. It would be a disaster."

Harpie was fascinated by his remark, even though the Robot was speaking for him, but the man looked and sounded human, and his demeanor made the reporter feel safer. "Maybe I should ask who you are and what you're doing on my planet," Harpie brazenly said. It wasn't courage that bade him to speak but a reaction of his inquisitive mind, and it frightened the reporter after he said it.

"I am Commander Assan, and my starship is exploring the universe for a suitable world for my people, the Di, to live. Our world is billions of years old and our sun is dying, and we need to find another planet on which to live. Earth is much like our planet, and is the closest one to us. We are very much like your people, whom we call the Pi. Long ago we came in peace, hoping to be accepted. But you attacked us for no reason, riding on large animals and shooting at us with ancient weapons."

Harpie recalled the Tiguan and Comanche legend Nathan told him about.

"They were the Tiguan and Comanche," Harpie answered. "They're no longer warlike."

"I know," the Robot replied for the man. "But now you send your swiftest fighter planes to shoot us down, and we have to take evasive maneuvers to avoid them. Many of Earth's countries have developed weapons that can kill millions of us in an instant. You are like we were centuries ago, killing each other until our Armageddon. We are an advanced civilization now, but there are fewer of us left on our home planet.

"Our people, the Di, were supposed to be the most Intelligent of all the creatures on our planet, Rau, but we were the stupidest. The crops would no longer grow in the soil we chemically contaminated for thousands of years, and our people starved. After our Armageddon, there was not enough arable land to grow sufficient food for all, and we ate most of the creatures that survived—the ones that flew through the air or roamed the grasslands. Our sea creatures died by the millions in our poisoned seas. Our rivers reeked with the stench of industrial discharges, and on some days our air was so polluted, our youngest and oldest could not survive. We had no recourse but to return to the rules that were laid down by the Master eons ago, but by then it was too late; our sun was dying."

"By 'Master,' do you mean God?" Harpie asked. "And by the rules, do you mean the Ten Commandments?"

"The Pi calls him God and believes this miniature planet is all that he created, Harpie Colcek. But to us he is Master of the entire universe, and no matter where mankind lives in the heavens, he cannot live in peace unless he obeys the Master's rules, or the Ten Commandments as you Earthlings call them."

"You seem to know a lot about my world for someone who has never lived here, Commander Assan."

"The Di have migrated and lived among you for generations, but you didn't know it. Stay seated; I'll be right back." The commander disappeared through another door but soon returned wearing a full body suit.

"Why were you naked?" Harpie asked.

"During our years of space travel, clothing becomes soiled with sweat and body oils, and so we must cleanse our bodies with a fine chemical mist while we are in our habitats," the Robot replied for the man. "That is why we are naked.

"The mist evaporates epidermal discharges and dead skin cells, and a central vacuum system then removes the haze. That way the habitats are always sanitized and never stained."

"Your lips don't move," Harpie said as he looked at the commander. "Does the Robot always speak for you?"

"Yes," Commander Assan replied. "When I speak directly to an Earthling, we both must wear a conversion helmet to understand one another—if we're on a planet. I can understand what you were saying to me, thanks to the Robot. You can understand me because the Robot can read my thoughts and convert them into English."

Harpie was dumbfounded!

"Follow me, Harpie," the Robot commanded, mimicking the commander's thoughts.

Harpie obeyed, and they approached one of the glass-covered coffins and peered inside at a naked young lady. "Won't she be upset if we see her naked?" Harpie asked.

"No," the Robot replied. "You'll learn why later. All these glass-domed abodes are hibernation facilities that we call habitats."

"I thought they were coffins," Harpie said. He sounded relieved.

"No," the Robot said. "They're miniature homes and are kept at a constant temperature of fifty-five degrees. As you can see, the passenger is securely strapped in place, and trace amounts of a sedative are intermittently injected to induce suspended animation, or therapeutic hibernation, as we call it.

"This keeps the passengers asleep and prevents them from shivering, medically reducing their metabolism to a state of slow motion known as torpor stasis. Therapeutic hibernation greatly reduces the need for oxygen, which is fed into the habitat through vents on the metal sides. The vacuum vents have a permeable membrane that filters out the carbon dioxide and the sanitizing mist that cleanses our bodies, but not the oxygen.

"All those lifelines you see are color coded so they can be quickly identified. Blue ones are medical monitoring cables that are attached to the electrodes stuck on her skin, and they monitor her metabolic rate, blood pressure, heartbeat, and other vital signs.

"The green catheter implanted in her stomach is attached to a feeding tube of the same color. Freeze-dried nutrients are mixed with water by a computer located in the food area, and mixture is then fed into a huge pressurized vat that forces the liquefied food into the feeding tubes.

"That yellow tube is a catheter, which has been inserted into her urethra so she can urinate, and the brown one has a tapered nozzle that is inserted into her rectum and held in place by that strap wrapped around her hips. When feces are detected by the sensor, it signals a distant vacuum machine and the suction empties the waste from her colon through the tube, which leads into the power plant.

There, all the bodily wastes are burned and pulverized and then blown into space."

Harpie was flabbergasted!

"Every twenty-four hours the chamber you see inside the habitat, which we call the drum, is rotated for one hour every day," the Robot continued. "The motion creates a centrifugal force that simulates gravity. This is very important, because at zero gravity bone density begins to deteriorate. When the passenger is awakened and tries to stand and walk, their bones would fracture if the simulated gravity had not occurred regularly."

"How come those wires don't get twisted when the drum rotates?"

"Because each drum is a self-contained module with its own monitoring device. If something goes awry, a red LED flashes on the outside of the habitat and an alarm sounds."

"Oh. What are those little red wires for?" Harpie asked.

"They are electrical stimulators," the Robot again answered for the commander. "They exercise every major muscle group in the body while the traveler is dormant. When they awake, their muscles will be strong and flexible, even though they have been in a state of torpor stasis for a long period of time."

Harpie's eyes kept darting back and forth between Commander Assan and the Robot. It was difficult to remember it wasn't the Robot talking, although it was putting the commander's thoughts into words, and Harpie occasionally responded to the commander's words while looking at the Robot. It seemed as though the Robot was a third person participating in the conversation.

"Now, Harpie, as I said"—the commander continued to think, and he reached out and turned Harpie's head so he was looking at him and not the Robot—"some of the Di has lived among you for generations. Molly, the lady you are looking at here, lived in New York for three years but decided to go home.

"She couldn't stand Earthmen and said they're liars, cheats, and are too bossy; she decided to go back and spend the rest of her life on

Rau. Molly made her way back here during the night and turned on her identifier so the Robot guards wouldn't laser her. We immediately put her in therapeutic hibernation. What people like Molly learn about Earthmen is how we learned so much about the Pi."

"I didn't notice her return," Harpie said. "Maybe it was because I kept dozing off and on." Then he asked, "How long does a Di remain in therapeutic hibernation?"

"It depends on their destination," he answered. "A year or two at a time. Others have traveled to distant galaxies and were in hibernation for as long as ten lightyears."

Harpie was astounded. "They're actually asleep for ten years?"

"Yes," the commander answered. "However, the computer wakes them up every two weeks for one day by suspending the sedation and raising the temperature inside their habitats to ninety-three degrees Fahrenheit. If they were sedated for longer than two weeks, their brains would become somewhat demented.

"Therapeutic hibernation allows us to pack the bodies close together, which saves weight and space, since no one—except the Robots—will be wandering around the spaceship. However, the commander can be awakened at any time by the Robot taking manual control of his habitat, just as he did when the guard Robot discovered you were on board."

"So the purpose of this hibernation is to save space and weight?" Harpie asked.

"Yes," the commander said, "but that is not the only reason. There are four-hundred days in a Rau year, which is thirty-three and one-third orbits around our sun, but we have no seasons like Earth. There are ten days in our week. There are twenty days in two weeks. Divide that into four-hundred days in a Rau year, and you get twenty days of being awake during a lightyear of travel.

"Since we awaken a traveler for one day every two weeks, a Di traveling for one lightyear will feel as though they have been traveling for only about two Di weeks. If they were awake the entire time they would go crazy with boredom on such a small spaceship as this and would be at each other's throats and consume too much of our food, water, and air. That's what happens when the Pi is incarcerated in your prison systems—they go haywire with boredom and do insane things to each other."

"You keep saying lightyear," Harpie said. "How fast does this spaceship travel?"

"Once we are outside a planet or a star's pull of gravity, we can almost hit the speed of light—nearly 186,282 miles per second. That is relativistic speed-speed close to the speed of light and it is generated by what is known as Photonic Laser Thrust, which is measured by clocks within the Star Voyager-the object in motion. The lasers bounce off highly polished surfaces within the spacecraft to provide the thrust."

Again, Harpie was astounded! "But you talk about one lightyear of travel. On earth, our nearest star is Proxima Centauri, which is approximately 4.22 lightyears away. That means a passenger would have to be aboard this spacecraft for more than four lightyears, which is far beyond one lightyear."

"That is true, Harpie, but the problem is that all space travel is so long and the distances are so great, we must run a shuttle service," Commander Assan said via the Robot. "The passengers that are born on Rau cannot tolerate such long and arduous journeys, and neither can Earthmen. We meet other spacecraft one lightyear out and dock, transfer passengers, and get resupplied. Those space stations are extremely large, much like the supply ships in your navy, when it is at sea.

"These intermediate space vessels are known as major supply stations, and they orbit selected stars. Travel to and from them and the planets must be precisely coordinated by computer if you are to intercept them at a certain point in their orbits, and because they circle certain stars these stations can be readily located in the vastness of the universe.

Some of the stars are so large that it takes several years to complete one orbit, and if you miss your intercept time by as little as several seconds, you can linger in space for several months or a year before docking. It has happened before, believe me; all the intercept times must be precise whether orbiting a star or landing on a planet.

"Those major supply stations are assembled in space and improved over a period of decades. Some become larger than many of the small cities on earth, and the crews manning these stations are known as the MSS. They are usually born on the station and most spend their entire lives in orbit. Some never set foot on a planet and never experience therapeutic hibernation. It is a decision they have to make when they are very young. When they die, the MSS are cremated, their bones pulverized by the power plant, and their ashes blown into space.

"Those who are wary of spending their lives aboard the MSS are transferred to Rau when they are thirteen years old, to let them decide if they wish to live on a planet. However, most decide to return to their original station a year or two later, because of their hatred of temperature changes, the solar winds, the food, the masses of strangers, and being confined to living in a tiny space called a home. The few who choose to stay on Rau are adopted by other Di families.

"The reason life aboard the major supply stations is so very attractive to the returnees is that it is a very controlled environment; the temperature is kept at exactly seventy-two degrees; there is no rain, wind, or snow; ultraviolet lamps provide artificial sunlight; and most crewmembers are strict vegetarians, as hydroponically grown food is readily available.

"For the omnivorous crewmembers, meat comes only in vacuum-packed containers, and supplies are limited because raising slaughter animals takes up too much time and space on Rau, where grazing meadows are very limited, and raising animals in a restricted environment like an MSS is forbidden by law. However, food fish are grown in large aquariums aboard the MSS, but meat remains a special treat, and the crews are allowed only two such meals a week.

"Garbage disposal can sometimes become a major problem since it piles up so rapidly. Unlike Earth's waste disposal methods that pollute the lands, seas, and space, Rau law now requires all refuse to be pulverized before being buried on the planet or blown into space. That is why Earth is becoming so polluted; we ceased that stupidity centuries ago, but it proved to be too little, too late. The Robots that run the refuse disposal plants are active around the clock—to use one of your earth terms. They wear out quickly and must be maintained and repaired frequently or replaced. Thus, working in the garbage disposal plant is not a coveted job for a Di who is an MSS technician!

"Because of the somewhat limited size of the MSS and the numbers of the crew, they become a very close-knit group, and marriages and divorces abound. Even with the advent of our advanced DNA testing, the group marriages in these small communes spurs incestuous relations between siblings and first cousins, even when the participants are aware of the DNA test results. It is a problem we haven't yet been able to solve."

Harpie was utterly amazed. *Such problems didn't exist on Earth,* he mused, *but the MSSs are not planets.*

"The passengers traveling to distant destination spend up to two weeks of vacation on the MSS each year," the commander continued, "since they have recreational facilities on board that we don't have on smaller craft like our *Star Voyager.*"

"The name of this spaceship is *Star Voyager?*" Harpie asked.

"Yes," the commander answered through the Robot, "but we are only one of many such shuttle spaceships."

Harpie was stunned by some of the things Commander Assan was telling him, and he didn't know what to say. Then he managed to ask, "Commander, one thing puzzles me. I could not hear *Space Voyager* land, nor could I see it. What kind of engines do you use?"

"We don't use engines," the commander replied. "We use converters. Earth space travelers still use ancient fossil fuel engines. Do you recall what the outside of the ship was like?"

"Yeah," Harpie replied, "the sides felt like tiny glass beads that are highly polished and reflective, like tiny mirrors. I could clearly see my own image in them when I got close to the ship."

"That's right. Each bead is a tiny converter, and their dispersal pattern points them in every possible direction to catch every beam or ray of light possible. They are composed of rather unique grains of sand that are exclusive to Rau and not found on Earth, and it is mixed with other minerals, many of which are native to Earth.

"That peculiar sand mixture possesses the ability to absorb photons, which are fundamental particles of radio waves, infrared rays, visible light, ultraviolet rays, and X-rays. In short, photons are a form of electromagnetic radiation that transmits light. All those rays are in eternal abundance throughout the universe, and they supply us with an inexhaustible supply of energy no matter how far we travel. That energy fires our photonic lasers and lift-offs and landings extract an enormous amount of photons. However, our ships can travel trillions of miles into space, running on the photons from starlight. That sand mixture is also an excellent heat shield that allows us to travel through dense atmospheres.

"That is also why you couldn't hear us. Can you hear light? Of course not, and you can't see us because the converters absorb or reflect the light waves. It is only when you are close to the spacecraft during daytime, when an astronomical volume of photons from sunlight is concentrated around the converters, that there is enough light left for the human eye to see. But the converters cannot readily absorb that massive volume of photons and some of the light waves bounce off, causing millions of those shiny beads to act in concert like a gigantic mirror that reflect a perfect image of what lies behind you.

At night, we are invisible to the naked eye of course, and yet the converters continue to absorb all those other types of rays so we still have power sources, but when we are in outer space the tremendous amount of star photons are reflected by the converters and makes us appear as an artificial light in the night sky.

"So now you know how and why the *Star Voyager* can travel at the speed of light, although it is barely detectable on your radar screens. That is because some of the radar's electromagnetic waves that strike the beads are converted into energy and therefore do not bounce back to the radar's antenna.

"Planet Earth is but a stop during what can be a very long journey. We can breathe the air here, tolerate your food and clothing, and our people can learn the languages. Some of the Di chooses to spend the rest of their lives here, but the elderly often prefer to return to die on Rau, believing they still have siblings or other relatives in residence there. However, most return home to an empty fold.

"Many of our youngsters choose to continue their trek by connecting with other scheduled flights migrating to destinations that are many lightyears away. There they hope to find a better place to live rather than choosing a warring Earth or staying on our dying planet. Those who start such a long journey at a very early age spend years in therapeutic hibernation and never learn to bond with others during their formative years.

"As a result, they never know what it is like to be in love, yet they still yearn for companionship, just as the children born on Earth do when they are neglected during their early childhood. It is not an ideal life for the Di or their parents, who are also space travelers. Earthmen have the choice of loving or not loving their children, but our neglect of those young space passengers is the only way our race can survive."

Harpie knew what he said was true and didn't know what to say.

"For those distant travelers, there are only a few fecund years to spend with a spouse and have significant time to raise children, learn a profession, and go on vacations. Remember—although you are in therapeutic hibernation, you continue to age, and years later, if these distant travelers choose to return to Rau, they discover things have changed considerably and that their relatives passed away decades ago. And think about this, Harpie Colcek: we have to limit therapeutic hibernation to ten years. We discovered that any time spent in hibernation beyond a decade causes passengers to become withdrawn, and our attempts to have them colonize a distant planet ended in disaster. Many of the travelers had grown too old to start over, and the younger ones aged and lost their desire to raise children. The colony died out because there were not enough suitable mates for the few children who were born there.

"The Pi is in its infancy of space travel and has glamorized it, mainly because it is relatively new to them. It seems as though everyone on Earth dreams of being an astronaut or a cosmonaut, but the truth is, once you leave the bonds of Earth or Rau, you are on your own.

"Time and distance become extremely boring. You can only have sex every two weeks, and you can look at the uninhabitable stars, planets, and asteroids for only so long. There are no movie houses, fast food restaurants, football and baseball stadiums, comics, television, or gambling casinos—except on the major supply stations. Most of the time it is just you and your fellow travelers jammed into a spaceship that is but a mere speck of light moving through a vast universe of time and eternity, while you waste years of your life in a torpor state of drug-induced unconsciousness, and when you awaken you hunger for companionship."

Harpie didn't say anything. He was disappointed, and at the moment he realized these people, who call themselves the Di, were every bit as human as he was, and the characteristics of planet Rau sounded rather earth-like. Then he thought of something extremely important, and he blurted out, "Sex, Commander, you haven't mentioned much about sex between the couples."

The commander took a deep breath and folded his arms cross his chest. "That took us decades to adjust to, and someday the Pi will run into the same problems. We weren't prepared for what happened, and when the Di went into space, they took their emotions with them.

"History tells us that during earlier flights, we sent only married couples on the multi-lightyear flights. That had worked relatively well on the shorter lightyear flights. However, during the longer multiyear voyages, when the spaceship reached an MSS, people were awake for as long as two Di weeks, and many problems arose. We discovered that the longer one spends in therapeutic hibernation without substantial sexual gratification, frustrations intensify, and spouses tend to drift apart—especially the younger couples, who have had no dating experience.

"While spending their two-week vacations on an MSS, jealousies and rage soared, when the men caught their wives having sex with the other passengers and vice versa. We had to deal with murders and suicides on board, and women clawing and maiming each other.

"In one instance, an angry male passenger killed several MSS crewmembers and wounded many travelers with an improvised knife. That man and his wife had been in therapeutic hibernation for six years, and during a two-week relief aboard the MSS, he went searching for her and discovered her having a threesome with a man and a woman. He went berserk and stabbed her and her lovers with a sliver of steel.

"After this dastardly deed, he was locked in a disciplinary cell without hibernation therapy and only had the Robot guards for company. After a few years of endless confinement and without seeing another living Di, he committed suicide. Those early Robots were not programmed to deal with such chaos, and jurisdiction for such crimes is still a problem for our court system."

"What did your government do to help solve the marriage problem?" Harpie asked.

"The Rau courts gave the spaceship commander the power to marry couples and the authority to dissolve marriages," Commander Assan said. "That helped somewhat, but it didn't solve everything. Simmering hatred amongst divorced couples can be very disrupting, even if they are awake for only one day out of twenty, and it is worse when they get to a major supply station. It wasn't working out, so we initiated group marriages. For example, everyone on this flight was group-married to each other, except for Molly here. However, it frequently happens that a man and a woman fall in love in the group marriage and don't want to have sex with the others in the group, and they can be ostracized unless they divorce the group and marry each other; anyone can change their marital status at any time during the flight. When Molly wakes up I'll marry her, since she is my only returning passenger-a woman thank goodness, and being married or divorced by the commander is just as acceptable to the Di as any human being married or divorced by any entity on Earth.

"Any child conceived on the flight is considered the son or daughter of every adult in the marriage group.

"The one major problem remaining is the babies."

"The babies?" Harpie asked.

"Five were born on this flight, but only one survived. See those smaller habitats over there? They're made for the babies born in space. Most of the women begin labor while in therapeutic hibernation. We wake them up of course, but they have very little bonding time, much less than they would have if the infant were born on a planet. Without that bonding, a number of the babies grew up to be megalomaniacs, which we determined is a defense mechanism of sorts, and twenty to twenty-two percent of them will grew up to be sociopaths or serial killers or experience other major social problems. The lack of bonding with one's mother seems to be a major factor."

An alarm sounded. The maintenance Robot sat at the computer keyboard and tapped in some esoteric codes, and Harpie saw five glass coffin covers open.

"These last five passengers have chosen to be discharged in Germany and have been trained in the language, customs, and dress of the German Pi," Commander Assan said, "or at least as best as we could train them. I'm sorry, Harpie, but they are going to need your car. It will save us a lot of time and effort. Please give me the keys."

"It's not my car," Harpie said. "It's a rental, and if you take it, that would be stealing."

"When your planet is dying, you must save as many of your people as you can," he said, "even if you have to lie and steal to save them. We have less than a century to do that and have already stolen many of the Pi's cars over the years, because the Di does not manufacture those ancient gasoline or battery-powered vehicles. Our cars travel on a cushion of air and power from cables buried beneath the road."

Harpie knew he was right. Saving lives was far more important than a rental car, and he handed the keys to the commander.

"You have made a friend, Harpie Colcek," Commander Assan said as he extended his hand, "and when a Di becomes your friend, he or she is your friend forever.

"Remember this: *Star Voyager* is but a very small part of a vast interstellar travel system of which the Pi know nothing. You are the only Earthling who has met the Di and the reason why we must keep coming here. Earth is like Rau in many respects, and it is our closest neighbor in this vast universe of time and space."

CHAPTER
4

Harpie Colcek made his way back down the trail toward the entrance to Caprock Canyons State Park. It was easier going downhill than up, especially since his backpack had been destroyed by the Robot's laser gun. When he got back to the parking area, he discovered his rental car was already gone, and a large patch of nearby snow was partially melted. It was obvious what had caused the thaw-it was the heat from *Star voyager*.

He walked to the emergency land line that connected him directly to the Texas Highway Patrol and he reported the theft,. Twenty minutes later a black and white patrol car marked *State Trooper* pulled into the park. His name tag read Robert Andersen.

"Was there any other vehicle in the parking in the lot when you arrived?" the trooper asked.

"No, Officer," Harpie answered.

"When did you get here, Mr. Colcek?"

"Yesterday around 4:00 p.m.," Harpie said.

"You mean to tell me that you spent all of Christmas Eve here alone?"

"Yes," Harpie answered.

The trooper was skeptical. "Where is your sleeping bag and camping gear?"

"I left it up on the plateau."

"Why?"

"Well, when I looking around last night, I saw this red beam of light hit my backpack and it exploded." Harpie could tell the trooper didn't believe him.

"Did you pay your three dollar camping fee, Mr. Colcek?"

"Yup," Harpie said.

They walked over to the after-hours self-pay box, and Harpie said, "I didn't have three singles so I put a fin in the lower slot."

The trooper produced a key and looked in the lower box. Sure enough, he found a five dollar bill.

"Show me where you parked your car," the officer said.

They walked over to the parking lot, and the officer abruptly stopped and said, "What the hell!" when he saw a place alongside the parking lot where the snow had melted. "The snow is eighteen to twenty four inches deep here. I wonder what the hell caused that big patch of snow to melt like that."

"I don't know," Harpie replied, "but there's another one just like it on the plateau."

"There's no way to get up to that plateau unless you're a rock climber or by helicopter."

"Oh yes there is, Officer Andersen," Harpie answered. "I hired Nathan, a Tiguan Indian guide, to take me there."

"So you know that old drunk who hangs around the general store in Quitaque?"

"Yup, he's the one who guided me up to the plateau."

"Show me the trail then," the trooper said.

Harpie nodded, and after the trooper checked in with his station commander, he opened the door to his patrol car and put on a heavy winter coat, hat, gloves, and snowshoes and retrieved a flashlight.

They walked past the sign marked Fern Cave, and soon the trooper could tell by the tracks in the snow that someone had recently been on the trail. *Maybe Mr. Colcek is telling the truth,* he mused.

It took more than an hour and a half for the men to struggle to the top, and Trooper Andersen's mouth dropped open when he spied a familiar-looking bare patch in the snow. Then he examined the broken thermos and shredded backpack, and he looked at Harpie as though he was dumbfounded.

"When I was a kid, my dad said my great-grandfather told my grandfather that this was a weird place," Trooper Andersen said.

"Yeah. Nathan told me Tiguan and Comanche legend has it that silver men's ghosts began appearing on the plateau about the time of the winter solstice, and they fired their weapons at the specters, but their arrows splintered when they hit the targets. The images fired back at them with long streaks of red lights that burned holes through the warriors and their horses. That's what happened to my camping gear."

Trooper Andersen felt the hair on the back of his neck stand up when Harpie told him the tale. Then he thought about his grandfather's story, and he remembered the winter solstice had begun a few days ago. "This place is giving me the creeps," he said. "Let's get the hell out of here."

After Trooper Andersen finished filling out his stolen vehicle report, he and Harpie rode in silence toward Plainview, where the Texas Highway Patrol Regional Headquarters was located.

"My great-grandfather was right, Harpie," the trooper suddenly blurted out. "There's something weird about that plateau. He told my grandfather about the Tiguan and Comanche legend, and he passed that lore down to my dad, who told me about it."

"Oh," Harpie replied, "I'm an investigative reporter, and I'm gonna find out the truth about that legend." *I don't dare tell him what really happened*, Harpie thought. *He might think I'm nuts.*

But then Trooper Andersen reached into his shirt pocket and handed Harpie his business card. "If you find out anything else about the legend or ever need help when you're in Lubbock or Plainview, you can call me at my private cell number."

The reporter nodded and thanked him, and stuck the card in his wallet. An hour and a half later, his brother, Jon, arrived at the police barracks to pick him up.

When they arrived back at Jon and Sue's house, Gloria threw her arms around Harpie and asked, "Are you all right?"

He nodded. "I'm fine."

But she could tell something was not right. He was different somehow and rather subdued. They sat around the Christmas tree chatting and opening their presents, and for an hour or so Harpie forgot about the *Star Voyager*.

That night, Harpie abruptly woke up in a sweat, and his sudden action aroused Gloria.

"What's wrong, Harpie?" she tenderly asked as she reached out and rested her hand on his shoulder.

He anxiously turned and looked at her. "You wouldn't believe me if I told you."

"Oh, Harpie," she replied, "I've always believed everything you ever told me."

"Swear to me that you'll never reveal to anyone what I'm about to tell you."

"You know I won't."

He anxiously looked at her and then exclaimed in a rather loud voice, "They're real!"

She drew back, and sounding very concerned, asked, "Who are real?"

"The spacemen!" he blurted out.

She looked incredulously up at him as she pulled back the covers and sat next to him on the edge of the bed.

"I was on their spaceship!" he cried out. "They're fleeing from their planet, Rau, because its sun is dying and the planet is polluted. Someday Earth will die that way too."

She didn't say anything, and for the first time in their marriage he knew she was having trouble believing him. But he kept talking anyway.

"The ship is huge, and they have Robots with laser guns. Other Robots interpret languages and care for the passengers that are kept in suspended animation, while they migrate to distant worlds in other galaxies or different countries on Earth."

She could tell he was extremely animated, almost manic. He wasn't the cool-headed Harpie she had always known and loved. That Harpie had always been her guardian, but now she felt as though she was talking to a stranger. Gloria realized it was now her turn to protect him—from himself and from others.

A bolt of fear rippled through her body when she whispered, "Oh, Harpie, if you ever tell anyone a story like that, they'll think you're crazy."

"I know," he said, "but it's all true, so don't tell anyone what I told you. If the FBI ever heard something like that, I would be put in prison for the rest of my life."

"I won't tell," she promised.

The more he said, the more frightened Gloria became, and they talked about his ordeal until the sun's rays filtered between the slats on the venetian blinds. She didn't doubt that something had happened to him up on that plateau in Caprock Canyons State Park—*but whatever it was,* she thought, *it's causing him to lose his mind. When we get home, I'll talk to Claude.*

At breakfast, Harpie was pale and subdued.

"Are you okay?" Jon asked.

"No," Harpie replied.

"You worried about the stolen rental car?"

"No. I know who stole the car, Jon."

"Don't say another word, Harpie," Gloria cautioned him.

"He's my brother and she's my sister-in-law," Harpie replied. "They're family—we can trust them."

"Who stole the car?" Jon asked.

"The spacemen did," Harpie blurted. Then he reiterated the story of his ordeal on Christmas Day.

Jon and Sue listened with incredulity to his story and kept glancing at Gloria to see if she was buying it; they could tell she wasn't.

"I wouldn't tell the police or the insurance company anything like that," Jon answered. "They'll think you've gone loony or that you had something to do with the theft."

"I didn't steal anything, and don't tell anyone else what I told you and Sue," Harpie said. "I especially don't want the FBI to ever hear anything about it."

"We won't tell anyone," they enthusiastically said in unison.

CHAPTER
5

When Harpie and Gloria arrived back in Denver several days later, he felt much better. They were far from Caprock Canyons State Park, and only his wife, his brother, and his sister-in-law knew about his contact with aliens from a distant planet.

The next day Harpie was getting ready to travel to Aurora, Colorado, to do an investigative story on a double murder that was supposedly gang related. He was closing the drawer to his desk and was about to stand up, when he saw Claude Hoskins and two other men coming toward him. It was Agents Halifax and Dubkowski. Harpie's heart palpitated, and he swallowed hard.

"These gentlemen need to talk to you, Harpie," Claude said.

"About what?"

"A certain rental car," Agent Dubkowski said.

"I filed a police report," Harpie answered.

"We know, Mr. Colcek," Agent Halifax said. "But we still need to talk to you."

"You can use my office," Claude told the agents, and a few moments later, Harpie sat in the editor's office with Claude, but the two FBI agents preferred to stand.

"We found the stolen rental car," Agent Halifax said.

"Great," Harpie answered.

"Not so great for you, Harpie!" Agent Halifax bellowed. "Interpol located the car abandoned in Berlin, Germany, in the afternoon of December twenty-fifth—the same day you reported it stolen, which was also Christmas Day here in the United States. Europe is only six hours ahead of us."

"International thieves are getting more sophisticated than ever," Harpie replied.

"International thieves my ass." Agent Halifax continued. "We have Trooper Andersen's stolen car report. It was only about 4:00 p.m. December twenty-fifth in Europe when you reported the rental as being stolen from Texas at 10:00 a.m. on the same day. There's no crime syndicate on the face of this earth that can transport a car from Texas to Berlin in that time frame."

"I can't explain that," Harpie replied. "You know where I was at the time. I didn't have anything to do with stealing the car."

"What the hell were you doing in Caprock Canyons State Park on Christmas Eve and Christmas Day anyway?" Agent Dubkowski said. "According to your probation officer, you were supposed to be spending the holidays at your brother's house."

"I did spend time with my brother and sister-in-law," Harpie replied. "I just needed a little time alone."

"A little time alone, huh?" Agent Halifax roared. "Your prints were all over that damned car, along with five sets of prints that are not in any database in the United States or Interpol. Here is your iPhone." He dropped it on the editor's desk. "There is nothing of interest to us on it. Who was with you, Harpie?"

"No one," he answered. "The prints probably belong to the thieves."

"We checked with General McCusker at NORAD," Agent Halifax continued. "Staff Sergeant Rebose swears he saw the Phantom Effect again on Christmas Eve, at exactly 23:55 p.m., the same time you were in Caprock Canyons State Park."

He looked at his partner in horror—he'd let the cat out of the bag by mentioning the name the Phantom Effect in the editor's presence.

"Is that where the foreign aircraft lands?" he asked, seemingly unperturbed by his verbal faux pas. "What country is it from, Harpie? Is it a threat to the people of the United States? Are they planting spies or assassins or weapons here? Are you being disloyal to your own country?"

Harpie remembered Commander Assan's words: "Sometimes you've got to lie and steal to save people's lives." Harpie thought, *The Di people come in peace, looking for a world in which to live, and they're just like us.* He knew if he told the truth and they believed him, the military might ambush the spaceship next Christmas Eve in Caprock Canyons State Park, but if he kept his mouth shut he could save the lives of those on board.

"I don't know what you're talking about," Harpie finally answered.

"Lift up your pants leg," Agent Dubkowski ordered him.

The monitor was still there. There was nothing they could charge him with to make an arrest and interrogate him further.

The agents left soon thereafter, and as they drove back to Lubbock International to return to Denver, Agent Dubkowski said to his partner, "How in the hell could they get a car from Texas to Germany within six hours of it being reported as stolen? There were only passenger jets flying out of Lubbock on Christmas Day, but not a single cargo plane."

"That's right," Agent Halifax answered. "Unless they stole the car as soon as Mr. Colcek parked it the night before. But even then, the two international airports nearest the park are Amarillo to the north and Midland to the south. Both are more than a hundred miles from Caprock. Even if the car was moving at a hundred miles an hour, it would take more than an hour to get to either airport.

"Then you would have to load the car on a cargo plane, fly across the United States and the Atlantic Ocean," Agent Dubkowski said, "and drive the car from God knows which airport in Germany to where it was abandoned in Berlin. The problem there is that there isn't any record of a single cargo plane flying out of either one those American airports on Christmas Eve or Christmas Day, and we know the drug cartels don't have any aircraft that size. The only possible way he could have pulled off that stunt is if Colcek is in cahoots with whoever is flying that super-fast aircraft NORAD calls Santa's Ghost."

"No," Agent Halifax said. "That rental car was tied directly to Harpie Colcek; it would be too easy to trace to him. The man is not stupid, but he knows more than he's telling us. I think he's discovered the landing site we've been seeking for the last fifteen years. We've gotta put a tap back on his phone."

"Yeah, he knows a lot more than he's telling us," Agent Dubkowski replied. "Maybe he's in with a crime syndicate. But we've gotta get the president's okay to pin something on his ass to get him back into federal custody, and then we'll find out what else he knows. It's a matter of national security."

"Once we arrest him," Agent Halifax said, "we've also gotta put the pressure on his wife, brother, and sister-in-law and find out if he's told them anything."

"Oh, Harpie," Gloria said, "what did the FBI want from you this time?"

"They came down to the office and accused me of having something to do with stealing the rental car."

"You didn't tell them that crazy story about the spacemen, did you?"

"No!" Harpie replied. He was shocked—he forgot the house and landline were probably being monitored again, since they suspected he had something to do with the rental car theft.

The agent, monitoring their conversation from the van parked down the street, noted their conversation and had it sent to agents Halifax and Dubkowski. But the story Harpie Colcek told about spacemen did not violate any existing laws, since he said it during a private conversation and was not spreading wild rumors. They still could not arrest him.

"Well," Agent Halifax said to Agent Dubkowski when he read the note, "a spacecraft would sure explain the Phantom Effect and how the car got to Germany in such a short period of time."

They looked at each other, and this time neither of them laughed.

Days turned into months, and Harpie was careful about what he did and said. Then, on the first of December, Harpie applied with his probation officer to again spend the holidays with his brother and sister-in-law, and permission was readily granted. It was too easy, and it made Harpie suspicious, but his reporter's driving spirit wouldn't give him any peace; he had to go. Gloria, however, declined and chose to spend the Christmas holidays with their children, Carrie and Jack, and their grandchildren.

Harpie parked the rental car near the restrooms in Caprock Canyons State Park, and in the light of the full moon he caught a glimpse of several vans stopping near the entrance with their lights out; he was being followed! He quickly deposited his three dollars into the top slot in the out-of-hours fee box so they wouldn't have any reason to

arrest him. Then he quickly made his way past the Fern Cave sign
and ascended the trail leading to the top of the plateau.

Partway up he stopped to rest and catch his breath. Hiding behind
a boulder, he looked down the trail. He spied at least a dozen men
before they realized they'd lost sight of him, and they dropped down
on to the snow. They were tracing his tracks, and several of the men
were heavily laden with some type of equipment. The sight spurred
Harpie onward.

He reached the top of the plateau and looked at his watch. There
was still more than an hour to go before the *Star Voyager* landed, and
all he could do was wait. *What would I tell FBI if they approached me
now? I'll have to tell them I'm doing my usual Christmas Eve meditation.*
But the posse remained hunkered down in the snow near an array of
boulders, and when Harpie started back up the trail, they continued
their surveillance. They were so intent on tracking Harpie that they
never noticed the lone figure peering at them from behind the rock
formation.

After what seemed like an eternity, Harpie searched the heavens
and spotted a glimmer of light rapidly moving between the stars, and
when he looked at his watch it was nearly 11:35. Twenty minutes later,
he felt a warm familiar breeze brush against his cheeks and knew the
starship had landed.

The frantic reporter rushed forward with his hands outstretched
and a few moments later felt the glazed sides of the spaceship. He
had to get inside before the Robot guards emerged and detected the
posse hidden behind the boulders near the trail; they wouldn't stand
a chance against the Robots' laser guns. He felt his way along the
edge of the craft to the steps. The door immediately opened, and he
scampered aboard.

The guard Robot was just heading for the open door to secure
the landing area, and it seized Harpie by his shoulders, paralyzing his
body and heightening his fear, while its red protruding eyes scanned
his retinas to identify him. Surprisingly, it recognized him, and led

him to the same room where he'd met Commander Assan last year. Harpie breathed a sigh of relief.

A man was awake and dressed, but it wasn't Commander Assan. "Welcome back, Harpie." The Robot interpreted the commander's thoughts as he extended his hand. "Commander Assan told us about you. You are our friend! I am Commander Toka."

"Nice to meet you," Harpie replied as they shook hands. "Where is Commander Assan?"

"He comes back every other year," the commander answered. "Remember—his ship needs one lightyear to travel back to the nearest major supply station, unload a few returning passengers, take on supplies, and after spending two weeks free time there, he must again travel back for another lightyear to reach this destination at Caprock."

"Doesn't he ever get to spend time with his family?" Harpie asked.

"No," the commander replied. "He has no family. When he decided to become a spaceship commander, he dedicated his life to saving thousands of his people. He can join a different marriage group on each trip for the love and sex, but believe me, it is life of loneliness."

Then Harpie remembered the real meaning of his visit, and he reached out and touched the commander's shoulder as he blurted out, "Don't let the guard Robot go outside; there's a posse waiting there. You've gotta get out of here! They know you're here, and I think they have weapons that can disable this spaceship and kill everyone on board."

"Who has the weapons?" the Robot asked.

Harpie looked at the commander and said, "The FBI and the US military. They believe you're part of a criminal syndicate or terrorist element from Earth."

The commander stared at Harpie in alarm and then glanced at the Robot. The mechanical man read his mental orders and quickly moved to a computer and tapped some keys with its esoteric markings. A moment later, Harpie felt a strange sensation, and in a panic, he bolted down the hallway, but the steps were already pulled in and the door was shut.

"Where the hell are you taking me?" Harpie shouted as he turned in horror and ran back toward the commander; he desperately wanted to get off. But then he abruptly stopped and his mouth dropped open when he encountered a lovely blonde lady walking toward him, carrying a suitcase. There was something familiar about her.

"Don't panic, Harpie," she said, trying to reassure him. "We're not going very far." He knew her from somewhere yet couldn't remember where and when he'd met her.

"You know me," she said, assuming he recognized her. "I changed my mind. I lived in New York for three years and was returning to Rau until I learned my parents had died two years ago."

Then Harpie remembered where he'd seen her. "You're Molly, the lady who was in the habitat when I came aboard last year," he said. "How did you get back here in a year?"

"When we were six months out when I learned about my parents' fate due to flesh-eating bacteria, the two crafts rendezvoused, and I got aboard this starship. I had no reason to continue on to Rau. Commander Assan told me about you. We're already landing, and I need you to give me a lift to Lubbock International Airport so I can catch a flight back to New York. We don't have much time. Are you ready?"

The door opened, and he felt a blessed relief as he jumped down into the snow, realizing they had landed next to his car.

"Aren't you cold?"

"No," she replied. "I'm just excited to be back."

Harpie started the engine, and they headed for the exit, and that's when they saw a group of Robots carrying one of the vans toward the spacecraft.

"Good grief," Harpie said as he braked. "They're stealing the FBI's vans."

"Yes," Molly answered with a laugh. "The commander is dropping a crap load of people off outside London and Paris, and they'll need the vans to get into the cities. Interpol will eventually recover the vehicles."

Harpie didn't say anything, but he knew Halifax and Dubkowski would soon be on his ass again. After the second van was aboard the spaceship, it silently lifted into the air, and Harpie and Molly headed for Lubbock International airport.

High up on the plateau, agents Halifax and Dubkowski led eight US marshals and six US Special Forces soldiers armed with infrared guided antitank weapons and night vision goggles, yet they somehow lost track of the reporter. They came to a place on the plateau where Harpie's tracks stopped. It was rather puzzling.

"What the hell," a Green Beret sergeant whispered. "No wonder we lost him. It looks as though he somehow got airborne!"

They were flabbergasted and shined their flashlights around the snow-covered plateau. They noticed the huge area of partially melted and compressed snow located less than a yard from where Harpie's tracks ended.

"He can't be airborne," another soldier said as he looked at the huge impression in the snow. "There's no flying machine on earth that big."

No one said anything, but they caught the gist of his implication; even agents Halifax and Dubkowski remained silent. They searched the entire plateau until the sun peeked from in between the clouds amassed in the eastern sky, but there wasn't any sign of the suspect.

"Maybe Mr. Colcek is right," Agent Dubkowski said to Agent Halifax. "Those criminals, or whoever they are, are getting more sophisticated."

"But then how did they get airborne?" Agent Halifax asked as they were hiking back down the slippery trail. "We didn't hear or see a helicopter or plane."

The mystery deepened when they found another patch of partially melted snow that bore the same huge imprint as the one they'd discovered on the plateau. Harpie Colcek's car was gone, and when they reached the entrance to the park they discovered their vans had been stolen. It was an embarrassing situation for federal officers.

"Son of a bitch!" Agent Halifax screeched as he threw his woolen cap down. "He's fucked over us again; that makes three stolen vehicles. We've gotta find a way to lock his ass up and find out what kind of aircraft lands and takes off without making a sound and leaves these damned impressions in the snow."

They were enjoying a Christmas brunch when there was a knock at the door. Sue Colcek answered it. Two men flashed their badges and pushed past her without being invited in and encountered their quarry enjoying a feast in the kitchen with his wife, Gloria, and his brother, Jon.

"We need to talk to you, Mr. Colcek," Agent Halifax said. "What the hell did you do with our government vans?"

"What," Harpie replied. "Those were your vans? Were you following me?"

"Yes, those were our vans," Agent Halifax tartly replied, "and yes, we were following you by monitoring your tracking device."

"The vans were stolen while you were in Caprock Canyons State Park last night, Mr. Colcek," Agent Dubkowski retorted.

"I saw two vans in the park when I was leaving," he replied. *I really didn't lie*, he thought. *The vans were being put inside the spacecraft, which was still in park when Molly and I were leaving.*

"Why the hell did you return to Caprock State Park on Christmas Eve again this year, Mr. Colcek?" Agent Dubkowski asked. "And at the time NORAD says they again picked up Santa's Ghost on radar!"

"I'm a devout catholic," Harpie answered, "and I told you before that I find solace there. I go there to meditate and celebrate the birth of Christ."

"We followed you to Caprock Canyons State Park and tracked you to the top of the plateau. You were alone then, but somehow you managed to elude us," Agent Dubkowski said. "How the hell did you get off the plateau without us seeing you?"

"I hiked off," Harpie replied, remembering Commander Assan's remark about lying to save lives.

"No, you didn't," Agent Dubkowski remarked.

"Do you think I suddenly grew wings or something?"

Agent Dubkowski shook his head. "Tell us how you really got off the plateau."

"I hiked off," Harpie replied again, trying to sound agitated. "I just walked down the trail, probably right past you guys."

"No, you did *not*," Agent Dubkowski angrily shot back. "Where are our vans?"

"Oh," Harpie said. "Not only did I sprout wings and fly off the plateau, but I performed another miracle and drove my car and your two vans away at the same time?"

"Well, we didn't see you once you got to the top of the plateau," Agent Halifax said.

"That's not my fault," Harpie said.

Agent Halifax said, "We parked near the entrance to the park, but when we got back your car was missing and so were our two vans. You must've had accomplices. That's also how you got off the plateau without us seeing you."

"A moment ago, you said I was alone, and I had no idea you were following me, so how could I have had the time to make arrangements to have your vehicles stolen?"

The agents knew he had a valid point; that kind of collusion took time.

"You had time," Agent Halifax said. "We didn't hike off the plateau until daylight."

Harpie angrily blurted, "Last year you accused me of stealing the rental car, which you found in Germany on virtually the same day it was stolen. I still think some crime syndicate stole it. Now you're harassing me about stealing two government vans! Why the hell don't you call Interpol again? The syndicate probably has those vans in Paris or London by now!"

The minute he said it, Harpie regretted it. He knew the agents would now check with Interpol, and when they found the vans near Paris and London he would be more than just a person of interest, maybe even be arrested. As soon as the agents left, Harpie made reservations to fly back to Denver the next day, but Gloria would return home on their scheduled return flight after the New Year. Next, he called his best friend, Monty Galbreth, and asked him to meet him at Denver International Airport. Then he cut the monitoring device off his ankle.

The agents knew there wasn't any crime in going to a secluded area to meditate—that was covered by the First Amendment—and they didn't find another soul on the plateau that night. At least they hadn't seen anyone else there, nor did they encounter anyone when they returned and found their vans missing. The haunting mystery was how Harpie got off the plateau without them seeing him. The agents knew he hadn't committed a crime, or at least they couldn't prove he did, yet they knew he wasn't telling the whole truth.

As they drove away, Agent Halifax said, "He gave us a subtle clue. Let's contact Interpol from the Lubbock office to see if they found either van in Paris or London. If they do, we'll know for certain Cap

Rock is the enemy's landing site and that Harpie Colcek is in cahoots with an international criminal element."

"No," Agent Dubkowski said, "if a criminal cartel is involved, we would never recover the stolen vehicles, because that's how they make their loot."

The next day, Interpol confirmed via the Prefecture of Police of Paris that they did indeed find one of the vans abandoned outside of the city, and the other one was recovered in London by the Metropolitan Police Service. Based on Harpie's statement, the FBI now had enough evidence to accuse him of complicity and duplicity in the theft of the stolen government vehicles, and a federal judge issued a warrant for his arrest. The monitoring device indicated he was still in Lubbock, and the agents raced back to Jon Colcek's home.

"Where is Harpie Colcek?" the agents asked Sue.

"He flew back to Denver this morning," she answered.

The monitoring device was traced to a ditch not far from Lubbock International Airport, and soon the FBI and the Denver police knocked on Harpie's door with an arrest warrant; no one answered. They kicked the door open and scoured the premises, and confirmed that he had not returned home, although they knew he'd arrived at the Denver airport around noon.

When agents Halifax and Dubkowski returned to Denver that afternoon, they went straight to the *Rocky Mountain Times* office and queried Claude Hoskins.

"I haven't seen Harpie since he went on vacation over the Christmas holiday," he told the agents.

Agent Halifax searched Harpie's desk but didn't find anything of import.

"Well," Claude Hoskins said, "that's two of my people who are now missing."

"Who is the other person?" Agent Halifax asked.

"Martha Spiller," Claude replied. "She went on vacation a week before Christmas and was supposed to be back at work today. It's only a matter of a day, but she doesn't answer her landline or cell phone and has no known relatives in Colorado."

"Did they work together?" Agent Halifax asked.

"Yes," Claude replied. "They're both investigative reporters. Harpie handles the heavy stuff like murder, Robbery, and kidnapping. Martha investigates women's issues like rape, celeb divorces, domestic violence, and child custody issues."

The agents ran a background check on Martha Spiller, but they couldn't find any evidence as to where or when she was born. There were no high school or college records and no medical history. The only records they could find went back ten years to the day she started working for the *Times*.

"She's got to be in on the plot," Agent Dubkowski said to his partner.

"Yeah," Agent Halifax, answered, "we know a lot of foreign agents have a fictional history of being born in this country, and when we vet them, their records go only as far back as the day they landed in Colorado or God knows where else. The one place we know their agents infiltrate this country is in Caprock Canyons State Park, and from there they probably migrate to the major cities like Dallas, Denver, Chicago, New York, and Los Angeles and assimilate into the populations. What I still can't figure out is why we couldn't see or hear a helicopter or a plane land when Harpie got off the plateau."

"I wish I knew," Dubkowski answered. "But now we gotta put pressure on Gloria Colcek and Jon and Sue Colcek to see how much he leaked to them."

Two weeks after Harpie disappeared, agents Halifax and Dubkowski knocked on Gloria Colcek's door.

"Have you found my Harpie?" she asked.

"No, we haven't found him yet, Mrs. Colcek," Agent Halifax said.

"I don't know what happened to my poor Harpie," Gloria said and she teared up.

"We're sorry, Mrs. Colcek, but did you ever hear of a coworker at the *Times* named Martha Spiller?" Agent Halifax asked.

"Yes," Gloria replied. "She works at the paper with Harpie and has for years."

"Well, Mrs. Colcek," Agent Dubkowski said, "Martha Spiller is also unaccounted for."

"Oh no," Gloria replied. "I hope nothing bad has happened to her and Harpie. They've worked together for so long and—"

"Mrs. Colcek," Agent Dubkowski interrupted, "she and Harpie went missing at the same time."

Her brow furrowed at his implication, but before she could speak, he said, "Has Harpie come up with any inane stories or such lately? I mean like something you would have a hard time believing."

Gloria's jaw dropped and she stared at him for a long moment before answering. "He hasn't been himself lately." Then she turned away; she couldn't look at them. Gloria knew she couldn't lie to the FBI, so she was about to betray the man she loved. "He came up with some weird story about being on a spaceship, and he talked about Robots and people from another planet."

"I'm sorry about all this, Mrs. Colcek, but people who intend to disappear sometimes come up with ridiculous stories like that," Agent Dubkowski continued. "Do you have any knowledge whether they might be involved with an international crime syndicate that's stealing vehicles from America and taking them overseas?"

"No, Harpie would never do that!" she shrieked and turned to face them.

Agent Dubkowski reached inside his jacket, removed a piece of paper, and handed it to her. "Did you know about this?"

She looked at the document with the Bank of Denver's heading; the account was listed in Harpie's name.

"It's for more than a million dollars!" she screeched.

"Do you see that $200,000 withdrawal?" Agent Dubkowski asked her.

She merely nodded, too shocked to respond.

"He made that withdrawal right before he disappeared," Agent Dubkowski said, "and purchased two tickets to Cancun, Mexico—one for him and the other one for Martha Spiller. They're on the run, and she's traveling under your name."

"How did she get on the aircraft without proper ID?" Gloria asked.

Agent Dubkowski again reached in his pocket and produced another document—a duplicate driver's license. It had Gloria's name and address on it, but the picture was of Martha Spiller.

"They never got on that aircraft," Agent Dubkowski told her. "We don't know where they are, and we don't have a copy of her passport yet, but we're working on it."

"I can't believe Harpie would do this to me. Not after all these years," she said as she teared up and handed the documents back. She sat on the sofa.

"We think Mr. Colcek concocted this whole fairy tale about space aliens to make you think he was having psychological problems. That way if his relationship with Miss Spiller doesn't work out, he'll have a perfect excuse to beg your forgiveness," Agent Dubkowski said.

"However, according to their friends at the *Times*," Agent Halifax said, "their affair has been going on for several years."

It was hard for her to believe what the agents were telling her, yet she saw the documents and knew they no reason to make up such a story. Harpie hadn't been himself lately and was either losing his mind or had concocted a story to end their marriage. *And where did he get all that money?* she thought. Either way, she knew their marriage was in real trouble.

Agent Dubkowski handed her a card and said, "If he contacts you, please call me at this number."

"I most certainly will," she snapped as tears streamed down her cheeks.

After they left, she called Claude Hoskins and told him what happened. He promised to stop over as soon as he finished giving instructions to his staff.

"I hated to lie and break an old lady's heart," Agent Halifax said as they drove away, "but if foreign agents are landing in the United States, they could be assembling nuclear weapons under our very noses. We have more than three hundred million Americans to worry about, so breaking one old lady's heart seems trivial compared to our possibly saving millions of lives."

"Yeah," Dubkowski answered, "and we have two simultaneous scenarios that could be linked. One is the possible nuclear threat to the United States, and the other is the existence of an international car-theft ring that has some ulterior motive for stealing cars but letting us recover them. Maybe they use them to commit crimes overseas and then abandon them. We'll have to check on it."

"Our New York offices have reported those same types of incidents in several other states," Halifax said. "It's imperative that we find out if they're using that same aircraft to plant alleged nuclear saboteurs all across the United States, and how they transport those stolen vehicles into other countries and why. Or maybe the two events are not even related."

They headed down to Lubbock to question Jon and Sue Colcek to learn what Harpie told them, if anything, about the Phantom Effect or a car-theft ring.

"Yes, he talked about an encounter with aliens," Jon Colcek admitted—he didn't want to lie to the FBI—and then described the details of the spaceship, the passengers, and the Robots.

"But Harpie had nothing to do with the stolen vehicles," he told them.

"Do you think his encounter with aliens is true, or do you think he concocted the whole story?" Agent Halifax asked.

"One of our ATCs saw that same faint blip on our radar for two consecutive years, and Harpie confided in me that NORAD sees them every Christmas Eve," Jon answered, "which leads me to believe there may be some element of truth in what my brother said."

The agents were stunned by his remark; Harpie had spilled the beans about the Phantom Effect—a top secret government phenomenon.

"Did you discuss this with anyone outside your family?" Agent Halifax asked.

"Yes, of course," Jon replied. "The other air traffic controllers, who were on duty on those two occasions, saw the blips on our radar screens too."

Agent Halifax stepped outside the home and spoke on the phone to his bureau chief in Denver. "Harpie told Jon and Sue Colcek about the Phantom Effect. Jon Colcek said a few other ATCs in Lubbock picked up the blips these past two Christmas Eves moments after they disappeared off NORAD's radar. Thus, Harpie's brother and sister-in-law believe that his story about space aliens might have some element of truth."

The bureau chief hung up and called the White House, and a few minutes later he called Agent Halifax back. "President Jamieson signed an executive order today, charging any person or groups of persons with sedition and possibly treason if they spread unsubstantiated rumors about extraterrestrials. That tale is causing worldwide chaos and fear around the globe. Protests about the lack of government security are breaking out in major cities around the world. Terrified citizens are buying up all the available supplies of potable water, toilet tissue, and foodstuffs or they're being looted or pilfered from the stores and warehouses.

"The president says, and I quote, "'A charge of treason may be warranted if the government can show beyond a reasonable doubt, that the conspirators have been spreading such rumors, and aiding and abetting foreign agents that have invaded the United States and are assembling or have assembled a nuclear device or devices on American soil; other countries are following suit.'"

"Therefore, based on what you've told me about Jon and Sue Colcek and their association with Harpie Colcek, there is sufficient reason to arrest them. They are helping to spread rumors about alien invaders, who we believe are really foreign government agents. Additionally, charge them with compromising top secret information concerning the Phantom Effect and allegedly aiding and abetting an international car theft ring.

"After you arrest the three of them, turn custody over to the CIA. Then track down the other ATCs who saw the blips on Lubbock's radar and arrest them too. Under the circumstances, the president assures me that their actions are causing a national and international crisis, so you won't need a writ of habeas corpus."

"Turn over custody to the CIA?" Agent Halifax asked. "Why?"

"Because the president says so, that's why, Agent Halifax!" the bureau chief replied and hung up.

FBI agents and the local police in Denver scoured the city and even spoke to Monty Galbreth, Harpie's best friend, but he couldn't tell them anything about the whereabouts of the fugitives.

CHAPTER

6

When Monty Galbreth picked up Harpie at Denver
International airport, the reporter told him the whole
story as they rode back into the city.

"Good grief, Harpie," Monty said, "the FBI questioned me about
you and Martha spiller right before I got here. Then there was a story
on the morning news that the president signed an executive order that
authorizes the FBI and local police to arrest anyone concocting and
spreading stories about space aliens invading the planet. They claim
the rumors are a hoax, but people are still panicking. Murders have
been committed by vigilante groups that believe their neighbors are
alien monsters in human form. There's looting, rapes, and Robberies,
and the National Guard is being mobilized."

"It's not hoax, Monty," Harpie replied, sounding a little annoyed.
"The existence of extraterrestrials is true, and I'm beginning to think
the government knows it. The president has probably sicced the FBI

on me again, and now I'm in real trouble; I removed my tracking device."

"Yeah, they're gonna be looking for your ass," Monty told him. "You've gotta find a place to hide!"

"I know, but where? I sure can't go home now or even call Gloria, because our phones are tapped. They'll trace the call."

"I know just the place. I'll drop you off at Saint Mary's. The sacristy there will be unlocked."

"Do you mean the Saint Mary's where I go to Mass on Sundays?" Harpie asked skeptically as he looked over at his friend.

"Yup."

"How do you know the church will be unlocked?"

"Please don't ask me. I'm sworn to secrecy."

"What if Father Gallagher catches me? What will I tell him?"

"He won't catch you or care. Trust me, Harpie."

"Okay. I've always trusted you."

"Good. Now when you get there, go to the sacristy, open the largest closet, and go inside. Close the door and crawl beneath the bottom shelf. Feel around on the right corner of the back wall about a foot off the floor until you feel a small hole. Put one of your fingers in the hole and push the button. This automatically locks the closet door, and an entrance to a crawl space will pop open. If it doesn't work, it means you haven't fully closed the closet door.

"After you crawl inside, close the door, and it will unlock the closet door. There are chairs and water in there, and some dried food and crackers in case you get hungry. Above all, don't go anywhere until I come back and get you."

Harpie was stunned, wondering what was going down with the church and his best friend, but he didn't say another word until Monty stopped the car in front of the church.

"Thanks, Monty," Harpie said as they shook hands.

Harpie rushed to the side entrance to the sacristy; the door was unlocked. He did as Monty instructed and soon stood inside the hidden room and looked about. It was rather large, and he wondered why there were so many chairs scattered about. There was a refrigerator with bottled water, and next to it was a small pantry filled with the snacks Monty told him about. A half dozen filing cabinets lined the walls, along with several high chairs for infants, a rack of what looked like used clothing for men and women, and a playpen for toddlers. Toys were scattered about, and a large TV occupied a remote corner of the room.

Harpie looked at his watch and saw it was almost 1:00 p.m. The hours slipped by, and Harpie turned the TV to a news channel and was shocked when his picture flashed across the screen, along with that of his coworker at the *Times*, Martha Spiller. They were now on the FBI's Most Wanted list! The media showed scenes of rioting and looting going on around the globe, and a number of murders committed by people who believed their unsocial neighbors were aliens in disguise.

Harpie just sat there, stunned by the broadcast and horrified at what he had caused by simply telling the truth. Once or twice he thought he heard low murmurings, and in one instance he heard something hit the wall. He frantically jumped out of the chair, thinking it was the FBI breaking down the crawlspace door, but no one was there.

Finally, about 6:00 p.m. the small door popped open, and Monty Galbreth crawled into the room.

"What kind of a place is this?" Harpie asked.

"It's a safe haven for illegal aliens entering the United States, who are looking for a better life," Monty answered. "Father Gallagher has been running it for more than twenty-five years and has placed more than half a million immigrants with sponsors from other churches all across the country. The FBI and ICE have no idea this sanctuary is here. We can literally make people disappear into nearly every state in the union, and we can make you disappear too, Harpie."

"What is your role in all of this?"

"I am Father Gallagher's lieutenant, second in command, and have been since he started this program," Monty proudly answered.

Then the door from the closet in the sacristy opened again, and a man, followed by three little girls, a boy, and a woman crawled into the room. They looked fearfully at Harpie and then Monty.

"*Siéntate, por favor,*" Monty said in perfect Spanish, and the six Guatemalan aliens immediately sat.

A few moments later the door opened again, and Father Gallagher entered the room. When he stood up and saw Harpie, he got a horrified expression on his face. "What's he doing here?" he anxiously asked Monty.

"He's on the run from the FBI, Father," Monty said. "We need to find him a sponsor."

"Why are they pursuing you, Harpie?"

"I'm wanted for sedition and treason, Father," Harpie said, and told him about the newscast.

"I hate the FBI," the priest said. "They and ICE keep searching for us, but so far they haven't got anything on me. Of course, if they discovered this place they would shut down our operation and throw me in jail."

Father Gallagher unlocked one of the file drawers and withdrew several manila folders. "I have to make some calls to line up a sponsor for you and this immigrant family, Harpie. It may take several days to find one and make the arrangements. We'll need some money though—five-hundred bucks; do you have any?"

"Not much on me," Harpie said, "but I have an ATM card. The FBI and the local police are probably monitoring their use."

"I know, and you can't go out, Harpie," the priest said. "It would be too dangerous. The FBI and the local police are probably searching the city for you. Tell you what I'll do, Harpie. I've got plenty of church funds available for the undocumented alien program. I'll fund you for now. Give me you ATM card number and the PIN. A priest in Kansas City knows a guy who makes phony Credit Cards and ATM cards. My friend will have him make up a duplicate of your ATM card and draw the cash out to reimburse the church, and also make the FBI think you're heading toward the east coast."

Harpie gave Father Gallagher his ATM card and the PIN, and after the priest took his picture, he patted Harpie on the shoulder and then was gone.

"Come on, Harpie," Monty said, "I'll show you and this family where to get some sleep."

He led them to the darkened end of the waiting room and opened a door that looked like the other wooden panels nailed to the wall. Inside that room were other alien families. Harpie realized where the noise and murmurings originated. *More immigrants coming on board*, he thought. *Just like the Di.*

"These folks have sponsors and are waiting for their shuttles to arrive," Monty said. "When a bed becomes available, adults can get up to four hours sleep, but the kids can sleep longer. We'll have volunteers bring in fresh food and drinks after dark."

Harpie noticed they all had to share one bathroom. Then he walked with Monty back to the waiting room; it was time for him to leave.

Harpie looked at his watch; it was 10:00 p.m. Then, the door leading to the closet in the sacristy suddenly opened, and a dark-haired woman crawled into the room.

When she stood up, Harpie's jaw dropped. "Martha Spiller," he almost shouted. "What the hell are you doing here?"

"Oh, Harpie," she said, "I'm so glad you escaped."

"Escaped?"

"Yes, from Caprock Canyons State Park. I was there when the FBI and the soldiers were tracking you."

"What were you doing there?"

"I want to go home to Rau."

"You're a Di?"

"Yes," she replied. "Aren't you?"

"No," he said. "But I met Commander Assan last year and learned he only comes every other year, yet those new Robots recognized me. How come you didn't leave on the shuttle?"

"I was climbing the escarpment, following in your tracks, and was almost to the top when I heard the sounds of a group of men behind me. Some of them were soldiers and had these terrible-looking weapons. I hid behind some boulders and they passed me, but I heard them say your name. That's why I thought you were a Di too."

"So you missed the spaceship shuttle?"

"Yes. I knew you must have warned the commander, because I felt a warm breeze and realized the shuttle took off immediately," she said. "While the men searched for you and the shuttle on the plateau, I hiked back down the trail, but the shuttle had already been there and gone, and I took shelter in the ladies' room. The FBI men were furious when they returned and discovered their vans were missing. About an hour later, several other vans arrived and picked them up.

"I was frantic and hungry and cold. I started walking toward Quitaque, the nearest town, when a state trooper stopped and cuffed me, and made me get into the back of his patrol car. His name tag read Robert Andersen."

Harpie knew who he was, but he didn't say anything.

"'You just came out of the park,' the trooper said and then asked me my name.

'We've had vehicles stolen from there—do you know anything about them?'

'No,' I said.

'The FBI has a warrant out for your arrest, Martha Spiller!'

'What for?'

'Aiding and abetting a car-theft ring, and spreading false rumor about alien spacemen, Miss Spiller,'" he replied.

"I was so scared I couldn't answer him, Harpie."

"'What were you doing in the park, Martha?'" the trooper asked me.

"I was so frightened that I started crying, knowing he was going to arrest me and the CIA would take me to the Place."

"'I just want to get on the shuttle and go home,' I said. 'The CIA is going to send me to the Place.'

'What do you mean by the Place?' the trooper asked me.

'It's where the CIA holds anyone who claims to know anything about space aliens or a project called the Phantom Effect,'" I told him.

Harpie still didn't say anything.

"'Where is your home?' the trooper asked me.

'On Rau,' I said rather meekly. He looked at me rather amazed, and then said, 'Do you know a guy named Harpie Colcek?'

'Yes, I know Harpie Colcek,' I said. 'I worked with him at the *Rocky Mountain Times.*'

'You're one of them, aren't you?' the trooper asked me.

"I didn't answer him."

Then he said, "'My father was right—the legend is true.'"

"He got behind the wheel of the cruiser and didn't say anything for a few moments. Then he said, "'There is something that has always puzzled me about the legend. How come the Comanche arrows splintered when they hit the silver ghost-men?'

'They're not ghosts or men,' I said, 'they're Robots that are made out of a mineral that is harder than titanium.'"

"He immediately did a U-turn and drove me all the way back to the Plainview terminal so I could catch a bus ride to Lubbock International Airport.

"'When you get back to Denver,' the trooper said, 'go to Saint Mary's Catholic Church on Zenobia Street and ask for Father Gallagher. At this point, it's merely speculation on the part of law enforcement, but we believe he's helping smuggle illegal aliens into the country, although we can't prove it. Maybe he can help you.'"

"That's how I found this place, Harpie. I've already spoken to Father Gallagher. He's getting me forged driver's license and birth certificate, just as he does for the illegals."

"Good," Harpie replied, "he's getting me papers too. Now tell me about the Place that you so fear so much."

"It's located in Dallas and is a maximum security prison," she replied. "That's where the CIA imprisons anyone who claims to know anything about what the government calls the Phantom Effect, and they inject them with all kinds of drugs, trying to erase any memories or fantasies they may have of Rau or spaceships or aliens. They call it a truth serum."

"So," Harpie replied, "the CIA knows about the spaceships and Rau?"

"Yes and no," she replied. "Apparently, they don't have anything to validate our existence or they won't admit it, but too many drugged prisoners have told them the exact same things."

"Why would they do something like that?"

"I think they're afraid we might be telling the truth, Harpie. Other Di has told them we're an advanced civilization, and they fear we want to take over Earth. But we have no intention of doing that; we just want some place to live. We could help Earth a lot, especially with the treatments we have discovered for most of the major diseases that are still plaguing this planet."

"I know," he replied. "How did you find out about the Place?"

"One of the Di was in that prison for more than ten years, and he confessed everything about the Di and Rau. But the drugs eventually caused him to become so harmless and demented that the warden had him committed to a state mental institution. However, after several years of being off the drugs, a lot of his memory of Rau and his family returned. He feigned his incapacity and eventually escaped and made his way back to Caprock. He no longer had his identifier and had to get on board the spaceship before the Robot guards mistakenly killed him."

"I don't know where we can go from here," Harpie said. "The FBI or the CIA will never stop searching for us. They'll put us in that prison for the rest of our lives—or maybe kill us in the process."

"I know the perfect place to go," she answered.

"Where?"

"You can come to Rau with me. There are other shuttle spaceships the government hasn't discovered yet," she said. "Since the spacecraft I'm talking about has never been fired upon, there's no need for Robot guards. The spaceship lands near Lake Placid, New York, at 10:00 p.m. every June fifth.

"Other returnees have followed this pattern; we can get a flight from Denver to New York City and then Albany International, and then catch the bus up 187 to exit thirty at Witherbee. We can hire a car there to take us to the John Brown Farm State Historic Site, where the *Space Explorer* lands every other year."

Harpie was dumbfounded. He didn't want to go to Rau, yet he certainly didn't want to be imprisoned at the Place either—just the thought frightened him. He anguished at the idea of never seeing Gloria or his children or grandchildren again, but his fear of being incarcerated for life drove him onward.

"How long does it really take to get to Rau?" he asked.

"More than four lightyears."

"What?" Harpie nearly shouted. "I'll be fifty-eight years old by the time I get there."

"I'll be fifty-two," she replied. "That's what you and the Pi have to understand. Space travelers spend years in therapeutic hibernation; life is short. You must make good use of every minute you are awake. But there is good news too. Our advances in science and medicine have extended the average life span of most people on Rau to at least 110 earth years and sometimes longer."

At 11:00 p.m. that evening, Father Gallagher returned to the secret waiting room, where Harpie, Martha, and other immigrant families were waiting.

"I've got IDs for you and Martha," he told Harpie. "Here are your forged driver's licenses and birth certificates. Harpie, your name is now Harold Miller, and Martha, you are Marion Keller."

Harpie felt as though a ton of weight had been lifted off his shoulders, and Martha was delighted and relieved.

"I loaned you the $500 fee for expenses as I said I would for these forged IDs," the priest told Harpie. "I did the same for you too, Martha. I also took the liberty of withdrawing enough of the church's money to purchase ten prepaid credit cards valued at $300 each; they are untraceable. Here are five for each of you. Kansas City is already making arrangements to work on your ATM cards.

"I managed to get sponsors for you both, and those credit cards should be more than sufficient to get you to where you have to go. Harpie, a Montana rancher will harbor you in exchange for your labor and a cowboy's paycheck. Martha, you've been accepted into a convent in Saint Louis, Missouri."

"Thanks, Father," Martha said, "but we've decided to go to Rau."

"Rau?" the priest asked. "Where's Rau?"

Harpie reiterated the story of the spaceship, Commander Assan, the Robots, and the passengers from Rau, the dying planet. Then he told the priest how the US government suspected it might all be true, but was covering it up to curb the mass hysteria all over the world. The details Martha told Father Gallagher about the Place were frightening, and he believed her.

But then the priest said, "There's no such thing as spacemen or a place called Rau, Harpie."

"It's true, Father," Harpie answered him. "I was on their spaceship."

"Lying is a sin in the eyes of God, Harpie!"

"No Father, I—"

"I'm warning you, Harpie! You need to go to confession and say your penance. What you're saying about another planet being inhabited by humanoids is an insult to the Bible and the teachings of Jesus Christ."

"But Father Gallagher, I was born there and lived most of my life on Rau," Martha said.

"There is only one world, Martha, and that is this planet, Earth, the one God made in six days and rested on the seventh! Adam and Eve were the first humans he created; there is no world called Rau. It is merely a figment of your imagination."

"But, Father," Harpie replied, "if God made Earth in six days, maybe he made other worlds in six days too."

"You're bordering on blasphemy, Harpie!"

"But I was on their spaceship. I talked to the commander; I saw the passengers and the Robots. They are from Rau, and they're looking for a new home. They are immigrants just like the families you're harboring here."

"Blasphemy, Harpie. You're a blasphemer!" the priest shouted.

At his angry outburst, the immigrant children fearfully huddled about their parents, burrowing their heads into their mother's breasts or their father's shoulders, not knowing what made the priest—their rescuer—so angry. This strange country and its bizarre language only served to heighten their fears.

"Get down on your knees and say the entire rosary, and beg God's forgiveness for your blasphemy and lies!" the red-faced priest shrieked.

"But, Father," Harpie said, "if I did that knowing I was telling the truth about the Di and Rau, I would be lying to myself. That's another kind of lie, Father, and God doesn't like lies of any kind."

"You're trying to destroy the validity of the Bible and undo all the things Christianity has done for mankind for more than two thousand years. Since you will not fall on your knees and tell God you're sorry and beg his forgiveness, then you both must leave here! I will not shelter the devil's advocates in the house of the Lord. Now get out!"

With their new identities, they had safe air passage to New York City and then Albany, where they rented an apartment until June 4th. Then they rode the bus to lake Placid and hired a car to John Brown Farm State Historic Park. They toured the 244 acre facility once known as Timbucto and learned that was it intended to be a safe haven for runaway slaves during the Civil War, just as they were now fleeing imprisonment from the Place.

Later that evening the pair waited in the open meadowland just west of the historic site, and at exactly 10:00 p.m. they felt a warm gentle breeze.

"*Space Explorer* has landed," Martha excitedly said.

"Will these Robots know me?" Harpie asked.

"Yes. Once a Robot reads your retina's image, the info is transmitted to a universal database, much like the Social Security Administration recognizes your social security number when you access their system."

After they climbed aboard *Space Explorer,* a Robot scanned their retinas with its red binocular-like eyes and then led them down the blue LED-lit passageway to the commander's office. There, a multitude of the glass-covered coffins had opened, and a thousand immigrants prepared for a new life on Earth.

The commander's name was Robbie Eshwon, and he welcomed them aboard. Then the Robot quickly led them to side-by-side coffins, where they stripped naked and then inserted their feet into the recesses in the sides of their adjacent habitats and climbed aboard.

Harpie's heart pounded with anxiety about the trip and the loss of his family, yet he had to look. As he was putting one leg into the coffin, he turned toward Martha's habitat and caught a full frontal view of her nude body. She was beautiful, and was facing him, waiting for him to see her naked, and she smiled at him and then blew him a kiss.

"I'll see you in two weeks, Harpie."

He nodded and swallowed hard. Harpie wanted to linger and gaze at her beautiful form, but the mechanical man forced him to lie down. The Robot hooked Harpie up to the monitor and saw his rapid heart rate, and a moment later it expertly inserted a catheter into a vein in his left arm.

A few moments later Harpie blinked, and the last thing he remembered was a shiny metal skull with a pair of red protruding eyes peering down at him.

Harpie suddenly opened his eyes. The glass canopy above him gradually came into focus, but he was not afraid; a warm stream of air raised his body temperature. The glass top slowly opened, and he spied a Robot leaning over his habitat. It unbuckled the straps holding him in place and then removed the belt from around his hips and pulled the tube from his rectum. It then removed the catheter from his urethra, the jejunostomy feeding tube, the tabs connected to the muscle stimulation wires, and those monitoring his vital signs. The catheter in his left arm was disconnected last, and a few minutes later Harpie's mind cleared. The Robot helped him sit up. Then it inserted its feet into the recessed steps and effortlessly lifted him out of his habitat. Harpie stood on the deck on wobbly legs for a moment, and then the Robot bade him to sit in a chair next to Commander Eshwon.

"You will state your Earth wife's name and repeat three times, "I divorce you," the commander said via the Robot.

Harpie was shocked. "I don't want to divorce, Gloria. Catholics can't divorce according to the laws of the church."

"There are no Catholic laws in space, Harpie," Commander Eshwon replied. "On this ship I am the law, and I can assure you it will be a long and lonely voyage if you remain single!"

Harpie felt a gentle hand touch his shoulder.

"If you don't divorce Gloria," Martha said, "then you cannot make love for five years. You cannot even join a group marriage on this ship. When you get to Rau, you must then find and court another woman, but even then, you must still divorce your Earth wife.

"If you decide not to divorce Gloria, I must seek membership in the group marriage aboard this ship and mate with various companions who might find me attractive, Harpie. I don't want to do that because I've always been fond of you."

Harpie was floored by her remark. But then he became fully aware of her exposed breasts, which were mere inches from his face, and when he dropped his eyes and viewed the rest of her naked body, his penis hardened. He looked back up into her eyes as his face burned with embarrassment.

Martha smiled and said, "It's in the meds, Harpie—an aphrodisiac made from a unique fungus native to Rau. They give it to every male on board whether they're married or not, because after years in therapeutic hibernation, many men become impotent—use it or lose it.

"If you don't divorce your Earth wife, you can still go the bridal suite alone and masturbate for the next five years. They have all sorts of sex toys, vibrators, and lifelike dolls made of latex. Of course, when everyone on board sees you heading for the suite by yourself, they'll know what you'll be doing. Believe me when I tell you that you're heading for a very different world than Earth."

Their conversation wasn't confidential, and Harpie saw other couples holding hands as they headed toward the nuptial suites, and he noticed their smirking expressions as they passed.

They were all naked, and he flushed again and looked at Commander Eshwon, who merely shrugged and said, "The choice is up to you, but others who have chosen the single-person option become the saddest and loneliest people in the universe. Over time, you'll most joyfully divorce your Earth wife and join a group marriage."

Harpie though about his remarks for a few moments. *No real sex for almost five years?* he thought. Then he panicked when Commander Eshwon turned to shut down the marital database app on the computer.

Harpie blurted, "Gloria Colcek, I divorce you; I divorce you; I divorce you."

"Okay," the commander said. "Your verbal divorce decree is in the system. Now you can join a group marriage or marry an individual woman."

"I'll marry Martha," Harpie quickly replied and looked back up at her, but she merely folded her arms across her chest and averted his eyes. Harpie was puzzled and he looked at the commander and said, "What?"

"Well?" the commander said.

"Well what?" Harpie asked.

"Don't you think you should propose to her or something?" Commander Eshwon asked. "We may not be Earthlings, but on Rau we do harbor some very similar traditions."

"Oh. Well, yeah," Harpie said as he looked at Martha, who was still staring into the distance. "Martha Spiller," he asked on bended knee, "will you marry me?"

"Yes, I will marry you, Harpie Colcek," she cooed as he stood up and she threw her arms around him. "I can see you are embarrassed, but you'll get used to all this nakedness. After a while it will mean nothing to you, when you see everyone is undressed. There are simply not enough facilities on board to wash thousands of loads of laundry over such a long period of time. Nudity is the only practical solution, and we must be naked for the entire trip. But don't forget, the converters will keep the temperature at a comfortable seventy-two degrees in the marriage suites for the duration of our flight."

"Your proposal and her acceptance are now in the legal database," the commander said. "As the commander of the *Space Explorer* and by the power invested in me by the government of Rau, I now pronounce you husband and wife. You may kiss the bride, Harpie."

"The Robot has already started the timer," Martha said after they kissed. "Our twenty-four-hour honeymoon has twenty-three hours and fifty minutes left on the clock. When an alarm sounds, it means the lifeline computers that control all the functions of our habitats will be restarting, and we must return to therapeutic hibernation for another two weeks. If you miss the deadline, the computer shuts down the data needed to keep your personal habitat functioning, and you'll spend twenty days alone with the Robots. For food, you must manually mix and eat the same bland nutrients that flow through the feeding tubes. The diet is nourishing but tastes awful."

She seized his hand and they headed for their assigned bridal suite, but Harpie stopped momentarily and peered out one of the several portals they were passing; the stars were extremely large and amazingly bright. Harpie was unconscious when they'd begun the trip, and as he peered at the amazing universe outside the *Space Explorer*, it suddenly dawned on him where they actually were.

"Hey," he screeched, "we're in outer space!"

Everyone who heard his remark laughed and kept on walking.

"Yes," Martha replied and then embraced him. "The *Space Explorer* took off as soon as our habitats were occupied and sealed. After a few minutes, we broke free of Earth's gravitational field, and we are now hundreds of millions of miles from Earth, heading for the center of the Galaxy of the Milky Way."

Harpie's throat suddenly felt very dry and his head was spinning, but Martha's caress soon put him at ease. She again pulled him toward their temporary quarters. But he stopped once more at the last portal and peered out for a few moments to satisfy his intense curiosity.

For the first time ever, Harpie was able to gawk at the white dwarfs, giant reds, quarks, super-luminous supernovas, and magnetar stars. Their brilliant, swirling blues, oranges, greens, purples, magentas, reds, and other combinations of amazing colors emitted by the exploding novas were mesmerizing. Harpie had never seen such brilliance before; it was almost blinding.

A veteran traveler, who noticed Harpie's fascinated stare, peered out the portal with him. "Some of those heavenly orbs and odd-shaped galaxies, with their exploding spheres, are tens of thousands of times larger than the world we're leaving behind, my friend. Some are no longer in existence and haven't been for thousands of years, but their light waves and X-rays are still traveling through the universe and will continue on that journey for what is eternity to us mortals. Our converters on *Space Explorer* will absorb some of those photons and convert them into thrust.

"The red color, known as the redshift, has the longest length of all the light waves and provides the most energy. Perhaps one day it and all the other light colors will be absorbed by the crushing gravity of the black holes that are found throughout the universe, or they might fall victim to the pull of a supernova or such."

Harpie listened to his captivating tale until finally Martha said, "Let's go, Harpie; we're wasting time. You'll be surprised how quickly this one day out of twenty passes by."

As the months and years passed, Harpie was glad he took Martha's advice and married her. He was in love with her now, and the mind-shattering loneliness of the time and distance of space would have been unbearable without her love and companionship. Martha was also right about another thing too; the one day out of twenty they were allowed to be awake passed swiftly, and for the majority of that time they now clung to one another and made love multiple times.

At the end of every lightyear, they switched spaceships and spent two weeks aboard a major supply station. The respite turned into an annual honeymoon. The humungous MSSs were also heated by converters, but they were also full of warm and cool areas, and they were grateful to be fully clothed in the silk-like clothing that was designed for space travel. Life was wonderful again for them, and they were safe from prying eyes and their fear of the FBI and the Place.

Harpie's fascination with the passing universe had petered out; everything outside the *Space Explorer* now looked the same, but he never tired of seeing Martha's long, dark tresses or peering into her beautiful brown eyes. During their waking periods, they sometimes clung tenaciously to one another to endure the ungodly loneliness of their billion-mile journey. The memories of his former Earth life and his wife, Gloria, and their children, were fading with time and distance, although he never forgot them completely. However, he realized his dreams were merely reminiscences of the past, for his family was now hundreds of millions of miles away, living on a miniature planet he once knew as Earth.

CHAPTER
7

After traveling at the speed of light for almost four and a quarter Earth years, they landed on the planet Rau. Harpie was now fifty-eight years old and Martha was fifty-two.

Harpie stopped near the exit hatch, scared and shaking. "Where are we exactly, Martha?"

She drew him closer and felt his body trembling as she whispered, "Don't be frightened. It's safe here. This is where I was born."

"But where are we among the stars?" he asked as the other passengers filed past them.

She gently grasped his head between her hands and softly answered, "We are still in the Milky Way, on an exoplanet in the constellation known on Earth as Centaurus. Earthlings call it Proxima b, but my people, the Di, call it Rau; we talked about all of this, Harpie; remember?"

As they exited the spacecraft, he looked up and exclaimed, "Rau has three suns!"

"No, those are our moons, and they're always visible."

Martha chuckled when he said, "But it's daytime, so how come the moons are out now? And how come you told me Rau had five moons?"

"It is eternally daylight here, since Rau doesn't rotate on its axis. As for those moons, I wanted to save some surprises for you. We used to have five moons. Then a huge asteroid struck one of the moons we called Lia, and the resultant explosion also destroyed Tia. We called them the Two Sisters, since they were about the same size and looked as though they were side by side. The results of the impact caused terrible rauquakes and floods, and a devastating dust cloud blocked out the sun for almost nine months.

"Millions of Di drowned in the floods or were swallowed up in the rauquakes. Some were crushed by falling buildings or buried beneath the huge mountain ranges that collapsed, while others seemed to suddenly erupt from nowhere. The cataclysm isolated millions from the rest of the planet; the temperature dropped to less than forty degrees Fahrenheit, and millions of our young and elderly died from hypothermia or starvation. When the dust cloud finally disappeared, we discovered that our population had dwindled from about three billion Di to fewer than two billion."

"When did that happen?"

"A millennium ago. Rau has not yet fully recovered. Millions of acres of land are still not arable or are buried beneath the ruins of our collapsed mountain ranges."

Harpie felt somewhat relieved upon hearing the asteroid struck a thousand years ago. "Well, your moons look a little dull compared to Earth's full moon at night."

"That's because Rau's sun has only about fourteen percent of the mass of Earth's sun and is only fifty-five percent as hot. Earth's sun is about ninety-three millions miles from the planet; our sun is only five percent of that distance. Although your sun is hotter, our sun's close proximity keeps our temperature in a range of about eighty-six to one-hundred-four degrees Fahrenheit on one side of the planet."

"What?" Harpie asked.

"Rau does not rotate on its axis; it's locked. It's just like your moon is to the earth—the same side of Rau always faces the sun, because one axial rotation of Rau is equal to one orbit around the sun. The same is true of the moons. The same sides of the moons always face Rau, just as the same side of Rau always faces Proxima Centauri, our sun."

"And so?" Harpie asked.

"The part of Rau that faces the sun is eternally light and warm; the other side is perpetually dark and frozen. Rau is one and a third times larger than Earth. However, it has no axial tilt, so we have no seasons. Our sun is slowly dying, and ice is beginning to form at the poles, like those on Earth. We never had that happen until about a century ago." What she was saying was hard to believe, and then she said, "Now turn around and look at our sun, Harpie!"

Harpie did and his jaw dropped. "It's so huge."

"It appears to be ten times larger than Earth's sun," she said. "Earth is approximately ninety-three million miles from its sun, but Rau is only four million, six hundred thousand miles from our sun, which the Pi calls Proxima Centauri. That's why it appears to be so large, but it's also much cooler than Earth's sun, because it is a red dwarf star."

Harpie was so awestruck by her knowledge that he blurted out, "How come you know so much about the stars and planets?"

"When I lived on Rau years ago, I was an astrophysicist," she replied. Harpie's jaw dropped; "what!" he exclaimed.

She only smiled and then said, "Near as our scientists can figure, in about two hundred years, life on Rau will become unbearable for the Di, and already the temperature is slowly cooling. In about two Earth centuries, crops grown in our fields will begin to fail, as the sun cools even further, and the wind, which is caused by the sun warming the ground, will cease to blow. Right now it drifts from the warm side of Rau to the cold side, but its speed is slowing.

"The border between the warm and cold sides, known as the ring, is where the wealthy live. It is eternally dawn and sunset there, and the weather is the most Earthlike because of the drifting wind, which makes it the most habitable part of Rau. Of course, it's also the most expensive place to live and is also why many of the Di chooses to emigrate to Earth. You have days and nights there, so the people can live virtually anywhere on the planet, which makes Earth a rather unique place in the universe.

"Centuries from now all our lakes, rivers, and seas on the warm side of Rau will chill and then begin to freeze and the planet will become uninhabitable. The entire process may take eons, but Rau is destined to become a black dwarf star, and all life here will cease to exist, just as it will happen on Earth someday. But don't worry, Harpie, you and I will be long dead before all that happens."

Harpie was too stunned to say anything. *An astrophysicist*, he mused. *I'm married to genius!*

"This cooling has already happened to many other planets in the galaxy of the Milky Way," she continued, "and we know this thanks to the Di heroes who spend their entire lives in space. For trips to more distant galaxies, whose time travels exceed the lifespan of the Di, we invented super-Intelligent computers and Robots. They pilot those spaceships that explore distant planets and mine the minerals on those distant stars that are not found on either Rau or Earth."

The thought of Earth and Rau dying was horrifying to Harpie, and he thought about his family and quickly changed the subject. "What do you call the moons?"

"The big one we call the moon, just like on Earth. The one in the middle is known as the Little Sister, because she was smaller than the two that were destroyed by the asteroid. As you can see, the third moon is bigger than Little Sister, and we call it Big Brother. When we finish breakfast, I'll drive you downtown to solve your language problem and show you our urban farms."

"Urban farms?"

Martha smiled and said, "You'll see."

They watched a super large tractor tow *Star Lighter* away. It was their last shuttle ride, and Harpie suddenly felt alone; his only means of returning to Earth was being taken to an unknown destination, and Martha sensed his alarm.

"After every voyage, the spacecraft is inspected, repaired, and remodeled on the inside, and updated with the latest technology. The outside will be inspected to see if it needs to be repaired, but the beads will remain untouched. They are made of glass and can last for as long as a million years. Even the Robots must be inspected and repaired if needed, and their programing will also be updated, so *Star Lighter* will be available for another voyage within a year."

The information made Harpie feel better.

They spent the night in the quarters specifically meant for those departing from or arriving on Rau; everything in the hotel was so very Earthlike to Harpie. Even the restaurant she chose for breakfast proved to be like Earth's, including the booths and tables, and when he scanned the menu, Harpie decided to order two goobers, which Martha told him were equivalent to chicken eggs on Earth.

"I wouldn't order two though," she said. "The chickens that produced them have been genetically bred and fed, and they're almost as large as the emus in Australia, so their eggs are very large."

When his order arrived, Harpie was amazed at the size of the egg. The yolk was the size of a saucer, and the egg white covered the rest of the plate. The toast looked like white bread but tasted much different.

"The bread is made from genetically engineered grains and is very nutritious," Martha said when she noticed his inquisitive expression. She smiled and said, "You'll get used to the food, honey."

He turned his nose up some of the other foodstuffs that came with the meal, because the way they were prepared looked so foreign to him, although those that he did sample were rather tasty. Then, he learned from Martha that all the crops were organically grown.

"They have to be. Our scientists have concluded that our civilization is more than fifty-five-thousand years old, and since all the crops we grow are not native to Rau, we concluded that the earliest Di settlers migrated from another planet. We have no idea which one, although they must have brought the seeds and plants with them.

"While the soil was still pristine and agricultural production peaked, Rau's population exploded much like Earth is experiencing right now, with the influx of the Di and its own horrific birth rate. Famine soon spread throughout the planet, and we turned to chemicals to increase production. However, the fertilizers poisoned the soil over the centuries. We didn't know at the time that our sun was slowly dying, and its ultraviolet rays, which plants need to grow, was nonexistent. However, our agricultural science kept increasing productivity by artificial means, and we were able to feed more people, but again it caused the population growth to spiral out of control. We had to initiate stringent birth control measures to prevent food shortages and starvation, which included tubal ligation or vasectomies at a child's birth in order for the race to survive."

Everything was so confusing for Harpie; however, Martha managed to explain things to him in English.

"What do you call your native language?" he asked.

"I've told you a hundred times, Harpie: Stritz," she said and laughed. "You Earthlings don't have very good memories, do you?"

Harpie laughed, since he knew she was smarter than he was.

"After breakfast," she said, "I'll solve the language problem for you."

"Oh, yeah—Stritz—that's right; and you're going to solve my language problem just like that?" Harpie asked.

"Yes," she said, and although he still looked skeptical, she smiled again and almost whispered, "You'll see, sweetie."

"What other languages are spoken on Rau besides Stritz?"

"None. There is only one universal language."

"What? Almost two billion people live on Rau, and they all speak the same language?"

"Yes. According to our history books, after the apocalypse, the nations on Rau formed a confederation and created a universal language. The elderly had a terrible time learning the new words that were composed of excerpts of all the tongues on Rau, but the children thrived on it. It made life and travel so much easier."

"That's unbelievable," Harpie said.

"Yes, it is. Since then, knowledge from one culture was rapidly incorporated into another, and we made significant advances in medicine, health, and mutual understanding. We have not had a war on Rau in more than five hundred years. Believe it or not, the asteroid catastrophe that struck us millennia ago helped to unite the planet. It was a matter of survival for us all."

"That's amazing," Harpie said.

"Yes, it is, when compared to Earth's wars. We have no large standing armies; there are no guns; no warships; and no bombers and fighter aircraft. A lot of our routine police patrols are done by Robots that are armed with lasers. There is no police brutality, since the Robots have no emotions and everyone is treated the same. The most sophisticated Robots are programmed to perform surgeries, and some others are designed to do the more mundane tasks such as cooking, cleaning, and doing the laundry—if you can afford one."

"That's hard to believe." Harpie gasped. "Robots doing surgery?" A few diners turned their heads at the sound of his strange language.

"How many countries are there on Rau?"

"Just one," she replied.

Harpie seemed skeptical.

"By international agreement, all the cultures remained intact along with their borders," she continued without him interrupting, "except for the language, and by global agreement, all the countries became provinces under the confederation.

"If you want to run for public office, you must register with the Political Action Committee and get a predetermined number of signatures. There are no political parties. As determined by law, every candidate running for office receives equal media time on TV, audio, and the newspapers, free of charge; no one needs to raise money. The numbers of candidates are limited, and the first several candidates to get the proper number of signatures are on the ballot. This gives the poor as well as the rich an equal chance of being elected, and the number of wealthy citizens serving in the government has dropped dramatically.

"There is a government in place in each province that is known as the Lower House and Lower Senate, a president, and a Lower Case court system. They are subject to the rule of the Supreme Federation, which equates to the United Nations on Earth.

"It is composed of a Supreme Senate and a Supreme House, which are composed of members from every province on Rau, and they are nominated and voted in by the people of each such jurisdiction, and they make international laws.

"The Supreme House has representatives from each province, and the number of representatives depends upon their population-just like your country on Earth. They are limited to six two-year terms. The Supreme Senate has two senators from each province, and terms are limited to two six-year periods. There is a Supreme Executive branch too, and the president has a powerful advisory staff composed of one member from each province. The president is limited to two three-year terms. We also have a Supreme Court system that interprets the law and serves the same length of terms and receives the same salary as a Supreme Senator, and each justice is subject to the same rules as everyone else in the government.

"Any politician convicted of a crime at any level of the government is banned from politics for life and a prison sentence is mandatory. The length of incarceration depends on the nature of the crime. There's no such thing as lobbyists on Rau either, thus corruption is kept to a minimum, and any citizen who is convicted of trying to influence the vote of any member of the government by a bribe of any sort is subject to five years imprisonment for each offense. The same punishment is administered for any politician involved in the plot.

"Political figures are elected to serve the people, not the other way around, as is now being done on Earth, and once a politician reaches their term limits, they can never again serve in any capacity in the government. Unlike the American congress and the other Earth governments, the rules of conduct, salaries, and medical and dental benefits are the same as the benefits for the populations at large and last only for as long as they are in office. Then they must get a job or continue the career they had before being elected to public office.

"There are no dictators allowed in any province on Rau. When we got rid of all the dictators, all wars ceased, and as I said, we haven't had a war in five hundred years."

"I wish all that were true of our governments on Earth," Harpie said.

"Yes, but on Rau, the government has been in place for almost eight hundred years."

Harpie looked around the restaurant as he picked up his breakfast fruit drink that was as common as coffee and tea on Earth, and he realized something seemed amiss. "What other races are there on Rau besides the white race?"

"None. And there is no white race."

"Well, your skin always looked just a wee bit tanned," Harpie said as he laughed, "but you are definitely white."

"No. Ever since our Armageddon the Di has intermarried, because there was either a shortage of men or women in every province. All the races that survived are now mixed. Therefore, we have no racial prejudice by a majority race and no minority leaders stirring up trouble to keep them wealthy and in power. Earth is still evolving in that respect."

"I kind of like Rau's idea on that matter," Harpie replied.

When they finished eating, Martha asked him, "Are you ready to go?"

"Go where?" Harpie asked.

"First I'll inquire about a house for us to live in, and then we'll go to the licensing bureau."

"For my driver's license?" Harpie asked.

"No," she said and then laughed. "For your general license."

"My general license?"

"I'll explain it in a few minutes." Martha reached out and lifted a strange-looking instrument hanging from an ornate hook on the wall.

Harpie thought it was part of the restaurant's décor. It looked like a pair of old-fashioned opera-house glasses with a beaded chain attached to a hook. She put the lenses to her eyes and Harpie heard a distinct beep.

"Okay," she said, "we can go now." She stood up to leave.

"We didn't pay," Harpie said.

"I just did," she replied. "I used the homer."

"The what?"

She sat back down. "I keep forgetting you have never lived on Rau before, and I'm sorry. On Rau there is no need for money or credit cards of any kind. Everything is done by debits and credits via a homer.

"Look," she said as she seized the homer again, "when I put the homer to my eyes and press this button on the handle, it scans my retinas and sends the data to the Central Financial Agency here in the Megapolis. When it recognizes my retinas, it pays the tab punched in by the waiter or waitress and adds a tip, which means credits for the restaurant, a ten percent tip for the waitress or waiter, and debits for me. Retina scans are as accurate as fingerprints.

"While I am searching for a job, the CFA tracks on my expenses, and when I start working again it eventually uses my work credits to pay my bills. No money is exchanged, just debits and credits."

"What gives you an incentive to get a job and go to work every day then?"

"Well, of course it's the debits and credits, but we discovered ages ago that the menial tasks can be done by the poor and uneducated Di or a Robot," she said. "And since the destitute have always been with us and always will be, they will do the unskilled jobs a live Di was meant to do.

"On the other hand, an Intelligent Di, without an advanced education degree, as well as an educated Di, will gravitate to a job they love to do, and they eventually must find one, because they know they owe debits. However, once they find what they like, they stick with that chosen profession because they love it, and they derive a great deal of personal satisfaction from it because they're good at what they do.

"They work long hours and pile up millions of credits, some of which they donate to help the destitute and disabled. Their incentive is love of their occupation and not money, and no one gets bombarded by requests for credits from charities. Believe me, it took a long time for us to adjust to that kind of lifestyle, but in the long run it works well.

"Parts of all earned credits are taxed and go to run the government, social programs, and research, but that levy is relatively cheap since we have no enormous military expenses or huge political salaries or retirement benefits to pay.

"Another benefit of our credit system is that no one can steal your identity, because the retina scans are unique to each individual. Therefore, unlike Earth, there is no need for credit cards, no money to be stolen from you, no scams on your computer, no need for PINs or passwords, and Robots are programmed to be CPAs and are available to everyone as financial consultants. Laws have also been enacted so the elderly don't get ripped off by unscrupulous salespeople.

"Other than credit, crime on Rau is almost nonexistent; there are no banks to Rob; most of the criminals are the ones who steal credits. They're not arrested unless they steal by threatening a victim's life and force them to look into a homer and transfer credits to a particular account. That is a capital crime, and these people are prosecuted and sent to work in the mines on another planet. The nonviolent felons become credit slaves.

"A criminal, via their retina scans, becomes restricted to the bare essentials, such as food, water, and a minimal amount of clothing. They must report to a probation Robot for nine of the ten-day Rau week, where they do menial tasks until every credit they have stolen is repaid, including a hefty credit fine. There are very few repeat offenders.

"The credit system has also wiped out the need for life insurance and saves the public from having to deal with the big insurance companies that used to steal billions of credits from them by not paying out legitimate death claims.

"The Requiem Agency handles all funeral costs, which is funded by a small levy on all earned credits, and there are no expensive funerals; all the bodies are cremated because cemeteries take up too much space on Rau.

"There is also no need for medical insurance. Any Di can be treated at any medical facility they choose. It takes some of your credits, but everyone pays the same flat rate, whether it is to treat an illness or to undergo surgery, and there are no copays or out-of-pocket expenses either."

"What about sex crimes?" he asked.

"Sexual assault is almost unknown here, Harpie," she answered. "Although it's rare, those who are convicted of such violent felonies, such as murder or rape, are banished to a remote but habitable planet for life. Rapists are castrated. Men go to one planet and the women to another. Robot guards run the prisons there and are in everyday contact with the inmates, and they cannot be bribed or killed. There are no visitors, drugs, or alcohol either."

"Sounds like hell," Harpie said.

"It practically is. The prisoners slave in the mines to provide minerals needed by the good folks that still live on Rau. Life is harsh on those remote planets, and some prisoners die within the first five years. Those who survive the mining ordeal never return to a life of crime. The violent felons, who receive life sentences, know what banishment to the mines mean and most prefer to be euthanized; it's the cheapest way out for the government too.

"If a citizen wants to have sex, they can go to what we call a 'comfort house'; it's legal. There patrons scan in with a homer that brings up their medical records to determine whether they are free of sexually transmitted diseases. The comfort men and women must update their health status every single day and undergo a monthly medical exam by a qualified doctor and body fluid specimens are taken daily prevent the spread of STDs and to ensure the public's trust.

"A comfort man or woman who cannot pass the health tests has their licenses revoked immediately. Their names are removed from the homer scanner until the problem is taken care of by a qualified physician. Then and only then can their license be reinstated. If you are a patron, but your medical record indicates you have a sexually transmittable disease or are a wanted criminal, you can't even get into a comfort house.

"If you pass the medical records test, then you can choose a comfort woman or a comfort man, and you must scan the homer to give the comfort people credits, which they must share with the licensed comfort home owner."

"How has that all worked out?"

"Not well in some cases," Martha said. "Cheaters get caught when their spouse scans their daily credit and debit reports, since it identifies the specific comfort house involved, the date, and time. There are as many female cheaters as male cheaters. That report is enough to dissolve a marriage instantly in court. It can be a real mess, especially where children are involved."

"I'll bet," Harpie said. "Just like on Earth."

Then she said, "Anyway, FYI, every city block has cameras to monitor what goes on twenty-four-seven, and Di policemen and policewomen monitor them and can dispatch a Robot cop in seconds. You can't outrun a Robot cop; they can run at speeds up to fifty miles an hour for at least a hundred Earth miles, and they can lock their lasers on to a fleeing suspect and zap the nerves in their spine; it paralyzes the criminals for a period of up to several days or weeks, depending on their physical condition."

"Are the actions of Robot cops ever investigated?"

"A review of the incident is made and a software change may be initiated if necessary."

"Are there car chases here?"

"If the suspect manages to get into an autocar," she replied, "the Robot cop simply flips a switch on the laser gun, points it at the car, and fires. A hidden transceiver detects the signal and shuts down the inductor, and the car is brought to a standstill; the doors lock automatically and alert the Rau police dispatcher. When the Robot cop signals the dispatcher that he is at the felon's auto, the dispatcher taps in an arcane code peculiar to each autocar and the left door pops open. So far no one has ever evaded or escaped from a Robot cop, at least as far as I know.

"The Robot cops don't get a salary or receive any benefits, and they patrol until their parts wear out. When that happens, each Robot has a data bank that assesses its performance and signals a dispatcher that a particular cop is no longer fully functional. The mechanical cop is then summoned to headquarters and 'decommissioned' after transferring all its stored data concerning its beat, the local registered felons, and such to a new Robot cop. Then the worn-out Robot is unceremoniously retired to the junk pile. The parts are eventually recycled and a new robot cop is created."

As they left the restaurant, Martha walked over to a small kiosk-like structure and pulled a compact pouch off the rack. "Whenever the sun flares, it ejects electrons and protons at super high speeds and temperatures," she said. "These flares are known as the solar wind. They can be lethal on Rau and cause cancers that cannot be controlled or cured by modern medicine.

"When the proton and electrons of the solar wind become dangerously high, monitor satellites that orbit Rau detect them and activate the sirens in every city and town on Rau and alert TV and radio stations. The sound is three loud blasts that continue for five minutes; you must immediately open this pouch and don the solar suit. There are many of these kiosks around the city, but it is a smart idea to carry a suit with you—it saves time spent searching for a stand, and sometimes there are no outfits left by the time you get there; time of exposure is very important."

Harpie shook his head and thought, *There's so much to learn about Rau*. He looked up and noticed strange flying machines leaving multiple vapor trails as they crisscrossed the sky above the city, and he stopped. "What are those things?"

"Those are private autoplanes," she replied.

"They don't have wings, and they're not making any sound."

"They don't need any wings, just tailfins. They're rocket propelled and fueled by hydrogen. The engine extracts hydrogen from the air when the atmospheric moisture condenses on to a series of metal plates that are negative and positive electrodes. The resulting effect, known as electrolysis, separates the water molecules into hydrogen and oxygen. These gases are then stored in separate metal tanks.

"When these two gasses are again forced into the firing chamber, an oxidizer—an igniter—is introduced, and the resulting explosion generates a tremendous amount of energy. The two gasses change back into an extremely hot and rapidly expanding water vapor that escapes from the rear engine nozzle and propels the craft. That's why you see so many vapor trails. Those condensation trails replenish the moisture in the atmosphere so it can be reused by other aircraft. A similar method is used to break down the oxygen from our exhalations in our spacecraft. We literally break the oxygen molecule away from the carbon one-just like a tree does and then breathe the recycled oxygen. To preserve water, heat is used to vaporize the water from our body fluids, and then a series of filters are used to remove any solids-and presto you have purified drinking water or water for the food from the feeding tubes in our habitats."

"You seem to know a lot about everything," Harpie said. "It's almost embarrassing for a man."

"I grew up with it,' she said and then laughed. "My father was a mechanical engineer. On Earth, men build all sorts of cars or airplanes as a hobby. My dad built homemade rocket planes-that was his hobby. When you grow up around someone like my dad, you tend to learn a lot."

"Wait a minute," Harpie said. "How come I can't hear the sounds the engine makes when the igniter is introduced into the firing chamber?"

"Because the thrusters are lined with echo chambers that are connected to one another by a series of channels, the echoes cancel each other out. When the autoplane reaches its destination, the computer signals the engine to shut off the back nozzle and open a nozzle in the front to reverse the forward momentum; that slows the aircraft down until it stops it in midair above the designated landing site. The computer then completely closes the front nozzle and pressurizes the lateral nozzles located on the underside of the fuselage, and they safely lower the rocket to the ground. At the same time it extends several large spring-loaded landing legs to cushion the landing."

Harpie waited a few moments longer, transfixed by the wingless aircraft silently soaring through the cloudless sky. Some looked as though they were mere yards apart. Other Di looked up to see what Harpie was staring at and then smirked and kept walking.

"Who is flying those rockets?" Harpie asked.

"Multimillioncreditaires," she replied. "You could fly them too, since you will have your general license; but they're not flown by a Di. They're totally controlled by onboard and air traffic control computers. All you have to do is get in and input your destination into the computer and away you go."

Again, Martha could tell Harpie was enchanted by it all, and she was delighted. *I hope he'll stay for good*, she thought and smiled. But she knew he might find the advanced technology too intimidating, and might return to Earth. In fact, she knew Harpie had retained some of his earthly possessions.

From the restaurant, they walked another half a block to an entrance. "Are we taking a subway?" he asked.

"No, there are no subways, buses, or passenger trains on Rau. For trips of just a few hundred blocks or so, you can take an autocar and utilize the local streets. If you're going any farther, such as across town or to another nearby province, you can take an autocar and use the Fastway.

"To go to distant provinces, you must take the autoshuttle plane, which is akin to Earth's airlines. Those aircraft are usually flown by Robots, but intercontinental flights are manned by Di pilots."

Harpie was too flabbergasted to say or ask anything. When they got to the bottom of the steps, he discovered a vast open expanse of underground roadway and got his first glimpse of what Martha called an autocar.

"This can't be your car," he said. "You were on Earth too long."

"No, it is not mine. No one on Rau owns an autocar. They belong to the people. You just pick out an available autocar, identify yourself with its homer, and bingo, you can be on your way.

"When you get to your destination and want to return, you again pick any available autocar, and presto, you have a ride home. There's no such thing as stealing a car and no insurance to pay. All the cars are insured by the manufacturer and the government. If an accident does occur, which is extremely rare, the government has set rates to pay the victims or their families, so no greedy or crooked lawyers are involved."

Masses of autocars were parked on each side of the roadway. They came in a variety of colors and all had an upper glass dome, hinged down the middle. Both sides lifted up after Martha opened a small compartment and peered into the homer. The bottom half was made of metal and a small door opened on each side so they could enter, but Harpie refused to get in.

"Where are the wheels?"

"The autocar doesn't need any. It rides on a cushion of air. The lift is provided by four rapidly spinning multi-bladed fans, and a pulse-timer inside the inducer signals the buried power grid when and where to move the autocar forward."

They got in. The dome closed and the metal doors shut.

"We're taking a two-seater, because it takes fewer credits than a family sized autocar," she said. "We're heading for the General Licensing Bureau. It's about a two-hour ride."

"How far away is it?"

"About six hundred Earth miles," she said.

"Are you telling me that you're going to drive six hundred miles in two hours—in city traffic, no less?"

"No, I'm not driving, and we're going to take the Fastway."

He looked at her. "Well, I can tell you I'm not driving!"

She laughed and said, "You'll see."

"Just how big is the Megapolis?"

"Twelve-hundred miles across."

Again, Harpie was amazed. "A city twelve-hundred miles across?" he asked incredulously.

She only nodded and smiled, and then tapped in an esoteric code in Stritz, and the vehicle lifted up off the roadway and started forward.

Harpie cringed. There was no steering wheel, no brake pedal, no ignition, no turn signals, no seatbelts, and no white or yellow lines on the road. He didn't see any traffic lights either; it was frightening.

"How come I can't hear the motor running?"

"It's an electric motor," Martha said.

"This car runs on batteries?"

"No. There are super-high voltage and amperage cables buried beneath the road's surface, and that inducer I was telling you about is mounted beneath the car and absorbs the electromagnetic radiation, which powers the electric motors for the lifting fans. The electrons radiating from the high voltage cable magnetizes the inducer, and as the current moves along the cable it moves the autocar with it.

"The glass dome and the titanium-plus metal are super dense to protect our central and peripheral nervous systems from any damage that could result from the impinging electromagnetic waves from the cable. They also protect us from the stellar and solar winds, so you don't need a solar suit while you're inside the car."

"How come the electromagnetic waves embedded in the roadway didn't hurt us as we walked to the autocar?"

"Because the induced magnetic waves are not activated until someone activates a homer on the car, gets in, and closes the doors."

"What happens if I walk toward a car that someone else has gotten into and the doors close?"

"The electromagnetic waves are only activated in the area directly below the inducer, and no place else," she answered.

Harpie was so amazed that he could only stare at her as the car began moving. "How fast are we going now?"

She looked at the dashboard. "About the equivalent of seventy-five Earth miles per hour; that's the speed limit on city streets."

Suddenly it appeared—a vehicle heading at them at a high rate of speed; they were going to be T-boned, and it was too late!

Harpie slammed his right foot down on the nonexistent brake pedal, and his hands reached out to grasp the imaginary steering wheel, to no avail! His face turned ashen, and his heartbeat pulsed in his throat while his feet pushed him harder against the seat; his mouth was agape in terror.

The vehicle missed them by mere inches! "Relax, honey," Martha said as she squeezed his arm. "The computer's driving the car."

"But that car almost crashed into us!" he shrieked.

"No, sweetie," she said. "Do you see those poles with the small flashing lights? They're sensors that are connected to the Centralized Traffic Computer that measures the speed and distances between us and the cross traffic. It can handle trillions of bits of data per second, and thus keeps a minimal distance between us, the cross-traffic, and the car in front of us.

"Once our car's in motion, it won't stop or slow down until it gets to the destination I entered in its computer. That's why we don't need traffic lights or traffic Robots, and there's no such thing as a speeding or parking ticket in the Megapolis either."

Harpie was still ashen, and sweat ran down his face. Martha smiled and leaned over and hugged and kissed him. "Do you see that tunnel entrance coming up there?"

He was still too frightened to answer.

"That's the Fastway entrance," she said.

When the induction cables beneath the roadway ended, the car coasted the few remaining feet into the Fastway tunnel, and Harpie felt his body press hard against the back of the seat.

"We're now traveling at three hundred miles per hour," Martha said. "That's how we'll make the Central Licensing Center in about two hours."

"What motor are we using now?"

"None. The autocar fits snugly into the tunnel, and at every one-and-a-half mile interval there is a solar-powered electric motor with a powerful multi-bladed fan sucking all the air out of the tunnel; we're actually traveling in a vacuum tube that's buried underground. It's a giant-sized version of the vacuum cleaner hose used on Earth.

"By the way, if you have to pee, there's a relief tube beneath the dashboard. The one with the narrow elongated cup is for a man. After you stick your penis inside, you have to squeeze the tube shut to prevent back splatter. It's a one-size-fits-all cup. The other with the small reservoir attached is obviously for a woman. She pushes it up against her vagina and holds it in place until she's done."

"Isn't a public relief tube rather unsanitary? I mean, you don't know who used it before you and whether they had any kind of disease."

"No," she replied. "Look again and you'll notice the head of the tube is housed in a metal box with a door. The line is connected to the inducer, which gets extremely hot and works in several cycles. After you finish urinating, return the cup, and close the door, a red LED light comes on to indicate that the hose and the head are being sanitized. The inducer vaporizes the urine and forces it back into the tube and cup to sanitize them. When the vapor cools it drains back into the inducer, where it is vaporized again and blown out through the exhaust vent into the atmosphere."

"Well," Harpie said, "it still sounds unsanitary to me."

"Not so much so if you remember your history lessons," she replied. "Before the advent of modern medicine, fresh urine was used as an antiseptic on the battlefields of Earth and ancient Rau."

Harpie knew she was right and didn't know what to say.

"If you need to make an unscheduled stop for any reason," she continued, "you simply punch in the desired exit number on the dashboard screen and the computer will steer your car off the Fastway and onto the local street where you want to get off."

As they sped along, the only thing he could see were the flashing white sides of the tunnel that seemed to be pressing against them, and he swallowed hard when he realized their autocar was rapidly closing the distance with the car ahead. His right foot again searched for the invisible brake pedal in an attempt to slow down the autocar. Martha saw his reaction and smiled. Then he twisted around in the seat and saw another autocar about twenty feet behind them, and he abruptly turned back and stared at Martha, who seemed totally unconcerned.

"This is nothing," she said to reassure him. "During heavy traffic, the autocars are literally bumper to bumper at three hundred miles per hour."

"Do you ever have accidents in here?" he asked rather timidly.

"No. Obviously, there are no passing zones either, so we have no road rage. Whenever there's a malfunction in the giant motors or fans, or the computer detects a software problem, all the autocars slow down to the same speed at the same time but keep moving. Usually it takes less than a few seconds for the computer to locate a software problem and correct it, and presto, you're back up to top speed again.

"If there's a hardware problem, we maintain the lower speed in that section, but we still have enough momentum to get past the downed suction link in a matter of seconds. The spare hardware parts are plug-in types and are mounted on flatcars located at various intervals along the outside of the tunnel. It takes less than half an hour to replace them."

They rode in silence for a few minutes, and Harpie noticed that the glass dome of the autocar ahead of them had suddenly turned dark.

"It's for privacy," she said before he could ask her what happened. "Kind of a boring view isn't it?"

"Yeah. After a while, looking at the sides of the vacuum tunnel is kinda like looking at the stars from a portal of the spaceship. Wanna listen to the music channel?"

"No," she said. "I have a better idea."

She reached out and touched something Harpie couldn't see, but suddenly the back of their seats collapsed and the glass dome turned opaque, and he laid there astonished while she pulled off her skirt and panties and flung them to the side. He was both amazed and mortified, and he sat up to make sure no one in front of or behind them could see into the autocar, but the darkened glass obscured everything.

"I never had sex in a vehicle that is moving at three hundred miles an hour with no one driving!" he screeched.

"Oh, and you never joined the mile-high club when you were back on Earth?" she cooed.

"No," he anxiously replied.

"Well I'm gonna take your mind off all your concerns, Harpie," she said to tease him, "and you'll be joining the three-hundred-mile-an-hour autocar club on Rau, honey, and very soon."

A few minutes later Harpie forgot the autocar was moving at three hundred miles per hour and that no one was driving.

"Yes," he finally agreed as he rolled on top of her, "this is far more interesting and pleasant than listening to a music channel."

CHAPTER
8

When they got to Central License processing, they abandoned the car where it stopped in the parking lot. "It's okay," Martha assured him after he asked how they park the autocar.

"I set the timer on the parking app. After the doors are closed for several moments, the car will automatically search for an empty parking spot."

The entrance to the building had no doors, and after they entered, Harpie sat before a voice-actuated computer, and Martha tapped a nondescript icon on the touchscreen for him.

"That will convert English into Stritz," she explained.

When it came to the question of his marital status, and he answered yes, the digitized voice said, "Your spouse must now look into the homer." Martha did.

"Now the applicant must look into the homer," the voice commanded him, and Harpie complied. He heard a beep, and the digitized voice said, "You will now report to the west side of the license processing building for driver training."

"When Commander Eshwon married us," Martha said, "all that personal information he asked you for was transmitted to the Civil Intelligence Bureau. The General Licensing Center computer then cross-referenced that info you just gave it and got a match. If you weren't married to me, that Robot cop over there would be escorting you to police headquarters, where a Di officer would be questioning you about your legal status here."

"You mean you get illegal aliens here on Rau too?"

"Yes. The Di who visit us from other provinces and run up foreign deficits must be authorized by their home province. Once a debit link has been established to their account via a homer, they must look into it again and press the button to pay the bill. That interval is when they leave the establishment without paying, and they can cheat that way for days or months at a time. But soon or later they get caught, and the penalties are harsh."

Harpie followed the instructions in his driver training class, and an hour later the Di instructor said, "You are now a licensed driver and flyer."

Harpie looked at the Robot cop, but it didn't say anything else, so he asked Martha, "Where's my license, and how much does it cost?"

"It's in your head, Harpie," she said and then giggled. "Or rather, in your eyes. If a Robot cop stops you, it scans your retinas and within seconds knows everything about you, including if you are a licensed driver, a legal resident, and if you have any outstanding arrest warrants. The province can afford to pay for your license because the Robot cop instructors and patrolmen don't get a salary or benefits. Oh, by the way, you're a legal resident now because you're married to me, a Di person."

"That's unbelievable," Harpie murmured. They walked out of the licensing center and found an autocar parked nearby.

"Wanna drive?" she asked and laughed.

"The computer drives," he said and put his eyes up to the homer anyway; the glass dome lifted its sides up, and the metallic doors popped open. Harpie was delighted.

Martha gave him the common Stritz code to input and said, "Now, we're going to solve your language problem, Harpie."

The car zoomed down the roadway, and soon they were again zipping down the Fastway.

"Where are we going now?"

"The Megamall," she replied.

Twenty minutes later the car dropped them off at the entrance to the mall, and before they got out of the autocar, Martha tapped in another code. A few moments after they walked away the empty car drove through the garage until it located a vacant parking spot.

The mall was so gargantuan that it was almost impossible to walk and find what you were looking for in a timely manner, and Martha led him to where the electric carts were assembled. The service was free, so there was no homer on the cart. After they climbed aboard, she opened up a computer app on the screen and scrolled down until she found the list of electronics stores. Then she touched the screen again, and the metal seat belts encased their torsos and the driverless cart took off and roared up to fifty miles per hour. Five minutes later it came to a smooth stop in front of a sprawling outlet store.

"We need a conversion helmet," Martha told the young Di clerk in Stritz, and he showed them several models.

"These are similar to the ones commanders Assan and Eshwon use," Harpie said.

"Yes, but these are not nearly as sophisticated; try this on."

She said something to the clerk, and he reached below the counter and retrieved his own conversion helmet. "Ask him—in English— how much it costs," she told Harpie.

He looked incredulously at her but then asked the clerk in English, "How much does this conversion helmet cost?"

The youth replied in Stritz, and Harpie looked at Martha and shrugged, but then he distinctly heard a digitized voice inside the helmet answer, "Thirty-five hundred credits for item number 6303," and his jaw dropped.

Martha said, "The reason for the slight delay in his response is because the helmet transmits your voice to the language conversion center, where it's converted to Stritz, and then transfers our native tongue to that small antenna on his helmet. Then, of course, his reply is converted to English and is received by the antenna on your helmet."

"But where did your people learn the English language to begin with?"

"The Di has been migrating back and forth between Rau and Earth for several centuries now, Harpie; remember? We've stored in our conversion centers the languages of nearly every culture on Earth, with the exception on a few isolated tribes in South America and Africa. We also know the tongues of other worlds, which the people on Earth don't even know exist yet. We can't move to those planets because the environments are too harsh. It will take the Pi a thousand years to learn what the Di knows at this moment. Scientists on Rau could teach your people so much, if only mankind wasn't so paranoid, greedy, and fearful of the unknown."

Harpie didn't know what to say.

"Oh, by the way," she said and then chuckled, "congratulations! You now owe the Central Financial Agency thirty-five hundred credits, and that means you won't be leaving Rau anytime soon. If you looked into the homer and tried to get on an interstellar shuttle without paying off your debits, a Robot cop would be paying you a visit before you got aboard."

She seized his cheeks between her hands and then kissed him. "I'm sorry, but you can't leave, at least not until you pay for your conversion helmet."

Then Martha reached into her handbag and withdrew what looked like an iPhone. She looked at the small screen and said, "We can go home now. The Housing Commission found us a place to live."

"The government found us a place to live?"

"Yes. The government and the real estate industry. I requested permanent housing for us, and the Housing Commission put it into their database."

"What is that thing you're holding called?"

"It's my witcher. It's very similar to the iPhones used on earth. That's the only thing Earth has that's similar to a witcher."

"Oh," he said. "Where are we going to live?"

"Our address will be 1122 Zenoid Place. A young couple abandoned it yesterday and are now on a ten light years voyage to another planet."

"Which planet are they headed for?"

She shrugged. "Take your pick." "There are an estimated two hundred billion stars in the Milky Way, and more than forty billion are earthlike suns. That means there is the possibly there are more than 8.8 billion planets that might be comparable to Rau and Earth."

The Housing Commission Robot gave them the door code so they could inspect their new home at 1122 Zenoid Place. It was beautiful and completely furnished.

"There is no such thing as a key on Rau," Martha informed Harpie. "Everything has a code. There were so many things about Rau you have to learn, just as I had to learn so many things about Earth, and I had to learn them quickly to maintain my false identity."

"What's this house made of?" he asked her.

"It is a substance much like the Styrofoam you have on Earth. The walls are fifteen inches thick and are covered by a super-hard and dense mixture of sand and epoxy. It's very cheap to cool or heat this house. As you now know, our sun is a flare star, and when there is an eruption, this external construction material also protects us from the resulting solar winds and X-rays, which are much higher than those that strike Earth."

Harpie put his conversion helmet on and asked the Robot, "How much is the mortgage?"

"There is no such thing as a mortgage," the Robot cryptically answered. "The cost is five thousand credits a month."

"The people indirectly control all the housing, and no one compiles equity in a home," Martha explained. "No one is homeless here, and our monthly rates are dirt cheap compared to Earth's mortgage and rental rates. People here move frequently to get into an upgraded home. This is especially true for the older folks. When they reach age seventy-five, they can retire and live in the last house they occupied free of charge for the rest of their lives—which includes the utilities."

The Housing Commission Robot had retrieved all their personal information from the Civil Intelligence Bureau and seized control of Martha's witcher. "Look into the camera," the Robot commanded." It then scanned their retinas and matched them with the ones from the Central Licensing Commission. The Robot clerk informed them that the home had been updated within the last five years, so their move-in basis was as-is.

"We need the language conversion box activated," she told the mechanical clerk, and it was so noted. Then they took possession; it was as simple as that!

The kitchen looked strange to Harpie. The first thing he noticed was that there were no handles on anything. "How do you open the refrigerator door?"

"It's voice actuated," she said, noting Harpie was wearing his conversion helmet.

"Open the door," Harpie shouted in a stentorian voice, and the refrigerator door and every cabinet, closet, and exterior door in the house opened at once.

Martha was in stitches and couldn't answer at first. "No, Harpie." She kept laughing. "You have to be specific. Say, 'Open the refrigerator door.' Now tell the computer to close all the doors."

Before he obeyed her directions, he noted the young couple had left plenty of food in the refrigerator, and then he shouted, "Close all the doors," and every door that had opened automatically closed. Harpie shook his head.

"How does it distinguish commands from ordinary conversation?" he asked. "For example, if we were sitting at the table and I said, 'When we're finished eating, open the refrigerator and put the leftovers away'—how would the sensors know it was just our conversation and not a command?"

"By your proximity and the level of your voice. And you must be specific. If you stand close to the refrigerator and speak in a normal tone and say, 'Open the refrigerator door,' only the sensor in the refrigerator will pick up the sound."

Later, Harpie found the bathroom and sat on the commode, and when he was finished relieving himself he realized there was no toilet paper. There was a tap on the door.

"If you're looking for toilet tissue," Martha said, "there isn't any and it hasn't been available on Rau for more than a century. There aren't enough trees growing on Rau to meet the demand."

"Well now what?" Harpie asked. His face flushed; it was embarrassing. *I don't know enough about Rau yet to even wipe my own butt.*

"Look to your right and down," she finally said after she stopped laughing. "See those buttons on the right side of the commode? Toilets on Rau have built-in bidets. The one marked with something that looks like the letter F is the cleanser; push it once if you're a male and twice if a female. If you push it twice a sprayer comes up in the front as well as the rear." He pressed it once and felt a small stream of warm water impact his anus.

"When the water shuts off, press the button that looks like the letter O."

He did, and a warm stream of air soon dried his rear end, and when he stood up to pull up his pants, the toilet flushed automatically.

"There's so much I have to learn," he quipped, "and it looks like I'll have to be potty trained all over again." They both laughed.

As they were entering the Saturn restaurant to eat dinner that evening, a shuttle landed nearby, but only the commander got off. The spaceship was now empty except for the Robot crews that remain aboard. All the Di passengers had been outbound to another world, and there were no returning passengers. But now crowds of young adults, many with children, lined up to get on the passenger list that would be stored in the spacecraft's computer for next year's trek, after the spaceship had been repaired and remodeled. When the list was full, those without reservations got on the standby waiting list, hoping to fill any cancellations so they too could leave Rau.

"Since Rau's population is decreasing at a rapid rate as the younger generation heads for distant planets in other galaxies," Martha said, "food and housing are becoming easier to find. The landers, farmers to you Earth people, have also been migrating in large numbers. But it doesn't make much difference, since the amount of arable land, which lies only between our massive rock formations, has also been shrinking for decades. We had to turn to urban farming in order to survive."

"Urban farming?" Harpie asked.

"Yes," she replied. "Tomorrow I'll take you on a tour of one; it's free."

The next morning they took an autocar downtown so Harpie could tour an urban farm. The building that offered free tours was several hundred stories high, and they took an elevator to the fourth floor. Harpie listened to the lecture via his language conversion helmet.

The tour guide said, "Normally it would take two acres of land to feed a family of four for one year, if they ate meat, dairy, and eggs. However, due to advances in agricultural techniques, we can now feed that same family on the equivalent of a quarter acre on an urban farm.

"As you may be aware, most of the plants grown here are not native to Rau, and because our planet does not spin on its axis it does not generates a magnetic field, which produces the ultraviolet rays that are so essential for plant life. When our ancestors migrated to Rau from a planet with a magnetic field, they brought much of their flora and fauna with them, and we were forced to invent the lights you see overhead; they emit ultraviolet A and B rays that are a form of electromagnetic radiation. These artificial rays fool the plants into believing they're in natural sunlight and cause them to emit a sort of 'sunscreen' to enhance growth, color, and taste. It helps the seeds to germinate faster and prepares them to withstand higher doses of the A and B rays, which we intensify when they become seedlings.

"There are six levels of racks on each floor, and each has millions of plants that grow rapidly in a year-round environment that is made possible by these artificial lights. The ultraviolet light-emitting bulbs are imitation suns that never set.

"Currently, about eighty percent of food plants grown on Rau come from urban farms like this one, and because we use hydroponic and hydromorphic techniques to grow the plants, we use just ten percent of the water an outdoor farm would need to grow the same amount of crops. Our transportation costs are minimal too, since most of the population on Rau now lives in the big cities, not far from where the food is grown."

Harpie was amazed at the huge size of the vegetables and berries being grown by using these advanced farming techniques. Many of those floras were also native to Earth. He saw hundreds of indigent Di workers harvesting the crops and among them were the infamous criminal credit hackers. They were wearing orange suits marked with a CS on the back of their shirts that identified them as credit slaves.

Other workers were packing the harvested crops into baskets before placing them on conveyor belts. At the end of the line, others were stacking the produce-laden hampers into hundreds of waiting driverless autotrucks that would soon be bound for local markets. The trucks were loaded fifty at a time, and as soon as one fleet was loaded and pulled away, another took its place. It was a bigger and faster operation than anything Harpie had ever seen on Earth.

"Most of our diet is vegetarian, chicken, seafood, and white pork meat," Martha said. "Earthlings eat a lot of fats and carbohydrates, and millions of them are obese, causing untold health problems and driving up medical costs. Did you notice that almost none of the Di is overweight?"

"No I wasn't aware of that," he said.

"That's why our medical costs are lower. Our children are imbued with facts about healthy diets and living habits while they are still in what Earthlings call grammar school. Everyone must be trained about the benefits of a daily exercise program that is suitable for them, and there are hundreds of fitness centers located all over the city. Those who do not follow a daily regimen are identified by an annual physical exam, and may have their health benefits curtailed, unless a disease is detected. Thus, most the Di adhere to the appropriate fitness regimen identified in their early childhood."

To show him the advances Rau scientists had made in medical field, Martha took Harpie to the General Medical and Oncological Research Center, where Dr. Rita Cathay was conducting a tour. Some of the pharmacological names could not be translated into English, so Harpie was rather left out in the cold in that regard.

"We have a vaccine for nearly every major disease known on Rau," Dr. Cathy said, and Martha whispered to Harpie that many of the illnesses on Rau were the same as those on Earth.

"As soon as a child is born," Dr. Cathay continued, "blood draws and samples from the placenta and unbiblical cord are sent to the lab, and we label and preserve their stem cells for future treatments. After an in-depth analysis of its DNA is completed, the parents then know what series of vaccines the baby needs immediately and those needed at specific ages throughout the child's lifespan; the timing of those injections is rather important.

"Their analyses also determine what foods, ointments, and soaps this person would most likely be allergic to, and which ones could possibly cause cancer over time due to the genetic makeup peculiar to each child. We now have proven that heredity plays a key role in all diseases, as do carcinogens, which we have learned to eliminate at the source.

"The result of this early childhood analysis is that diseases such as cancer, heart disease, stroke, diabetes, chronic pulmonary obstructions, infections, cirrhosis of the liver, and tuberculosis are now virtually unknown in adults on Rau. Congenital defects cause us the biggest problems."

Harpie was fascinated by and stunned at some of the revelations. *If only there was a way to impart that knowledge to Earth's scientists!*

"Addictions to opioids and other addictive drugs have been virtually wiped out too," Dr. Cathay said, "since the medical records of every Di are immediately available to physicians in every province on Rau, which means a patient cannot go to multiple doctors to shop for additional prescriptions for the same medications. But most important of all is that all new manufactured drugs must be non-addictive.

"We must also give due credit to our Financial Credit System. It's extremely difficult to launder large amounts of illegal drug sale credits or debits, because your retinas are scanned by homers for every deposit and withdrawal anyone makes, limiting the number of financial accounts to two per each Di helps prevent criminals from opening multiple accounts."

Martha drove Harpie to a factory were the autocars were made, and they stood behind glass walls and watched the assembly line move quickly and efficiently. There were no people in the factory; it was totally robotic.

"Where are the Di workers?" Harpie asked.

"There are none," the Robot conducting the tour replied. "The entire Di crew responsible for this operation controls everything from their home computers. They never need to come here except in dire emergencies, and most glitches can be handled with software solutions.

"They have no daily commute; no time card to punch; and they can work any hour of the day or night; the quality and quantity of their work are evaluated by a computer. By the end of each shift tour, a Di working from his or her home knows exactly how many credits they have earned, all the debits they owe, how much goes into their pensions and saving accounts, and the amount of vacation hours they have accrued."

"I though Robotics drove most of the population from the workforce," Harpie said to the tour Robot.

"It did initially," the Robot replied, "but the paucity of jobs made everyone train longer and harder. Today, seventy percent of the Di population holds degrees in engineering or computer technology. Twenty percent work in the medical field and research, and five percent work in other miscellaneous fields, such as astrophysics, the arts, and writing. The remaining five percent is composed of those who couldn't cope, and they comprise the indigent work group."

Harpie watched a driverless truck back up to a crane that unloaded the dense metal sheets and glass domes. Another machine picked up one of the metal sheets and fed it into a rolling press machine and moments later the metal body of an autocar emerged out the other side.

A Robot, standing near a feed-in assembly line conveyor belt that contained a number of titanium chassis with the inducers attached, slid one under an adjacent body, while another Robotic machine picked up the dome and set it on top. As the assembly line moved onward, another Robotic arm pressed a drill-like device against the glass. The heated heads softened the dome at various intervals and then embedded an equivalent number of rivets into the glass before it hardened again and secured the hinge to the dome. As it neared the end of the glass dome, the head of the device rotated, and the same Robotic arm moved in retrograde and welded the other side of the hinge to the metal body.

Then the dashboard, with all its wireless electronic components, was attached to the metal body through the uplifted dome doors, and finally the seat frames were welded to the floor. The entire process took fewer than fifteen minutes. *No wonder there are always plenty of autocars available*, Harpie mused.

A year passed by quickly, and Harpie secured a job as a reporter on the *Ronnett*, one of the largest newspapers in the Megapolis. His main assignment was to focus on climate change, wrought by the fading sun, and he traveled to the poles several times to witness the increasing mass of the polar icecaps. The polar caps were still minute compared to Earth's, but it was big news on Rau, and each time he saw them, Harpie grew more and more homesick.

On several occasions he managed to linger in a small hotel in the ring, the land bordering the warm half and the cold halves of Rau—the eternally warm and frozen hemispheres.

The warm part of the ring, which faced the sun, was a land of perpetual daylight, where the climate was most similar to Earth's climate. The mild temperature was due to the warm breeze drifting in from the sunny side of the planet. The cold half was a world of eternal darkness, where the temperature lingered at four hundred degrees below zero.

Harpie learned the ring was the most densely packed population zone on the planet, and there was no available housing on any province bordering it unless the occupant or occupants of a house died. The ring was also where the megacreditaire Dis somehow managed to congregate.

"One day our sun, a red dwarf star, will become a white dwarf," Martha told him one evening as they ate dinner. "And when it cools completely, it will become a black dwarf—a dead planet—or perhaps a neutron star."

But Harpie wasn't paying much attention to what she was saying. He was thinking about Earth, and Gloria, the wife he had divorced, and his children, Carrie and Jack—and his grandchildren. The grand kids were very young when he left Earth, and he knew they wouldn't remember him.

Martha noticed his melancholy mood. "You miss your Earth family, don't you?"

He couldn't reply. Harpie didn't want to hurt her.

"I know how it feels. My husband died, and our children have gone off to other worlds; I will never see them again. I don't have a single relative left on Rau—you're the only one left here that I love. If you go back to her, there will be nothing left for me to live for on Rau."

Martha turned away, and he could tell she was wiping the tears from her face.

"I'll never go back there without you," he said as he placed his arms on her shoulders. "I love you."

She turned to face him. "I love you too, but you won't be happy if you stay here. I'm fifty-three years old now, and you're fifty-nine. We've been gone from Earth for almost six years, and by the time we get back there, eleven years will have passed. Things must have changed by now and will change even more before you return.

"Gloria has probably remarried, as you have; your grandchildren will be teenagers. By the time we reach Earth, I'll be fifty-eight and you'll be sixty-three. That's one of the drawbacks of space travel; you waste a lot of your life in therapeutic hibernation, an unconscious state. I don't want to sleep away fifteen years of my life."

"Not fifteen years," Harpie retorted. "It would only be ten years."

"No, you forget I spent nearly five years getting to Earth the first time and almost five years getting back to Rau."

Harpie didn't know what to say, and he silently cursed his editor, Claude Hoskins, for sending him to Cheyenne Mountain in the first place. He wished he'd never heard of the Phantom Effect!

"And don't forget about the Place in Dallas," Martha reminded him. "Once you get there and the FBI catches you, the CIA will keep you drugged out of your mind for the rest of your life!"

"Well," Harpie finally said, "I can't leave Rau anytime soon. I still owe the Central Financial Agency fifteen hundred credits for my Language Conversion Helmet."

She looked at him rather apprehensively but then said, "If you really want to go back, I can transfer credits from my account and help pay off your CFA debt."

Harpie was delighted. Martha tapped in a code in the financial app on her witcher and then looked at a several different location. "Several shuttles are getting ready for another trek to Earth," she said. "The commander must grant you priority status, since you were originally from Earth. Once you leave Rau, he can grant you a divorce from me so you can join a group marriage."

"I'm not interested in a marriage group, Martha. I want you to come with me."

"I can't," she replied.

The weeks and months passed quickly, and they compiled thousands of pages of instructions and documents so Harpie could take them back to Earth with him and solve many of the medical and agricultural problems there. On the day he was to leave Rau, Harpie woke early and was surprised to see Martha was already up. He quickly dressed and went into the kitchen. Breakfast was on the table, and he called out her name, but she was not at home.

She must be out doing her morning run, he thought, *although it is rather early.*

Then he noticed something rather unusual. She had left her witcher on the table; she had never done that before, and he got a horrible feeling. Harpie scanned the messages, but they were all in Stritz, and he didn't know her arcane code to convert Stritz into English. He put on his conversion helmet and tore out of the house and down the street until he spotted a Robot cop.

"What does this mean?" he asked.

The Robot cop eyed him suspiciously for a moment and then scanned the messages, and a moment later its digitized voice said, "She has an appointment at the Requiem Agency today at eleven thirty."

"What the hell is the Requiem Agency?" Harpie asked.

There was the usual slight delay, while the Robot deciphered his English. "It is the place where the Di goes to be voluntarily euthanized," the digitized voice answered.

"Euthanized?" Harpie screeched. "Yes, now I remember. Is that legal for a perfectly healthy person to do?"

"Yes," the Robot cop answered. "Volunteering to be euthanized is legal on Rau after an in-depth consultation with a licensed psychiatrist."

"What is the location code of the agency?" Harpie nervously asked.

He heard the answer in his conversion helmet and sprinted for the nearest autocar, and the Robot cop quickly caught up with him and handed him Martha's witcher. Harpie found a newer model autocar and looked into the homer.

After he got inside, he shouted into the voice-actuated computer, "Take me to the Requiem Agency," but nothing happened. Precious moments were slipping by. He searched the array of icons on the screen until he recognized the autocar's voice converter icon, and soon he was whizzing toward the center of town.

Harpie ran up the steps into a huge waiting room. There were hundreds of people gathered there, some saying their final goodbyes to their ill or aged loved ones. Martha wasn't in sight, which meant she was already in a chamber. He looked at his watch; it was 11:25! He ran toward the five chambers in the next room, when suddenly a powerful force grabbed him from behind.

"My wife's in here somewhere," Harpie shouted to the Robot cop. "She's changed her mind. Her name is Martha Spiller Colcek."

The Robot and Harpie ran to different chambers, and soon the Robot shouted, "Over here—number five."

Her name was flashing on the monitor above the door; her death was imminent. Harpie recklessly dashed inside, just as the thick colorless poison began flowing through the plastic catheter into her arm. He ripped the needle out and the clear fluid dripped onto the floor, and as he felt for a pulse the Robot wheeled the gurney out of the chamber.

"Where's the antidote?" he anxiously asked.

"There is none," the Robot answered.

Harpie immediately pulled her off the gurney and sat on the nearest chair with Martha on his lap; her pulse was weak and racing; she had been drugged to ease her journey into eternity. Anxious minutes passed, but then she blinked and reached up to touch his face, and the anxious crowd that had gathered around them burst into cheers.

"What the hell did you think you were doing?" Harpie asked her as his tears dripped on her face. She couldn't talk for a few moments, but then she hoarsely whispered, "I became so distraught, Harpie. My children and all my relatives are gone, and my mother and father died in in each other's arms in one these chambers. You were the only one left here that I love, and when you decided to leave, I never felt so alone in all my life. I just wanted to die."

"I would never leave you, Martha," he promised her.

"What about Gloria?" she asked.

"That was over a long time ago."

"I couldn't stand it—I thought you were going back to her, Harpie. That's why I couldn't go back there with you," Martha said as she wept.

"No, I'm not going back to her, and I have no one on Earth I can turn to either at this point either."

She nodded and put her arms around his neck.

"Let's go back to Earth together," he said, "and dedicate our lives trying to convince the Pi of the Di's true intent, and we'll show them all those documents and studies we copied of Rau's advances in medicine and the other sciences. It would be a world-changer and could save millions of Pi and Di lives in the process—if you'll finish translating them into English."

Martha merely nodded again. She was still too drugged to do much else.

"Do you remember the IDs, birth certificates, and the driver's licenses Father Gallagher gave us?" he asked. She nodded slightly again.

"Well, I still have them, and a fistful of American dollars," he said. "When we get back to Earth, I'll be Harold Miller again, and you'll be Marion Keller. It worked when we got our airline tickets to go to New York, but we gotta be very careful for a long time. As you know, Earth people are very skeptical about the existence of aliens and too scared to accept radical innovations, even in the light of prima facie facts and evidence."

CHAPTER
9

The *Star Warrior* spaceship passengers had were already filled all the available habitats, but *Galactic Stalker* had two cancellations. Since Harpie was an Earthling he had priority, and because they were married, Martha was allowed aboard too.

After *Star Explorer* stealthily landed at the John Brown Historical Site in New York in the middle of the night, Harpie Colcek and Martha Spiller thanked Commander Eshwon again, and then assumed the identity of Harold Miller and Marion Keller. They grabbed their luggage and walked to the limousine and taxi stand, and rode to Lake Placid, where a bus marked Albany was already boarding passengers. They reached New York City later that day and waited at LaGuardia Airport until their scheduled flight left for Denver at 4:00 a.m.

It was dawn by the time they arrived in downtown Denver, and Harpie whispered to Martha so the young taxi cab driver couldn't hear him, "Good grief, Denver has grown exponentially in eleven years."

"Yeah," Martha replied. "I wonder how many more thousands of the Di lives here now."

The taxi dropped them off at Saint Mary's Catholic Church on Zenobia Street, and Harpie tried the sacristy door; it was unlocked. They went into the large closet and closed the door, and Harpie got down on his hands and knees and found the hole with the button inside. The door popped open and the lights came on. They crawled inside, only to discover the room was empty. There was no water in the refrigerator, and the snack cupboard was bare. Harpie remembered the secret door in the back of the room, and he quietly opened it, but all the beds were empty. It seemed a little stuffy, and when Harpie turned on the lights and ran his hand across the top of a dresser, it was dusty.

"This place looks like it hasn't been used for a long time," Harpie said.

"It's hardly been used in the last three years," a familiar voice echoed through the empty room.

The pair abruptly turned around. His hair was thinner and had turned white, and Harpie saw wrinkles in his face that weren't there eleven years ago. "Father Gallagher!" he exclaimed.

The old priest squinted as he gazed at his face until Harpie blurted out, "It's me, Father—Harpie Colcek!"

The priest's mouth dropped open and he drew back, his face paling as he stared at the intruders. After his initial shock subsided, he said, "The FBI lied to everyone, Harpie." He reached out and seized Harpie by the shoulders. "They said you and Martha Spiller were killed in a shootout in Lubbock, Texas."

"They said what?" Harpie asked.

"Your pictures appeared in the *Rocky Mountain Times* and many other papers across the country. They said you both had gone crazy; that you claimed to have met aliens from outer space and you had to be stopped, because your maniacal rantings created a pandemic of fear that was flooding the world!"

"Obviously they lied," Harpie replied. "Why did they do that?"

"It was a trick," the priest answered. "If they made it known you were dead, it proved you both were really only humans and hoped it made the turbulent world settle down; it did. They even held mock funerals for you and Martha. They probably hoped the news would make you grow careless so you could be apprehended. Then they arrested your brother, Jon, and his wife, Sue, saying they were an imminent danger to the United States."

Harpie was horrified.

"They're confined at that undisclosed location in Dallas," Father Gallagher said as he released Harpie's shoulders, "along with a few air traffic controllers the government claimed were also spreading tales about UFOs and alien monsters that were invading and conquering the world and enslaving the survivors."

"They're in the Place, Harpie," Martha fearfully cried out as she seized Harpie's arm, "where they drug prisoners out of their minds, just as they did to the Di man I told you about, remember? He was the one they sent to a mental institution, but several years later he regained his senses and escaped!"

Harpie remembered their conversation and was even more dumbfounded.

"That's not all," Father Gallagher said as he sat on the side of a bed. "About a year after your so-called death, Claude Hoskins converted to Catholicism, and I married him and your wife, Gloria." He looked into Harpie's eyes and said, "Everything is such a mess."

Harpie plopped down on the bed next to the priest and then looked up at Martha and said, "I'm not surprised. They were always fond of one another. I married Martha."

There was a moment of silence, and then Harpie asked, "So my children and grandchildren also think I'm dead?"

The priest merely nodded, and Harpie bowed his head.

Martha immediately sat next to him and put her arm around his shoulder. There was another long moment of silence, and then Harpie changed the subject. "What happened to all the illegal aliens you used to run through here, Father?"

"Well," the priest said, "after America built the wall and hired all those new border agents, the illegal alien flow slowed to a mere trickle. Then, after the president gave the Dreamers a path to citizenship, the illegal immigrant influx stopped completely, and their families turned on the Mexican drug cartels and the coyotes and smugglers; the drug trafficking ceased too. But I'm sure the FBI and the CIA are still searching for you both."

Harpie asked about his best friend, Monty Galbreth. "Monty was your lieutenant, Father, so what is he doing these days?"

"He is also in that prison in Dallas," Father Gallagher said. "The FBI got him on tape picking you up at the Denver airport when you returned from Lubbock years ago. They charged him with aiding and abetting a fugitive. No one has seen or heard from him since, and his wife eventually divorced him and remarried outside of the church."

Harpie was still shocked about Jon and Sue's incarceration, and now he felt guilt-ridden about his best friend's imprisonment. "It's entirely my fault, Father."

"By the way," the priest asked, "where have you two been hiding these past eleven years?"

"On Rau," Harpie answered.

He expected a rash reaction from the priest, but he was older and wiser now. "Ever since I banished you from Saint Mary's because of your belief in space aliens and the other worlds you thought God may have created," the priest said, "I studied astronomy. So tell me about this place you call Rau."

"Rau is an exoplanet in the Alpha Centauri star system," Martha proudly answered. "Earth people call our sun Proxima Centauri, the third star in Centaurus, and Rau is what earthlings call Proxima b."

After Martha gave him a lengthy explanation of life on Rau, they retired to the waiting room, and the priest sat on one of the chairs while Harpie removed the numerous photographs of Rau from his luggage. The documents and studies proved their advancements in technology, science, medicine, and social issues.

"We need these," Harpie explained to the priest, "if we are ever to convince the Earth people of the existence of the extraterrestrials and their advanced civilization."

The pictures of the three moons of Rau, the gigantic fruits and vegetables, and the autocars and rocket planes were what impressed Father Gallagher the most, as were the alleged cures for many of the diseases that still plagued Earth. It was obvious he was astonished, yet he remained ominously silent.

Then he looked at Martha and asked, "God? Does the Di believe in God?"

"Of course," Martha replied.

"Did Jesus also appear on Rau, and was he also crucified on these other planets that you claim exit?"

"We believe he didn't have to," she answered. "It took a catastrophe, but Rau learned to live by the Master's rules—the ones you call the Ten Commandments. But Earth was still heading in the wrong direction, particularly concerning human rights, and it needed help in addition to the Master's rules. We believe help came in the form of the Incarnation—Jesus Christ, the son of God, was made man. However, the Di Bible, which is thousands of years older than Earth's bible, says that when God drove mankind out of the Garden of Eden, he pulverized the entire planet, and its fragments became the universe. Earthmen call it the Big Bang Theory.

"But God was merciful and banished the descendants of our first parents to other planets, and as punishment for their sins he turned them into ignorant savages. They had to learn everything from scratch, including such simple things as making a fire.

"The Pi believes the Garden of Eden was located on Earth, between the Tigris and Euphrates rivers, in what is now present-day Iraq, because that land is the most fertile soil on earth. But the Di knows this isn't true. "

Father Gallagher didn't say anything. The photos looked authentic, and the couple seemed sincere enough. They even told him about how the spaceship, *Space Explorer,* took them on the final leg of their journey back to Earth at Lake Placid. They showed him the pictures of Commander Eshwon, the lines of coffins used for therapeutic hibernation, and the Robots. They also told him how the *Star Voyager* alternately landed at Caprock Canyons State Park every other Christmas Eve and that another one landed there on the year in between.

"These flights are what the US government calls the Phantom Effect, because they didn't know what they actually were," Harpie said.

Father Gallagher knew they were telling the truth, but it was frightening for a man who had dedicated his life to the church and his belief in the teachings of the Old and New testaments. The traumatic reversal left him stunned and horrified, and he became deeply distraught.

"We need a place to stay," Harpie said. "We're exhausted!"

"You can stay here for as long as you wish," the priest replied. "I'll have the Sodality ladies bring you some food and drink." He looked at his watch and said, "It's time for me to get ready to say Sunday Mass." Then he was gone.

After Mass, Father Gallagher retreated to the solitude of the rectory to think. The FBI never discovered the waiting room and the sleeping quarters where the illegal aliens once waited for their sponsors, so

Martha and Harpie were safe for the time being. *What they showed me and told me challenges everything I have believed in all my life*, he pondered. *They seem very sincere, and now I don't know what to believe.*

"If the world believes their episodic story," he said as he looked up at the crucifix on the wall in the study, "the book of Genesis and Adam and Eve could become a mere fairy tale, and Christianity might eventually cease to exist! The world may never again believe in one God and possibly will revert to paganism and idolatry. Riots might break out between those who still believed in the Creation and the atheists.

"Without the guidance of the Ten Commandments, it could initiate universal crimes that defy description. There is the possibly of mass rapes and murders without conscience. Adultery would be even more acceptable than it is today, and there would be no such thing as lying, and therefore an oath taken in a court of law would be meaningless; the proverb that 'right makes might' would never be beseeched again."

Father Gallagher strode to the cabinet containing his secret stash of liquor and poured himself a shot of Irish whiskey. The phone rang, but the housekeeper didn't work on Sundays, and he didn't want to talk to anyone anyway, so he didn't answer it. He gulped down the drink and then went into the library and pulled out a copy of the New Testament and began reading, but it didn't settle his conscience. It was a day filled with angst. He was torn between his lifelong religious beliefs and what Harpie and Martha had said and what he'd seen in the photos of Rau and the *Space Explorer*. That night as he said his prayers, he begged God for guidance.

At 3:30 a.m., Father Gallagher woke with a start. His heart raced; he was breathing rather deeply and was drenched in sweat. A frightening voice echoed in his mind: *Sinner; blasphemer!* It seemed to resonate from his subconscious mind. His symptoms made him feel as though

he was in his death throes, and soon his soul would be cast into the fires of hell for his sins! The priest rolled out of bed and onto his knees, and with his head bowed and his hands clasped in prayer, he begged the Almighty for forgiveness.

He confessed, "It was blasphemy for me to ever consider what Harpie and Martha told me is true." *The Lord has spoken*! he thought. "Dear Jesus, please forgive me," he cried as he knelt there, spreading his arms out in replication of the crucifixion. "I believe in you, Lord, and deserve whatever punishment you may mete out."

It took more than an hour of prayer and repentance before he calmed down enough to think straight. Harpie Colcek and Martha Spiller were blasphemers and had to be punished. The Lord had given him a sign—that terrible fear!

Their destiny and punishment must be meted out in a living hell on earth known known as the Place, he thought. *Someone has to pay a price to keep the Ten Commandments intact and to protect the church from harm.*

His shaking hands sorted through the telephone directory until he came to the blue pages with the government listings. The office had a twenty-four hotline, and without hesitation he dialed the number of the FBI office in downtown Denver.

At 6:00 a.m. Harpie and Martha woke in the hidden bedroom and then walked into the waiting room. The refrigerator was still replete with foodstuffs left by the Sodality members last night, but they wanted to freshen up before they ate. Harpie felt his two-day beard growth. They both needed to shower and change clothes, but the common bathroom had no bathing or shower facilities.

"I'll ask Father Gallagher if we can use the rectory shower," Martha said. She tried the trap door leading into the large closet in the sacristy, but it wouldn't budge. "The door won't open, Harpie," she said.

He tried it too to no avail. "That means the door to the closet on the other side is open or ajar; we're trapped. I'm surprised, because Father Gallagher has always been so careful about closing it completely." The thought made him feel rather apprehensive.

"Well," Martha said, "let's eat breakfast anyway. We can shower after Father Gallagher returns and closes the outer door." She turned to open the refrigerator door.

The entrance door suddenly opened and Father Gallagher entered, followed by a man in a civilian suit; he was holding a revolver.

"This is the FBI," the man shouted. "You're under arrest. Get face down on the floor!"

They obeyed, and the agent was followed by another man, who stood up and shouted, "Harpie Colcek and Martha Spiller Colcek, you're being charged with sedition and treason!"

Harpie's mouth dropped open. It had been more than eleven years, but he recognized agents Halifax and Dubkowski and realized Father Gallagher had betrayed them.

"Did you think I believed your ridiculous story about Rau," the priest bellowed. "God created this world in seven days. It is the only world he ever created."

The priest didn't know why, but now that he openly confessed how he honestly felt about the matter, he was relieved. *I have appeased the Lord*, he mused. Then he informed the two agents he had church business elsewhere and he left.

After the agents cuffed them, they forced them up against the wall and frisked them, even though Father Gallagher had assured them the fugitives were unarmed.

"I can't believe you're still assigned to the Denver office after all these years, Agents," Harpie said.

"We know more about the Phantom Effect than anyone else in the entire US government," Agent Dubkowski answered. "Our destiny is to remain here until the mystery is solved one way or another."

"If the Phantom Effect was the insertion of enemy agents into the United States," Harpie replied, "they would have attacked or sabotaged American interests or cities a long time ago."

"Maybe, maybe not," Agent Halifax replied. "But we can't take the chance; millions of American lives are at stake."

"Harpie Colcek and Martha Spiller Colcek," Agent Halifax said as he looked at their credentials, "you've been using someone else's identities—another felony." He called the office on his iPhone, and a few minutes later he turned toward the fugitives and announced, "Both Harold Miller and Marion Keller have been dead for more than twenty-five years. Who got these forged identities for you?"

"Father Gallagher," they said in unison.

"We're not surprised," Agent Halifax answered. "We were so anxious to nab you two that we didn't ask Father Gallagher what the purpose of this hidden room was."

"He's been using this place to smuggle illegal aliens into the United States for decades," Harpie angrily blurted.

The two agents were dumbfounded, until Agent Dubkowski said, "The FBI and ICE have been searching for this sanctuary for years, but we couldn't find it when we did our initial inspection of the church. We knew Denver was the hub of the operation, but we could never find cause to get a search warrant, and then out of the clear blue sky we get a call from Father Gallagher.

"It seems you challenged his basic belief in God and the Creation at a time when the illegal alien intrusions are at a virtual standstill, so this place no longer has any real use for him."

The pair sat in the waiting room while the agents searched their luggage and were shocked when they discovered the photos of Rau and the technological, scientific, and medical documents.

"If you come from another world," Agent Dubkowski asked Martha, "how come some of these documents are written in English?"

"Martha spent months converting them from Stritz into English," Harpie answered, "but we didn't have enough time to decipher them all."

"Stritz?" Agent Halifax asked.

"Yeah, Stritz," Harpie answered.

"You mean Martha can convert all this gibberish into English, Harpie?" Agent Dubkowski asked.

"It's not gibberish," Martha retorted, "it's Stritz, the universal language of Rau."

The agents looked at one another but didn't reply, and Harpie got the feeling they were growing uncertain as to whether they were telling the truth.

"We've gotta get these photos and documents to the FBI lab in Washington to determine if they're authentic," Agent Halifax said to his partner. "We'll take these two to downtown headquarters. But first I want to see what's in these filing cabinets. Agent Dubkowski, go get Father Gallagher and tell him to bring me the keys."

"They're the records of all the sponsors and parishes in the United States that have helped smuggle immigrants into our country over the past twenty-five or thirty years," Harpie said.

"If that's true, we've finally nailed him," Agent Halifax replied. Agent Dubkowski was gone for more than ten minutes, but Father Gallagher was not in the rectory or the church.

"His housekeeper says he usually goes to the Denver General Hospital or the Institute of Mental Health on Mondays," Agent Dubkowski said, "and won't be back until this evening."

"Well, as soon as he returns," Agent Halifax said, "we'll place him under arrest for smuggling aliens into the country and aiding in human trafficking."

Then he looked at Harpie and Martha and said, "Our sting operations netted a few unscrupulous sponsors he recruited, and they confessed they sold some of the younger women to several major crime syndicates. Those unfortunate women are now sex slaves and are scattered across nearly every major city in the country. The info in these files may help us track down many of the criminals and free their victims."

"Aiding human trafficking was not Father Gallagher's intent," Harpie retorted.

"We know that," Agent Halifax said. "His heart was in the right place, but the road to hell is sometimes paved with the good intentions of those who operate outside the law."

Agent Halifax then called his office, and Agent William Voyavich, an image interpreter expert, arrived an hour later. He looked at the photos with a magnifying glass for more than half an hour and then proclaimed, "I can tell you right now that all the photos I've looked at so far are not doctored prints."

"Are you sure?" a dumbfounded Agent Halifax asked.

"Yes. I've spent more than twenty-five years in photo interpretations in the military and the FBI," Agent Voyavich answered. "The lines in these photos are sharp and the images are crystal clear. There's no unusual shading or shadows. However, I've never seen this kind of photographic paper before; its topnotch stuff, whatever it is."

"It's made out of a highly processed mixture of sand, clay, and wood," Martha said.

The three incredulous men glanced at her and then at one another, and Agent Voyavich asked her, "Can you show us how to make this kind of photographic paper?"

"No. The clay with the particular molecular structure needed to produce that quality of paper does not exist anywhere on earth. However, we have billions of tons of it on Rau."

"Rau?" Agent Voyavich asked. "I never heard of it."

"You know it as Proxima b," Harpie said and laughed.

"It's an exoplanet that orbits Proxima Centauri, a red dwarf star, our sun," Martha said, "and it's slowly dying. That's the only reason we migrate here."

"Wait a minute," Agent Dubkowski interjected. "Proxima Centauri is the third star in the constellation Centaurus."

"That's correct, Agent Dubkowski," Martha answered.

"How do you know that, Robert?" Agent Voyavich asked.

"Well, I once I dreamed of being an astrophysicist," he answered. "However, grad school was highly competitive, and my math skills weren't exactly equivalent to Einstein's, if you know what I mean. So astronomy became my passion."

"That was my major in the Advanced School on Rau," Martha said. "A degree in astrophysics is as common on Rau as a liberal arts degree is on earth."

Harpie laughed and said, "She's smarter than all of us."

"If you're from this planet Rau as you claim," Agent Dubkowski asked, "how come we have never seen any of your spacecraft?"

"Your space technology is still in its infancy, Agent Dubkowski," she answered. "You can barely see our ships on your primitive radar, and Harpie is one of the few humans who have ever traveled outside your solar system. Our spaceships have traveled trillions of miles to other galaxies. Your most advanced satellites like Hipparchus can only measure the distance from the earth to the stars or other planets, and your Hubble spacecraft cannot even photograph Proxima b. The only reason you know Rau exists is because of the gravitational pull of the other stars in the constellation Centaurus."

"That's absolutely correct," Agent Dubkowski answered. "Your knowledge of astrophysics is rather impressive. But if your people travel trillions of miles to other galaxies as you claim, the crews would die of old age before they got there."

"The freighters that mine and transport minerals from other galaxies are not manned by the Di," Martha said. "They are manned by computers and Robots. The furthermost distance a Di has traveled in the universe is ten lightyears, and those passengers were in their teens or early twenties when they began their journey. We know some of them landed on a Rau-like planet in the constellation Cassiopeia, but after a dozen years we lost contact with them."

The group spoke for hours about Rau and its advances in technology, science, and medicine, and the three agents could only sit there, fascinated by what Martha was telling them, although they were still somewhat skeptical.

Finally, Agent Halifax looked at his watch, and said, "Father Gallagher should have been back by now."

Agent Dubkowski went looking for him and was gone for nearly an hour, and when he returned he informed them, "Father Gallagher never went to the hospital or the mental institute today. He took a noontime flight out of Denver to New York and is now on a direct flight to Rome."

"I should have known he'd be seeking refuge in the church," Agent Halifax blurted. "We don't have an extradition agreement with the Vatican City State."

"I guess it's a state department problem now," Agent Dubkowski said. "But the Holy See will never turn him over to us. They will view him as some kind of hero for having saved thousands of people from Mexico, Central America, and God knows where else, from living in poverty, although he knew many of them are a security threat to the United States."

"Well," Agent Halifax said, "as far as these two are concerned, we have orders from the president to turn custody of them over to the CIA."

"Not yet," Agent Voyavich interjected. "I want to learn more about these photos and documents. The photos are real; look at this picture—it shows three moons."

Agent Dubkowski retrieved the photo from Agent Voyavich. "Scientists have speculated for years that Proxima b had several orbiting bodies, and if this photo is real, it proves it could only have been taken by someone or something on Proxima b!"

The FBI agents were stunned. But they had orders to turn the pair over to the CIA. "If you do that they'll imprison us in the Place!" Martha shrieked.

There were rumors in the bureau about a secret CIA holding center, but no one had been able to substantiate the fact; it was classified top secret. Only the president and a few other select government officials actually knew of its existence and where it was located.

"Where did you hear about this prison you call the Place?" Agent Halifax asked Martha.

"One of our Di, named Shamon, was captured and spent ten years there," Martha answered. "The CIA infused him with so many mind-altering drugs to erase his memory that he became severely demented, and they confined him to a mental institution. Several years afterward he recovered somewhat and escaped."

"And just where is this prison located?" Agent Halifax asked.

"I don't know exactly where, Agent Halifax," she said, "but Shamon said the drugs didn't erase everything from his long-term memory. In one of his more lucid moments, fellow prisoners told him they were in Dallas and confined beneath a large government building. There is a park nearby named Trammell Crow and the Divinity River runs through it."

Again the agents were alarmed. They knew that area and realized that Harpie Colcek and Marth Spiller were probably telling the truth. Until now they could not validate the existence of a CIA prison known as the Place, let alone know where it was located. Yet they knew there was just one US government building near Trammel Crow Park—it was the largest post office in Dallas. However, this newfound knowledge of the location of a top secret government operation sealed their fate.

"In fact," Agent Halifax said to the two other agents so Harpie and Martha couldn't hear him, "we're in trouble for just knowing about it."

The three agents looked at each other with expressions of mutual alarm, and Agent Voyavich packed the photographs and documents back into the suitcases, hoping no one in authority would ever find out they knew anything about the Place.

Agent Dubkowski anxiously got on the phone and called the home office in Denver to inform his superior that they had arrested the fugitives. Then, as the president ordered, they turned custody of the prisoners, the documents, and the photos over to the CIA.

CHAPTER
10

They had been handcuffed and their ankles manacled for hours before the four stern CIA agents hustled them aboard a government jet in the wee hours of the morning. The plane was parked on the National Guard tarmac at Denver International Airport, and they were forced to sit in different sections of the aircraft so they couldn't see or talk to one another. Harpie told them they were both hungry and that he had to pee, but they paid him no mind.

Fewer than two hours into the flight, hoods were pulled over their faces and secured by drawstrings; it was hard to breathe, and Harpie couldn't see a thing. The anxiety-ridden prisoners realized they were about to land.

Then they were separated and forced to sit on the dual backseats of a stretch limousine. One seat faced the rear and the other the front of the limo. A CIA sat next to them. The dark-tinted windows prevented anyone on the outside from seeing the restrained prisoners

with hoods over their faces. A few minutes later the car stopped, and
Harpie heard a window being rolled down.

Someone said, "Thank you."

We're at a toll booth, Harpie surmised, *and I know Dallas-Fort
Worth International Airport has a parking fee; they're taking us to the
Place!*

The limo eased out on to the freeway, and half an hour later it
pulled into Trammel Crow Park. An agent got out and unlocked
the gate, and although the park was closed for repairs of the Sylvan
Bridge, the feds still had access.

The man opened the gate, and the limo drove up to a false
maintenance garage. The driver hit the door opener, and the car
disappeared inside. A moment later, Harpie could tell they were
driving down a ramp. The driver turned on the headlights and drove
into a narrow tunnel before stopping near a set of double metal doors.

Although the hood blocked out nearly every trace of light, Harpie
could tell they were on an elevator and it was descending. Seconds
later he heard a door open, and with agents on either side grasping
them by their arms, they stopped. Harpie could tell by the screeching
sound that it was a metal door. The agents said nothing but turned
them over to prison guards, who seized them by the crooks of their
arms, and then Harpie heard the door slam. They were led down a
hallway and thrust into separate cells. Their handcuffs and manacles
were removed, and when the guard jerked the hood off Harpie's head,
the intense light blinded him; he wondered how Martha was faring.

Martha was enduring the same kind of treatment, including a
humiliating and prolonged body cavity search by a snickering guard,
and as she squinted she could barely make out the number two
emblazoned on the upper left pocket on his uniform. The prisoners
would soon learn that the guards had no name tags; they were
identified by a number only and addressed each other that way to

conceal their true identities. They wore specially designed glasses to protect their eyes from the intense lights and to partially disguise their faces.

Harpie squinted for several minutes, but the lights were so bright that he knew his eyes would never adjust to such intensity. Still squinting, he scanned the room and saw it was austere, with merely a bunk, a metal commode, and a sink with a small plastic cup. His bladder felt as though it was about to burst, and on stiff legs he staggered over to the commode to pee and felt an extreme relief.

He kept his head down as he ambled over to the cell door and realized the hallway lights were dimmer than those in his cell. He peered out hoping to catch sight of Martha. But all he could see was a wide hallway, where other prisoners were roaming freely about, shuffling their feet and staring straight ahead; some drooled at the mouth.

Others crawled about on all fours, and he saw their knees sticking out through the holes in their worn orange jumpsuits; they couldn't stand up. Each had a number printed in black on the upper left side of their uniforms. They looked as though they hadn't showered or shaved in weeks, and their babbling sounds made no sense.

They're a mass of idiots, Harpie thought as he stared at them, and then he drew back in horror. *That could be me in a couple of weeks.*

The onset of fear set off a wave of panic, and in spite of the powerful lights, he hastily retreated to his bunk and sat. Then he went back to his cell door, just as a lone man came shuffling by, wearing the same type of orange jumpsuit as the other prisoners. Harpie wanted to talk to someone—anyone who could carry on an Intelligent conversation—but as he stared at the approaching man, he thought he knew him from somewhere. Something about his hair and gaunt look brought back a haunting memory even though a scraggly beard partially hid the outline of his face.

"Hey," Harpie squinted shouted with a trembling voice, "don't I know you?"

The man stopped and turned toward the sound of a familiar voice. Drool ran down his chin and jumpsuit before rolling on to the floor.

"Yah, yah," the man could only mumble in reply, and although the sounds meant nothing to him, Harpie remembered that tone from times long past. He pulled on the bars on his cell door even harder and tried to press his face farther into the space between them as he stared at the pathetic figure. The man's blank stare seemed to bore through Harpie as if he wasn't there; yes it was him. His brown hair and eyebrows had turned gray, and he was now somewhat underweight. Harpie hadn't seen him in more than eleven years, but he recognized him.

"Jon," he screeched, "it's me, Harpie—your brother!"

Jon stared at him for a brief moment, and for an instant a fleeting memory brightened the look in his eye, but when he tried to speak he could only babble. "Yah, yah." Then he turned and continued on his journey to nowhere.

"Jon, don't you remember me?" Harpie screamed through the bars as the man walked away. But the fading figure no longer paid him any heed.

"Where's Sue?" Harpie shouted.

Jon stopped and turned for an instant. The name rang a bell, a mere evanescent memory of a distant past, but that was all there was to it, and then he continued on his eternal trek walking around the cellblock. It was the only thing he could do. When he walked by again, Harpie screamed, "What the hell did they do to you, Jon?" But this time the figure in the orange jumpsuit had no reaction and continued walking, still babbling and drooling.

"He doesn't remember you, Harpie," a strange voice resonated from across the hallway.

Harpie looked to where a tall man with thinning brown locks and wire-rimmed glasses stood with his arms folded across his chest. The stethoscope hanging around his neck and the long white coat identified him as a physician.

"Who the hell are you?"

"I'm Dr. Stangle, the psychiatrist in charge of this unit. If you and your wife keep spreading stories about alien life on another planet, you'll both end up like your brother."

"You're a psychiatrist and you do insane things like that to people's minds?" Harpie screeched. "What the hell kind of a doctor are you? What did you do to my brother?"

"I'm just doing my job. Your brother was not very cooperative. He wouldn't tell us where you and Martha were hiding. People like you and your brother have spread panic around the world by swearing you've had contact with people from outer space, and your lies caused turmoil and fear beyond belief. A lot has happened since you went into hiding eleven years ago."

"I wasn't in hiding," Harpie insisted. "I was living on Rau with my wife, Martha."

But Dr. Stangle kept right on talking. "People were building bomb shelters of every imaginable size and shape, expecting an alien invasion at any moment, and hording foodstuffs, batteries, guns, ammunition, and toilet tissue. Many left their jobs to spend their final days with their families, fearing any day could be their last.

"In every country on earth, people were pointing their fingers at their neighbors, suspecting they were alien monsters disguised as humans. Consequently, people who were different, like autistic children, homeless adults and the mentally ill, were being murdered. There was a sharp rise in the number of rapes and Robberies too, since the criminals believed everyone would be dead long before they could be apprehended and put in prison. The home guard in every country on Earth was activated on several occasions to quell the riots and to patrol the streets in most major cities."

"But it's true," Harpie insisted. "I lived on Rau for more than a year. They're far advanced beyond life on Earth. They have miracle drugs and supersized plants and animals. The Di speaks only one universal language, and there hasn't been a war there for centuries. They have Robots that are so sophisticated they can do tasks as well as or better than humans."

Dr. Stangle watched Harpie and listened closely. Then he smirked. Those were the exact words of a prisoner named Shamon, and even the name of the planet Rau was the same. *I know for certain that Harpie isn't one of the Di,* he pondered, *which makes him a threat. In the morning we'll follow the routine anyway. Then I'll call the president. It's the only way I can hold him here. It's too risky to let the CIA transfer him to the federal prison at Fort Leavenworth, Kansas.*

It was a night of horrors for Harpie. He heard the cries and moans of the afflicted and the sporadic screams of those who woke from a hellish nightmare. "Where are you, God?" a voice echoed between the cells. "Please help me."

Harpie cringed; the pathetic sounds were radiating from all along the cellblock and were unnerving. His hands shook uncontrollably.

But the worst was yet to come, when the terror-stricken reporter heard the entrance door open. A CIA agent stepped inside, and the guard signed the custody exchange sheet. The agent escorted a prisoner inside. Her hands were cuffed behind her back, and two guards led her to a cell directly across from where Harpie was being held. He returned to his cell door.

They turned her so that she faced Harpie while they unlocked her cell, and his jaw dropped. "Molly?" he shouted.

"Harpie?" she answered. It was her—the one who was headed back to Rau from New York because she didn't like Earthmen, but she returned when she learned her parents had died from the flesh-eating bacteria. It was one of the maladies Rau scientists couldn't cure.

"Oh," the older guard said. "So you're a special friend of Harpie Colcek's, huh?" He snickered as he turned toward Harpie. "Well, don't worry, Harpie, old boy, we'll take good care of her."

With that he turned and ripped her blouse completely off, along with the rest of her clothes. She stood there angry and humiliated as he fondled her breasts and groped her private parts.

"Standard operating procedure calls for a complete body cavity search of every new prisoner," the older guard said. "Warden's orders. And you, cutie, are gonna get the most thorough body cavity search anyone ever had, and you know what I'll be probing with, don't you?"

Molly spit in his face!

"You'll pay for that, bitch!" he screamed as he slapped her across the mouth. Molly staggered backward and slammed against the cell door, blood dripping from the corner of her mouth.

"Leave her alone, you crazy bastards!" Harpie shouted from between the bars.

The older man, Guard One, turned toward him and scowled as he replied, "I can't touch you tonight, Colcek, but I've got something real special planned for you tomorrow night."

"He is not a Di!" Molly shouted.

"We know, he's human and you're not," the Guard Two answered, and then they pushed Molly into the cell and slammed her down on the bunk. Her female cellmate huddled in a corner with her arms wrapped around her knees and her head resting on them; she dared not look.

While the younger guard stood by holding Molly's orange jumpsuit, Number One proceeded to pull down his pants, and she spit in his face again. Infuriated, the man punched her in the face and head again and again and again.

"Stop it! You're gonna kill her!" Harpie shouted, but they paid him no heed.

The older guard raped her, and when he finished and was pulling up his trousers, he said to the other guard, "You can have her now."

The younger guard looked down at the prostrate form and placed his fingers on her neck. "Shit," he said, "she's dead."

His companion glanced down at Molly's naked and beaten body and then said as he looked back at the younger guard, "Dr. Stangle can always use another Di cadaver. But you can take her; she's still warm."

"I don't want to fuck a dead cunt," the younger man replied.

"Well, if you want a live piece of ass, go fuck the Colcek bitch," the older man replied.

"Okay, I will," Number Two replied as he flung the jumpsuit on the blonde-headed corpse.

"If you touch my wife I'll kill you!" Harpie screamed as he grabbed the cell door bar and shook it. Number Two snickered as he walked away.

Number One walked over to Harpie's cell and shouted, "Your wife isn't even human and you married her; that's bestiality! These Di apes are not human, and Dr. Stangle has proven it!"

"She is as human as we are!" Harpie screeched.

"You have the balls to compare me to a Di?" Number One raged. "I can't wait until tomorrow night! You'll be sorry you were ever born."

It was a terrible night for Harpie. He knew his wife had been raped, and he hadn't slept a wink. At 5:00 a.m., two guards escorted him to another part of the prison. En route he caught a glimpse of Martha, clad in an orange prison jumpsuit, being led into another room by two guards.

"Where are you taking me?" Harpie asked; the guards didn't reply, and he felt a rising sensation of fear. His heart was already racing and his face flushed when they opened a door to a room marked "Testing." He spied Dr. Stangle and another man sitting at a table.

"This is Mr. Tobias," Dr. Stangle said, "the polygraph examiner who represents the Department of Justice. He'll be giving you a lie detector test to determine the veracity of your answers. The test consists of a physiological recorder that assesses certain indicators of autonomic arousal; heart rate and blood pressure, respiration, and skin conductivity. An individual's cardiovascular activity is detected by a blood pressure cuff wrapped around the upper arm. Rate and depth of respiration will be revealed by a pneumograph belt wrapped around your chest. Skin conductivity, known as galvanic skin or electrodermal response, will be measured by electrodes attached to your fingertips."

They spent forty minutes going over the questions to be certain Harpie understood what was being asked.

Harpie sat facing away from the examiner and Dr. Stangle, and he answered the questions as honestly as he could. An hour and a half later the session ended, and Harpie was relieved, but the aloof Mr. Tobias gave Harpie no indication as to the outcome. Moments later the guards reappeared and escorted him back to his brightly lit cell.

"And the results are, Mr. Tobias?" Dr. Stangle asked.

"Well, I used the control questions test with questions designed to offset the effects of the threatening relevant questions. For example, one of the questions I posed to Mr. Colcek about his misdeeds was, 'Have you ever told a lie?' which is broad in nature and refers to his past life. I got a strong reaction because the control question arouses concerns about his past truthfulness. If one is telling the truth, he fears the control question more than a relevant question, such as, 'Did you ever live on a planet known as Rau?' But we get less of a response about the relevant Rau questions because he knows he's telling the truth. In Mr. Colcek's case, we had a minimal reaction."

Dr. Stangle asked, "So what is your conclusion as to the results of Harpie Colcek's polygraph?"

The examiner replied, "My conclusion is that he is telling the truth, just as I told you Mr. Shamon was telling the truth."

Dr. Stangle nodded. "Tomorrow we'll resume testing with the newly developed thioscopola."

"I've never heard of that one," John Tobias answered.

Dr. Stangle smiled. "It's a new composite drug derived from sodium pentothal and scopolamine; it makes them sing like canaries."

The next morning Dr. Stangle had Harpie lie on a gurney while he injected the thioscopola into the examinee's arm. In fewer than ten seconds Harpie was unconscious. But five minutes later he slowly opened his eyes; he became terribly frightened when he realized he was in four-point restraints. Harpie never felt so helpless in all his life.

Then Mr. Tobias asked him the same control and relevant questions he'd asked during their first session yesterday. Harpie's voice cracked, but he answered each question as honestly as his memory would allow.

An hour later the session was over, and Mr. Tobias removed the blood pressure cup, the pneumograph belt, and the electrodes from Harpie's fingers.

"He's telling the truth, Dr. Stangle," the polygraph examiner said in private.

Dr. Stangle confiscated the test results, and Guard Three escorted Mr. Tobias out the back door. He was not allowed entry to the prison proper itself; it was a top secret government location, where only the most trusted government officials were allowed access.

After Mr. Tobias left, Dr. Stangle removed the thioscopola tube from the catheter and quickly injected a mixture of endurol and midazolam. The beta blocker caused the doctor's smirking countenance to suddenly disappear, and hours later Harpie woke from the induced stupor and realized he was back in his cell, but he couldn't remember a single thing about his terrifying interrogation.

CHAPTER
11

"I'm telling you, Madam President," Dr. Stangle said on the phone, "Mr. Tobias's interrogation proved Harpie Colcek is lying."

"Are you absolutely certain of that?" Nancy Hamilton asked. She had succeeded President Jamieson, but retained him as warden.

"Yes, Madam President," he replied. "It took us months to break him down, but Mr. Colcek finally confessed it was all a hoax. Of course, his admission corroborated what we managed to wring from Mr. Shamon. Our tests also indicate Martha Spiller Colcek is also being deceptive. She's a tough one too, but we're still working on her."

"An FBI agent told the bureau he saw the photographs and documents taken from the Colceks," the president said. The agent allegedly spent years in photo interpretation and swore the ones he confiscated were not doctored."

"He lied, Madam President," the doctor replied. "The CIA confiscated those photos and proved they're fakes."

"But why would the agent lie about that?" the president asked.

"The CIA ran a check on all three of those FBI agents," Dr. Stangle said, "and we discovered they had savings and investments worth hundreds of thousands of dollars that went far beyond what they could afford on their salaries. It turns out they were in cahoots with Father Gallagher's illegal alien smuggling operations. He was paying them out of church funds for years to keep the operation going, and of course the church hid the Colceks at that secret location in Saint Mary's.

"That's why the government could never prove Saint Mary's was the hub of the smuggling operation," Dr. Stangle continued. "And when Harpie Colcek and Martha Spiller became fugitives, Father Gallagher paid the agents additional bribes so they wouldn't arrest the pair."

The president said, "I understand that, but how come those three agents suddenly decided to break up the smuggling ring and arrest the Colceks?"

"Very simple, Madam President. When the border was sealed off completely, the illegal aliens could no longer sneak into the country, and the church stopped funding the operation. The three agents decided the jig was up and allowed Father Gallagher to escape to the Vatican, knowing the United States has no extradition agreement with the Holy See. Those agents thought they were home free, since Father Gallagher would never report them, and Halifax and Dubkowski were certain the Colceks would stick to their illegal alien story."

There was an ominous silence on the phone, and then President Hamilton said, "Nice work, Dr. Stangle, but don't breathe a word about the FBI agents to anyone, and have the CIA issue warrants for their arrests; got it?"

"Yes, Madam President," he replied. "Oh, by the way, what do you want me to do about them once they're in custody?"

"They'll be your prisoners. Keep them in custody until after I speak to the Congressional Intelligence Committee, and then we'll decide what we have to do about the situation," she replied. Then she hung up.

Dr. Stangle smiled derisively. He was the warden and head psychiatrist at the Place and would remain so for the foreseeable future. The president didn't know the CIA had already arrested the three FBI agents days ago, and that they were already in his custody. Then he headed for his secret multimillion-dollar experimental research laboratory hidden within the deepest recesses of the post office building.

"We now know the MRIs we took of Martha Spiller matches the ones we took of Mr. Shamon years ago and the other five Di cadavers in the mortuary fridges," Dr. Stangle said to his five research scientists. "The Di has only one large kidney. There are no biliary trees either. Rather, the tissues of what resemble a human liver, pancreas, and gall bladders are fused, yet they somehow perform the same basic functions as the corresponding human organs do."

"Yes, Dr. Stangle," Dr. Michaels replied, "we determined that the evolutionary process of the Di differ somewhat from our own. However, the DNA results indicate we came from a common ancestry."

"You mean like Adam and Eve?" Dr. Stangle said and smirked.

"Not so funny anymore, Dr. Stangle," Dr. Freeman interjected. "Remember Martha Spiller told us the Di Bible is thousands of years older than our Earth's Bible? Well, their Bible says that when God drove humans from the Garden of Eden, he pulverized it and scattered the descendants of their parental heritage to different places in the universe, after reducing them to ignorant savages. They had to relearn everything from scratch, including a language and social mores."

"I'm a scientist, not a fool," Dr. Stangle answered. "I don't believe a single thing written in their Bible or any other bible. But what does fascinate me the most about the Di is that when we injected Martha Spiller with the thioscopola, it didn't affect her one bit. Somehow that permeable membrane surrounding the Di's brains filters out our mind-altering drugs. We must find out how it does that.

"Mr. Shamon, however, is another story. He was much older than Martha Colcek. Therefore, we can conclude that as they age, the membrane somehow begins to break down."

"Exactly," Dr. Michaels answered.

"The president has assured me," Dr. Stangle said, "that as long as she is in office, this prison will continue to exist to maintain global law and order. If we can solve the mystery of how that membrane and the rest of the Di's organs work within the three years she has left of her second term, we can prove they come from a planet that is still in an evolutionary process. We will become the most renowned medical scientists in modern history! Can you imagine the fame, power, and glory we will have at our fingertips, gentlemen?"

Not one of the five lab scientists showed the slightest reaction to his remarks; they feared him. He had absolute power over the entire prison, and several years ago one of their compatriots, Dr. Witherstein, who disagreed with Dr. Stangle's philosophy, said he wanted out of the program. Then Dr. Witherstein suddenly disappeared without a trace. The five research scientists were trapped here. It was obvious Dr. Stangle would never let them leave—they knew too much about the prison and this secret lab and the existence of extraterrestrials.

"Well, gentlemen," Dr. Stangle said. "I've got things to do, but I'll rejoin you later. Now get back to work; remember—we have just three years."

The door to the lab suddenly burst open and Guard One entered, pushing a gurney with a body strapped to it. The blood in her hair and on her face was plainly visible.

"She just went berserk, Dr. Stangle," the guard explained, "and we had to subdue her. Do you need another cadaver?"

"What was her name?" Dr. Stangle asked.

"Sue Colcek," the guard replied.

"No, we don't need her body," he answered. "She's not a Di. Cremate her, and after dark, scatter her ashes in the Trinity River."

"Yes, sir," the guard responded. He pushed the gurney through another set of doors leading to the onsite crematory.

After Dr. Stangle left, the five scientists anxiously looked at one another. They were now certain they knew what happened to Dr. Witherstein.

It was Christmas Eve, and the winter wind was sweeping across the top of the plateau in Cap Rock Canyons State Park & Trailway near Quitaque, Texas. State Trooper Robert Andersen was shivering, but not from the cold. He was afraid, but he knew what he had to do. He had never encountered extraterrestrials before, but he knew the Tiguan and Comanche legends were true, and soon he would be meeting the titanium Robots and the Di people Martha Spiller told him about years ago, when he apprehended her as she walked from the park toward Quitaque.

The FBI and the military had monitored this plateau on Christmas Eve for five years, hoping to apprehend the foreign saboteurs who were threatening the homeland, but to no avail. They did not see or hear anything and concluded that this was not the landing site and the large melted snow patches were merely a geological peculiarity of this particular mesa and the surrounding areas.

Trooper Andersen looked at his watch; it was exactly 11:55, and the cold wind suddenly turned warm. He knew it must be them, and he took a deep breath. A chill ran down his back as he courageously but cautiously stepped forward. In spite of the pale moonlight and the crested snow, he could hardly see anything. Then his shin grazed against something hard, and he stopped and looked down.

In the subdued light he could barely make out a white metal step, and a few moments later he was standing in a long hallway lit by a line of blue-tinged lights.

He reached for his pistol when he heard a strange sound behind him, and he tried to turn around, but a strange sensation prickled the back of his neck and his fingers froze on the handle of his weapon. *It feels like I'm having a stroke*, he thought, *but I'm still standing!*

A powerful force spun him around; he was staring into the red protruding eyes of a guard Robot. The trooper's pulse throbbed in his throat. The Robot was taller than the trooper's six-foot stature, and it held him semi-paralyzed while it scanned his retinas. But it didn't recognize them, and it released the human from his apoplectic state.

Trooper Andersen knew the steps had retracted and the exit door was shut. He drew his revolver, but an electrical jolt wrested it from his hand before he could pull the trigger. He didn't know how the Robot did that, and it paid him no further heed as it walked away with the weapon and beckoned him to follow.

A door slid open, and the trooper saw what appeared to be thousand glass coffins. A creature resembling a human turned toward them. The man looked at the Robot, and although it didn't have a mouth, Andersen's jaw dropped when it asked in a digitized voice, "Who are you and what do you want aboard my spacecraft?"

The man reached out and turned the trooper's head so that he was looking at him and not the Robot. *The Robot is somehow reading the man's thoughts and speaking in English for him*, the trooper realized. *The sound of its voice reminds me of Darth Vader from* Star Wars.

"I'm State Trooper Robert Andersen," he finally answered. "I'm a friend of Harpie Colcek and Martha Spiller."

"You mean Martha Spiller Colcek, don't you?" the man replied via the Robot. "Commander Eshwon married them."

"I had no idea they got married." He felt more at ease.

The Robot spoke for the man again. "I am Commander Assan, and any friend of Harpie Colcek is a friend of mine." They shook hands.

"So why did you come here, Trooper Andersen?" the commander asked.

"Harpie and Martha have been imprisoned."

"For what?"

The trooper kept his eyes focused on the man even though his mouth wasn't moving; it was all rather strange.

"He refused to betray your people by disclosing your landing site, and he tried to explain to the world that you're an advanced civilization and could help Earth solve many of its problems. He and Martha took many photos and documents from Rau to prove the things they were saying about your advanced civilization were true. But my sources tell me an evil, greedy man named Dr. Stangle intercepted them, and he's holding Harpie and Martha and certain Di and other Pi in a top secret prison known to the CIA as the Place. It is a chamber of horrors, torture, and death."

"How did you find out about this secret prison?" Commander Assan asked.

"My cousin Don is an FBI agent in the Denver office. They brought the prisoners there to turn them over to the CIA. When Don rifled through the evidence, he found my business card in Harpie's wallet, which I'd given him years ago after he reported his rental car stolen.

"Don called and told me they'd been arrested, and I knew where the CIA would take them. Martha told me about the Place years ago, when I apprehended her as she was walking to Quitaque after she missed the return shuttle."

The commander looked at him in disbelief, but then he realized the trooper risked his life to come aboard the *Star Voyager* before the guard Robot could kill him, so he wasn't setting a trap, and he made the Robot return the trooper's pistol.

The Robot was silent for a moment, and then it continued relaying the commander's words in English again. "I once told Harpie that when a Di becomes you friend, he is your friend forever! I must help him; he helped us."

They waited for more than an hour before Commander Assan received a reply from the Centralized Rau Defense Command. "I will remain on Earth for at least six months, and this plateau will be my base of operations. The Robot police contacted Mr. Shamon, who I got to know personally on his return flight to Rau years ago. He has mostly recovered from his abuse by Dr. Stangle and his cohorts, and he was able to pinpoint the exact location of the Place for us.

"We will free my friend Harpie Colcek and his wife, Martha, Trooper Andersen. I have fifty Robot soldiers on the way here to help rescue them. The Robots have been dormant for the last twenty-five years aboard a spaceship that was kept hidden behind an asteroid to prevent detection as it traveled throughout your solar system. They will arrive in three Earth days.

"Perhaps the time has come for Earth to have its Armageddon like Rau had, when an asteroid destroyed the sister moons Lia and Tia a thousand years ago. The survivors of that catastrophe came together after hundreds of millions of our people perished, and we came to realize that all we really have in life is each other.

"Earth is still a place of evil; the Pi never learned anything from the chaos caused by a few individuals with a lust for power, its eternal wars, tortures, murders, rapes, human trafficking, drug smuggling, greed, and the mere pittance it spends on the mental-health issues that plague every nation on Earth. If they addressed those psychological problems, Earth would go a long way toward solving many of its current difficulties."

Trooper Andersen didn't know what to say at first, but he heard every word he was meant to hear, even though the commander's mouth never moved. "What sort of Armageddon?" Trooper Andersen managed to blurt out.

The commander looked the trooper squarely in the eye, and Robert Andersen heard the digitized voice of the Robot say, "Every major power on Earth has an arsenal of atomic weapons pointed at one another. We were hoping peace will reign here for at least another fifty years, but it will not be so. That is why we no longer let our children migrate here; unfortunately, a few were born on flights to Earth. Only the middle aged or the elderly were permitted to emigrate to Earth, because they would have been dead by the time this planet self-destructs. Therefore, for the last fifty years, families with youngsters had to choose another world. We have seen this kind of confrontation on other planets that Earth now faces, Trooper Andersen. It is only a matter of time."

The trooper was stunned by what the Robot said, but before he could respond, the commander handed him a small black instrument. "This is your identifier. I didn't have a spare one to give Harpie Colcek, so I make sure to have a spare one on hand at all times. If you need to contact me here with any additional information or questions, push the button so the guard Robot won't laser you or anyone who comes with you. Do not disclose my location to anyone. You have made a friend, Trooper Andersen; goodbye and good luck."

General Louis Hammond looked at the screen in disbelief. He was the newly designated commander of NORAD, and it was the first time he ever saw what the Phantom Effect looked like on radar.

"I've been here for five years, General," Staff Sergeant Haliday, the radar operator, said, "and I've never seen the Phantom Effect except on Christmas Eve, and that was three days ago; now there it is again. But instead of dropping down below our radar net, this bogey keeps heading southeast. Wait a minute, sir, look; there's another one. They're both headed in the same direction."

"Major Dunn," the general shouted, "secure the complex. Colonel Hastings, get me the Chief of Staff on the line."

Almost immediately, the huge metal doors securing the Cheyenne Mountain Complex closed, and a few moments later Colonel Hastings handed the secure phone to General Hammond.

General Hammond said, "General Gonzalez, we've have an incident here. Two bogeys with the same screen blips as the Phantom Effect appeared out of nowhere and are headed southeast over the mainland."

"Are you sure it's the Phantom Effect?" General Gonzales sounded skeptical. "I thought that only happens on Christmas Eve."

"That has been the case for the last thirty-six years, sir," General Hammond replied. "But their angle of climb and speed indicate they are the same class of aircraft as Santa's Ghost. We got the Lubbock ATCs on the hook, and they confirmed that the bogeys dropped below their radar somewhere near the Dallas-Fort Worth area."

"They could be target cities," the Chief of Staff replied. "Did you scramble the F-35s from Lackland?"

"Yes, sir; they're already airborne and searching the area, but so far there's nothing to report."

"It could be the beginning of an enemy operation," General Gonzales replied. "Keep the F-35s in the area; I'll notify the president."

It was December 28, a beautiful day in Texas in spite of the season and the crisp air, and Dr. Stangle and his five research scientists were delighted. The chief of security phoned him last night that a new Di arrival, by the name of Molly Pittinger, had arrived last night and went berserk and had to be subdued; unfortunately, she was killed during the altercation.

"We have another Di cadaver to work on," Dr. Stangle said and smiled as he opened the mortuary fridge and looked at her blood-stained face and hair. "I can't wait to see what one of their fresh cranial membranes look like. They deteriorate rapidly after death."

The *Star Voyager* and the troop carrier with fifty Robot soldiers aboard had silently landed at Trammel Crow Park on the eastern bank of the Trinity River during the night. The park was closed to repave the road and bike paths, so no Pis were about, and Commander Assan sat monitoring the screen as the drone's camera scanned the area. At exactly 8:00 a.m., he saw a car matching the description of Dr. Stangle's limo enter the park and knew it had to be him and his research staff. Mr. Shamon's description of the area and his directions needed to find the hidden prison were obviously correct.

Commander Assan watched until the car disappeared through the gate and out of view just to be certain the occupants were heading for the prison. They waited until the chauffeur relocked the gate and drove the limo out of the park, and a few minutes later the force of soldier Robots, led by their blue-tinted platoon commander, headed directly toward the maintenance building.

The seven-foot-tall Robot soldiers marched with military precision, their titanium feet crunching the gravel, their metallic arms swinging back and forth in rhythm with each stride. They came upon the gate. It was locked, and although the stature of the soldier Robots dwarfed that of their leader, Commander Assan, he was their master. He turned and silently pointed to the lead Robot in the first column. It read his thoughts and stepped forward and raised its right arm, and a second later the laser bore through the lock securing the gate. The chain and lock fell to the ground.

The Robot pushed the gate open and the force marched onward. The leader Robot placed its finger on the electronic lock, and the door to the false maintenance garage opened. The troop marched down the ramp and through the tunnel and stopped in front of the elevator. Commander Assan waited until all fifty Robots fell into formation again in the prison foyer.

"Do not kill the guards," Commander Assan ordered. "Everyone is to be taken prisoner."

The fifty soldier Robots bowed in unison. The five hundred-pound Robots marched in perfect order down the hallway toward the cellblock entrance, cracking the ceramic tiles with every crunching step of their metallic heels.

The guard sitting at the desk behind the door heard the strange rhythmic sounds of their pounding feet and rushed to the peephole in the metal entrance door and saw a terrifying sight. He tore back to the desk and pushed the hidden alarm button just as a petrifying force buckled the steel door, and a heartbeat later he heard another terrifying sound as another impact tore it from the frame. It clattered to the floor, and a blue-tinted metallic monster with protruding red eyes stepped inside and stared at the guard, who fired twice at the fearsome intruder, but the bullets merely ricocheted off its titanium chest.

The monster pointed at him, and the guard felt a tingling sensation on his forehead and suddenly couldn't move. He could still hear, see, and think, but he couldn't move a muscle. The monster ripped the pistol from his grip and snapped the barrel and the handle off as though it were breaking a dead twig off a tree branch and then dropped the three pieces on the desk.

Commander Assan stepped inside, and the monster bowed.

The remainder of the force entered the cellblock and continued marching down the main passageway between the cells to where the remaining eight guards, who had been warned by the alarm, knelt or stood with the rifles drawn from the prison armory.

"Fire!" Number One shouted.

The noise was deafening, but the murderous lead enfilade merely ricocheted off the armor-like bodies of the soldier Robots and shattered into useless pieces of lead. Their titanium bodies bore nary a scratch, and not a single Robot was disabled, nor did the speed of the seven-foot monsters slacken.

As the force approached the terrified guards, they dropped their weapons and ran toward the lab where Dr. Stangle and his researchers were getting set to operate on the fresh cadaver of Molly Pittinger. The guards were rushing toward the lab in a futile attempt to escape through the back door, but the Robots pointed their metallic fingers in their direction, and the guards plummeted to the floor, paralyzed by the prickling sensation on the back of their heads.

Out of that titanium shield stepped Commander Assan, and he pointed at a prostrate guard on the floor. Number One suddenly stood up.

"You gave the command to fire," the blue-tinged Robot said for his master, "and I surmise you are the head of security. Where is my friend, Harpie Colcek?"

"He is in cage number five," Number One tremulously blurted out.

The Robot leader spun him around and grabbed him by the scruff of his neck and the seat of his pants and effortlessly carried him down the hallway toward cage five.

Commander Assan peered between the bars and barely recognized the emaciated figure sitting on the edge of his bunk. His filthy orange jumpsuit was worn through at the knees, and a scraggly beard covered his face.

Harpie sat there with his mouth agape and drool running down his chin and dripping on to his lap. He stared straight ahead, oblivious to his surroundings.

The pathetic images of the figures portrayed in a book Mr. Shamon gave him flashed to the forefront of the commander's mind. He recalled a man named Adolf Hitler and the words Nazi concentration camp, and he remembered the photos of those ghastly figures peering out from between the barbed-wire strands and the word genocide! The way Harpie looked now reminded him of one of those emaciated prisoners! The murders and treatment of the Di and Pi were similar to what had happened in those concentration camps!

"Open the cage!" he silently commanded the blue Robot leader when he realized what had happened to Harpie.

"Open the cage," the blue Robot said to Guard Number One, while he was still elevating him off the floor.

"I don't have the keys during the day," he screeched in fear. "I give them to Dr. Stangle as soon as he comes in."

"I want this cage opened now," the commander angrily thought in Stritz.

"Your wish is my command, Master," the blue Robot replied in the Rau tongue, and almost instantly four soldier Robots stepped forward and seized the two bars on each side of the cage door. They effortlessly pulled in unison and chunks of cement rained down on the floor as the steel bars were yanked out of the ceiling and the floor.

Commander Assan stepped inside the cage. "Harpie," he said, "it's me, your friend Commander Assan."

For the briefest of moments, something familiar woke in Harpie's mind, and he looked at the stranger standing before him. It was but a fleeting memory, and he returned to his stupefied stare as though his friend wasn't even there.

Commander Assan became even more infuriated, and he turned and looked at the blue Robot and it conveyed his thoughts in English. "Where is the antidote?" the Robot asked the horrified guard.

"It's in the lab. Dr. Stangle keeps it locked up," the frightened guard answered as he dangled from the Robotic arms.

The door to the lab opened, and Dr. Stangle looked up and pulled the surgical mask down. "Who the hell are you?"

"I am Commander Assan," the man replied, "of the *Star Voyager*."

Dr. Stangle's jaw dropped. The man's mouth never moved, but the strange reply was heard coming from somewhere outside the lab.

"You're trespassing on a US government classified location," the doctor shouted. "You are under arrest. Guard!"

The stranger walked over to the gurney and gazed down at the eviscerated body of Molly Pittinger. The digitized voice from outside the room said, "You didn't have to do this. Everything you need to know about the Di is in those documents and photos Harpie Colcek and Marth Spiller Colcek gave you."

"I tried to read those stupid things. They're nothing but gibberish," the doctor replied. "Guard!"

"Martha Colcek would have deciphered anything you didn't understand," the voice said.

"How can your voice answer me from another room?" the doctor asked.

"We are an advanced civilization," the voice said, "and we can do that and much more. We have the ability to help Earth solve many of its problems."

"I do my own research," the doctor answered. "This is the greatest discovery in the history of mankind. My research here will go down in medical history, and the fame and glory will be mine!"

"You and your guards murdered some of these people, Dr. Stangle!" the voice answered.

"People? These're not real people. Look at her internal organs," he said as he pointed at the partially dissected cadaver. "They are not fully developed—they're fused together, and she has a permeable membrane around her brain that differs from ours."

"We are human," the voice answered. "Our evolution took a slightly different path than that of the Pi, but we share a common ancestry."

"So," the doctor replied, "you're one of them. Don't you know what you are? The Di is the answer to what mankind has been searching for more than a thousand years. You're an intermediate step between the great apes and humanity, and the Di's underdeveloped organs prove it. The Di is the missing link, and I have three years left to prove it. Unfortunately, you are a Di and will become part of my solution. Guard!"

"Do you remember Dr. Josef Mengele?" the voice asked as Dr. Stangle turned toward the sound of the voice with a puzzled expression still etching his face.

"I don't know how you're doing that," he replied. "Your mouth isn't moving, but you're projecting your voice outside the lab. However, I will answer your question, Commander Assan or whoever you are. Of course I know of Dr. Mengele, you fool. He was a brilliant German physician and researcher."

"He helped murder thousands of people and performed horrible experiments on hundreds of others," the voice replied.

"I don't expect a subhuman like you to understand," the doctor retorted, "but that is how medical science advances."

"He too was an insane murderer," the voice answered.

"How dare you brand a man of my caliber as an insane murderer?" he angrily replied. "I'm doing this for the good of all mankind; Guard, where the hells are you?"

"You want a guard, Doctor?" the voice asked.

"Yes, I want the guard," he shouted back.

The light shining through the open door suddenly darkened, and a massive figure ducked under the doorframe and entered the lab, still holding Guard Number One by the scruff of his neck and the seat of his pants.

"It's not human," Dr. Michaels shouted as he and the other four staff members backed up against the wall.

The Robot's eyes protruded farther out of their sockets as it focused on Dr. Stangle's face, and then sunk back into the skull when it recognized his features from the portrait hanging in the prison foyer. The crunching sounds of its feet stopped when it reached the gurney separating them.

The physician could only stare up in awe at the massive hulk and the guard helplessly hanging there with a large piss stain in the front of his pants.

"Where is the antidote to the truth serum, Dr. Stangle?" the Robot asked.

Dr. Stangle looked at Commander Assan and shouted, "You'll ruin years of my hard work and experiments and set medical science back a hundred years, you idiot. You and your tin man can go to hell!"

Quicker than the human eye could follow, the metal monster released the seat of the guard's pants, and its Robotic arm stretched across the gurney and seized the doctor by the lapel. The doctor frantically stabbed at it with the scalpel he was still holding, when the Robot abruptly yanked him clear across the gurney and pulled his face close to the screened orifice from which the digitized voice emanated.

"I will ask you one more time, Dr. Stangle; where is the antidote?"

The doctor's mouth was moving but nothing was coming out; the scalpel dropped to the floor.

"Where is it!" the monster screamed.

"It's in the safe, the safe," the horrified physician blurted out in a high-pitched voice. "Fourteen left and seventeen right; twenty-seven left; thirteen right."

The Robot dropped both men to the floor and the doctor rolled backward and hit his head on the gurney wheel. He clutched at the painful bump, but neither man tried to get up.

"He made us do it," Dr. Michaels said as he looked at the Robot and then the commander. "And he murdered Dr. Witherstein because he wouldn't cooperate."

"I will take that under consideration," the voice replied. The Robot pointed to Dr. Freeman and read his name tag and said, "Open the safe and bring the antidote to me, Dr. Freeman."

When Dr. Freeman returned, the voice commanded, "Dr. Michaels, take a vial and syringe and meet me in Harpie Colcek's cage. The rest of you go about the complex and administer the antidote to all the other prisoners."

At that point the doctor and Number One tried to rise but were suddenly paralyzed as the blue Robot pointed at them, and the five researchers took off like a horde of rabbits fleeing a pack of hungry wolves. Moments later they stepped over the prison guards that were still lying in the hallway and set about the task of inoculating the remainder of the prisoners, while a team of the awesome Robots began tearing everything in the lab apart.

Dr. Michaels injected the antidote into his arm, but Harpie Colcek sat staring into space for almost an hour. Then he slowly became aware that his vision was clearing, and the migraine headaches he had endured for more months than he could remember began easing. He gradually stopped drooling and became aware of someone sitting next to him on the bunk. He slowly turned his head to peer at a somewhat familiar face and a seven-foot blue-tinged monster.

"It's me Harpie, Commander Assan," a digitized voice said.

From somewhere deep within the recesses of his mind he recalled that familiar voice. It was a digitized voice, and he stared in wonder at the figure, thinking he was hallucinating again as he had a thousand times since his incarceration. Harpie reached out to touch the man sitting next to him, and realized it was true—it was Commander Assan!

Harpie started sobbing; he was a broken man. The figure embraced him and the voice said, "It's really me, Harpie, your Di friend."

It all seemed unreal to Harpie, and he shook when he realized his dreams had finally come true.

"Oh, Harpie," he heard another voice say in perfect English. He would never forget that voice for as long as he lived—no matter what they did to him. He wiped the tears from his eyes and face, and standing on shaky legs, he shouted, "Martha! Martha!"

She stood there in her orange jumpsuit with tears streaming down her face, and he could clearly see her prisoner's number etched on the left side of her uniform.

"You look so good," the emaciated reporter exclaimed, "in spite of what they did to us all."

"The Di has a thickened permeable membrane that protects our brains and filters out toxins from the blood, including the thioscopola," Martha replied. "Our scientists determined the membrane somehow evolved due to the noxious clouds and volcanic eruptions that occurred thousands of years ago on our native planet.

"That is why they couldn't break me, and it took ten years to subdue Mr. Shamon, who is forty years older than me. Earthlings didn't evolve that way. Dr. Stangle and his cohorts kept telling me that they had erased all the memories you had of me," she said as she sobbed. "I was so afraid you wouldn't remember me."

He wanted to take her into his arms, but then she backed away and said, "They raped me, Harpie."

She looked back at him and cried out, "They raped every woman in this prison, and Guard Number One raped Molly Pittinger after he murdered her."

Commander Assan angrily bolted to his feet and left the cage.

The word rape conjured up a horrible nightmare for Harpie also. "I still love you. On my first night here, Guard Number One said he had a special treat waiting for me. The day after my polygraph they tied me face down on my bunk, and they took turns, painfully raping me with their batons."

They held their embrace, not realizing Commander Assan had left, but he returned a few minutes later with two new orange jumpsuits.

"We'll spend the rest of the day here," Commander Assan told Martha in Stritz, "while the Robots finish reducing this evil place to a pile of rubble. A thousand years from now an archeologist will discover the ruins and hypothesize as to what this place was all about.

"Then this evening, we'll be going to the White House to talk to the president before she presents her well-publicized annual budget to a joint session of the Congress. I want Earth's controversy over the existence of UFOs to end once and for all and let the world know we are a peace-loving race and mean mankind no harm."

Harpie did not have a conversion helmet, so Martha had to explain what the commander said in English so Harpie knew what was happening.

The researchers watched as Dr. Stangle and the guards were being herded by the soldier Robots out the back door toward the troop carrier. They had no idea where the Robots were taking them, but they were glad they weren't going with them. But the commander had kept his word, and although they had been forced to do Dr. Stangle's dirty work under the threat of death, they would be tried by a court on Earth. When the shift changed at 9:00 a.m., the Robots seized the daytime guards too, and the fate of the entire prison was sealed forever.

CHAPTER
12

"Gneral Hammond!" Staff Sergeant Haliday, the radar operator at the Cheyenne Mountain complex, called out. "Sir, those two blips we picked up on December twenty-eighth have left the Dallas area. All the airports on the East Coast are closed due to the winter storm, but we got a report from both Ronald Reagan International and Andrews Air Force Base in Washington, DC that they picked up two bogeys moving toward the capitol at supersonic speed, but they quickly disappeared off radar."

"Colonel Hastings," the general ordered, "notify General Gonzales that the bogeys are on the move again and probably landed somewhere in the DC area. Major Dunn, contact White House security."

"Yes, sir," both men responded and raced off to complete their assignments.

On that cold blustery evening in late December, the *Star Voyager* and the troop carrier *Galactic Guardian* silently landed on the snow-covered south lawn of the White House. Not a single person was wandering about in the twenty degree weather that felt like fifteen below zero when the wind blew.

President Nancy Hamilton sat at the Resolute Desk in the Oval Office, going over the speech that she was to deliver in her State of the Union address to the joint session of Congress at 7:00 p.m. There was a rap on the door leading to the south lawn, but she couldn't see anything.

It must be the wind, she reasoned. *Everyone is inside on such a horrible night.*

Then she heard the sound again and considered calling her security detail. But she didn't want to be an alarmist and instead walked toward the door and stopped midstride when she recognized Dr. Stangle peering through one of the window panes.

"I didn't request your presence in the White House, Dr. Stangle," she muttered as she cringed when the icy blast flowed through the open doorway. "I will be delivering my State of the Union address in half an hour."

She was about to close the door when another figure stepped inside. "Who are you?"

"Commander Assan," a strange-sounding voice answered.

"A commander in the US Navy?" she asked as she stared at his mouth; she didn't see his lips move.

"No, Madam President, I am the commander of the starship *Star Voyager.*"

This time she was certain his mouth didn't move, and it alarmed her. His gray hair was combed back in an old-fashioned hairdo known as a pompadour, and he wore a style of clothing she had never seen before.

She turned and took full note of Dr. Stangle. He wore an orange prison jumpsuit, and his face was as white as a sheet. Nancy Hamilton kept her eyes fixed on the doctor as she tried to close the door, but when she turned to see why it wouldn't budge, her jaw dropped.

A metal monster that appeared to be ten feet tall stood in the doorway, and she looked into the fiercest eyes she had ever seen. She took several steps backward.

The Robot stepped inside and with a backward push of its arm closed the door. At that point Dr. Stangle bolted for the secretary's office, hoping to escape.

The president watched in awe as the metal leviathan pointed a finger at Dr. Stangle, and he abruptly halted. Commander Assan looked at the Robot, and it bowed and said, "Yes, master." Then it bowed to the Chief Executive Officer of the United States of America and said, "Nice to meet you, Madam President."

An hour later, the joint session of Congress heard the Sergeant at Arms announce, "Mister Speaker, the president of the United States!"

President Nancy Hamilton stood before the cameras and the joint session of congress for more than an hour, presenting her proposal for the current year's budget. Then she announced, "My entire cabinet, the chief of staff, the directors of the FBI and the CIA, and the Chief Justice will please join me in the Cabinet meeting room immediately following this session."

Everyone sat around the table in the Cabinet meeting room, wondering why this unusual and unscheduled meeting had been called into session. The president arrived and stood behind her designated chair at the table.

"First of all, I want to thank you for being here, and I want to emphasize that this meeting is classified top secret. You will be surprised, but do not be afraid; these people are friendly, so remain in your seats."

The assembly looked about curiously and then at one another.

The door leading from the secretary's office opened, and a man clad in an orange prison jumpsuit walked in holding a strange-looking helmet under his arm. He stopped at the president's side and said, "My name is Harpie Colcek, and I have been on the FBI's most wanted list for more than eleven years.

"You must be wondering how I avoided arrest by such a fine organization for such a long period of time. Well, twelve years ago I was a guest on a spaceship called *Star Voyager* that started me on a journey that took me to a planet we Earthlings call Proxima b."

"I know who you are," the Secretary of Agriculture shouted. "You're that nut who started all those rumors years ago about space aliens, and it caused a lot of chaos in every country in the world!"

"Let him finish, Mr. Hage," the president said.

Harpie explained how he lived on Rau for a year and told them about the advanced civilization that had colonized Proxima b eons ago.

The Secretary of Agriculture interrupted Harpie again. "I'm sorry, Madam President, but I can't sit here any longer and listen to this garbage. This man belongs in a mental institution!" Then he got up and started for the exit door leading toward the hallway.

"If you leave, Mr. Hage, you will be fired," the president replied.

"My sincerest apology, Madam President," he said as he stopped and turned to face her, "but this man is making a fool of us all. He is a notorious liar seeking fame and fortune; I must go."

As he turned toward the door again, a strange voice echoed across the room. "You aren't going anywhere, Mr. Hage."

Everyone had been concentrating on the verbal exchange between Nancy Hamilton and Secretary Hage and didn't notice the door to the presidential secretary's office open or hear the approaching footsteps of the man who was now standing on the other side of the president. Everyone now focused their attention on him.

Locks of his graying hair were protruding from beneath the strange helmet he wore, and he wore silken garments and the epaulets adorning his shoulders were etched with strange golden symbols.

"Who the hell are you?" Mr. Hage asked.

The man removed the odd-looking helmet and said, "I am Commander Assan of the *Star Voyager,*" in that same strange voice, and suddenly everyone's gaze shifted back toward the secretary's office. The voice came from there and not from the man. They drew back in their seats when they spied a frightening seven-foot metal monster enter the room.

It resembled a man but had fearful red eyes that seem to be protruding from its skull. Its face was shaped like a human face, but it had no nose or ears, and a metal screen served as a mouth. Most of the people sat there stultified with fright, but a horde bolted from their seats and headed toward the door.

The monster bowed, and said, "Yes, master," and just as Mr. Hage's hand seized the doorknob, he and the fleeing throng felt a strange sensation on the back of their heads and froze in place. The frightened horde stood like statues chiseled in stone, and each bore a fixated stare that betrayed their horror and shock, while the staff and officials still sitting in their seats looked on in mortal terror.

"Get back to your seats!" the strange voice commanded, and the statue-like figures seemed to come alive again and readily plopped back in their chairs.

"Do not be afraid," the digitized voice said. "We come in peace and friendship."

The frightened public officials heard the rhythm of marching feet, and a few moments later the west side door to the Cabinet meeting room burst open. Forty-nine more soldier Robots quickly surrounded the mortified politicians.

"These are the soldier Robots of Rau," Commander Assan said via the Robot, "and they are our heroes. Several thousand years from now, when your Armageddon is but a few bytes in your historical database, you will send your soldier Robots into space to clash with the evildoers of distant planets. Human flesh and blood will not fight each other. The planet with the most advanced technology and the largest number and the most powerful soldier Robots will survive, just as the nations on Earth that have the most soldiers and the greatest firepower win wars. That is how my planet, Rau, remains free.

"The people on those other planets that evolved like Earth's humans will want to conquer the universe, just as today's despots in China, Russia, Iran, and Syria want to conquer your world; you must not let them win.

"You will even invent smaller Robots to do the most mundane tasks that humans do not want to do, and you will program Robots to police your streets and others to perform your most delicate surgeries."

The exchange lasted for almost five hours, while Commander Assan, Harpie, and Martha filled them in on the planet Rau, its people, and space travel.

In the wee hours of the morning, Diane Mandel, the CIA director, asked Commander Assan, "Where did you get those videos of Zhang Li and Sergei Sukov?"

There was a delay in his response while the commander and Harpie donned their strange helmets. The commander wanted his captive audience to hear an Earthly voice to calm them. It would be his words but Harpie's voice.

"We have been immigrating to other worlds and this planet for more than several hundred years," Harpie said, "and the Di, the people of Rau, have migrated to every major country on Earth. They assimilated into many cultures, but the Di never let their progeny forget their history and their roots. This imbued their heirs with the Master's rules; thus they were raised with a strong sense of right and wrong.

"Subsequently, these offspring worked their way into high government positions in many countries, and we got the secret tapes of those two dictators from those Di offspring, whose ancestors had made those two countries their homes. Now you know the intentions of those two dictators."

Then the president spoke. "But even if we warn our allies of the Sino/Russian pact and their intent to destroy the United States and its allies on July 4, 2051, which is the two hundred and seventy-fifth anniversary of our independence, we and NATO don't have enough ICMs to fully retaliate, nor a sufficient number of antiballistic missiles necessary to counter the combined threat of the Chinese, Russian, Iranian, and Syrian rockets.

"All the major wars that have ever been fought on Earth were precipitated by dictators like Genghis Khan, the Roman emperors, King George III, Hitler, Stalin, and Idi Amin—and now we have face Zhang Li of China and Sergei Sukov of Russia. If we have a nuclear war, hundreds of millions will die, Commander Assan. Will you help us defend the freedom and liberty of all mankind and destroy the dictators' armies or their will to fight?"

"I'm sorry, Madam President," the Harpie replied for the commander, "but I am forbidden by the Supreme Confederation from interfering in the political disputes or wars of a world that is not yet an interstellar force; your planet is still evolving-a new born baby in the history of the universe."

"But those dictators slaughtered millions of people, including some of Rau's ancestors!" the president retorted. "Are you going to let that happen again?"

"The atomic wars will be your Armageddon, Madam President," he said, "and every planet has a catastrophe of one type or another. The asteroid that destroyed Lia and Tia, the sister moons of Rau was our destiny-our Armageddon. Our near total destruction is what united the survivors on Rau. A thousand years after your holocaust, Earth's survivors will also unite and form some sort of a world confederation, where each country retains its own borders, culture and laws, and abolishes the power of dictators forever.

"Your United Nations is a feeble attempt to accomplish that, but it is a very weak organization, a tiger without teeth, and is therefore largely ineffective. The lust for world domination is a powerful temptation for dictators, and you must maintain peace through strength.

"Even if we interfered with your planet's wars, we cannot help. We haven't fought a war in more than five hundred years. Remember— Rau was almost destroyed by a huge asteroid, and we developed weapons that have powerful lasers that can destroy the asteroids that threaten our planet. They are weapons of mass destruction and are powerful enough to destroy a large building in the blink of an eye or a city in a matter of minutes. But the main lasers cannot intercept the vast number of supersonic missiles that will be airborne when the holocaust begins.

"But the root of Earth's problem, Madam President, is that dictators have banished one of the Master's greatest gifts: love. Love of God, their families, their neighbors, and their country. Life is and always will be a matter of the free will the Master gave each individual—the choice between what is good or what is evil. Even on Rau we're still working to resolve a few of those issues, Madam President. But despots have always chosen evil—the very antithesis of love—and its dark side is the murder and desecration of the most vulnerable human beings.

"Those evils are the most egregious violation of the Master's rules, and unfortunately millions of the innocent have always perished with the guilty in order to make things right! It is the price of freedom and liberty.

"My best advice to you at this point, Madam President," the commander continued via Harpie's voice, "is to allow Harpie and Martha Colcek to finish converting the documents they brought from Rau into English and several other major Earth languages. Then seal those documents in a time capsule, and bury it in a remote part of your country where a nuclear blast will not destroy them. Millennia from now a curious archeologist will stumble upon them, and a new world will begin to emerge from the ashes of planet Earth."

For the first time since Nancy Hamilton became president, an eerie silence pervaded the Cabinet meeting room. The cabinet and other government officials sat in stunned silence, and Commander Assan waited a few moments to let the sobering reality of what he revealed sink in before he spoke again.

"However, there is one small ray of hope for this planet," he said via Harpie, "and that is multilateral nuclear disarmament. I urge you to disclose Earth's fate to the United Nations, and tell them that if humanity does not eradicate every weapon in its nuclear arsenals and cease the human rights violations committed in those countries ruled by dictators, Armageddon will surely rein in every country on Earth."

"The Chinese and the Russians will never agree to that," the president said. "If you are forbidden from interfering militarily, will you negotiate with these despots on Earth's behalf? When they learn that you are truly an alien from Rau, it may be the lynchpin of peace on earth."

"The Supreme Confederation does not negotiate with dictators or terrorists," he answered. "That would be futile. But you must do your best and continue talking to them or at least try."

The president realized he meant the only hope the world had left lay in pleading her case before the United Nations.

"Remember," the commander said, "if you are not successful in your quest, you will have less than six months until the apocalypse. Whatever you do, do not reveal that you are privy to their intentions on July Fourth. They will merely slip their attack plan to an earlier day, like June fourteenth, your Flag Day." Then he tersely said, "Bring in the prisoner!"

The door to the secretary's office opened, and the blue Robot escorted a terrified Dr. Stangle to the commander.

"This man has made heinous experiments on Earthlings and the Di in the lab of the CIA prison known as the Place," the commander said.

"That's lie!" Dr. Stangle screeched. "I never harmed anyone."

"That prison was designed to confine the people who were terrorizing the world with rumors of aliens," the horrified president shrieked, "and was never authorized to be a human experimental lab." It was another stunning revelation for the Cabinet and other government officials; they never heard of a CIA prison called the Place.

Commander Assan nodded to the blue Robot that now stood near the secretary's office door, and a moment later three men entered the meeting room.

The president's jaw dropped and she gasped and blurted out, "Agents Halifax and Dubkowski, where the hell have you been? The CIA issued warrants for your arrests for corruption and collusion with Father Gallagher's smuggling ring, but you disappeared."

"Madam President," Agent Halifax answered as he pointed at Dr. Stangle, "he had us confined in that hellhole called the Place before you authorized our arrests. Like the rest of the prisoners there, he kept us sedated, and his guards murdered people they knew were aliens, as well as some American citizens."

"Why the hell did you do that?" the president asked.

"You don't understand, Madam President," Dr. Stangle replied, "they knew too much. They were going to spoil everything."

"How?" she asked.

"Well—" the doctor started to say.

"Because I authenticated the photos the Colceks showed us," the third man said, interrupting Dr. Stangle's response.

"Who are you?" the president said.

"I am former FBI Agent William Voyavich," the man replied, "and we three agents witnessed the rapes and murders of Sue Colcek and Molly Pittinger by Dr. Stangle's prison guards."

"Yeah," Agent Dubkowski said, "and Number One raped Molly Pittinger after she was dead, and then he snickered and said, 'Oh well, Dr. Stangle can always use another Di cadaver.'"

"That's a lie, Madam President," Dr. Stangle blurted. "Whatever research I did was for the good of all mankind."

"You're a liar," Agent Dubkowski shouted. "You did it for your own fame and glory."

"I'm on the verge of the greatest discovery of modern science," the doctor retorted as he looked at the president.

"What discovery?" the president asked as she stared at Dr. Stangle in disbelief.

"Molly Pittinger claimed to be from Rau. We arrested her, but she resisted and was killed. I did an autopsy to determine the cause of death and found she had the same internal organs as Mr. Shamon and Martha Spiller Colcek that we saw on our MRIs. I have absolute proof that these creatures that call themselves the Di are the missing link, the final stage of evolution that changed Cro-Magnon man, the earliest known *Homo sapiens*, into the perfect species, modern-day human beings, and that discovery was made in your lab, Madam President, to your great benefit!"

"I never authorized any such lab, Dr. Stangle and neither did my predecessor, President Jamieson." The president's gaze shifted from the doctor to Commander Assan.

"Internally, we are somewhat different from Earthlings," the commander said, still using Harpie as his interpreter, "because our evolutionary path differed from your biological journey. Our earliest ancestors evolved in a world that was drastically different from Rau and Earth. They endured a host of different challenges than those presented by this planet and our native world.

The climate there was different; they endured different diseases and the microbes that caused them. The atmosphere had a composition of gases that was unlike Earth's, and over the eons our ancestors adapted to the various poisons in the atmosphere surrounding their planet. Consequently, a thick, permeable membrane now envelops our brains to protect us from those gases and many other toxins, and the protection it affords differs from the membrane surrounding the brain tissues of the humans that evolved on Earth. Our membrane also filters out certain chemical infusions such as thioscopola."

"What is thioscopola?" the president asked.

"It's the truth drug administered by Dr. Stangle," the commander said. "If the victim is unaffected, he knows that person is a Di. If they become unconscious for a few minutes it means the drugs have penetrated the protective membrane and shocked the brain into a temporary but unconscious state; it means they're an Earthling."

"But to prove beyond a shadow of a doubt that they are a Di," Agent Halifax interjected, "he had to surgically verify it, and in order to obtain Di cadavers, he had them murdered!"

"It wasn't murder," Dr. Stangle insisted, "because they're not humans!"

"Agent Halifax," the president said as she glared at Dr. Stangle, "place this madman under arrest."

"I can't," Agent Halifax answered. "When we were arrested, the FBI director fired us, so officially we're no longer FBI agents."

"The hell you're not!" the president snapped. "Place this monster under arrest."

"How dare you insult a man of my genius and education?" Dr. Stangle vehemently replied as he stared back at the president. "I've made the greatest scientific find of the twenty-first century!"

"What the hell has happened to you, Dr. Stangle?" the president replied.

"He is what a human becomes when you give him absolute power over others," Commander Assan responded before Dr. Stangle could reply. "In his own right, Dr. Stangle is a dictator of sorts-and dictators answer to no one."

As agents Halifax and Dubkowski seized the doctor, Commander Assan said, "With all due respect, Madam President, the Supreme Federation has convicted and sentenced Dr. Stangle and his cohorts in absentia, since some of the people they have murdered were Di. According to the laws of the Supreme Confederation, they are convicted rapists and therefore Dr. Stangle and his cohorts must be castrated for those crimes. As for their murders of the Di, they will spend the rest of their lives slaving in the mines on Minerva."

"Minerva?" the president asked.

"Yes," he said. "It's a planet less than a lightyear away from Rau that is rich in minerals and plants not found on Earth or Rau."

The president was shocked at the sentence to be meted out for the crime of rape, but she knew she was powerless to prevent Commander Assan from retaining custody. To save face she said, "Very well, Commander, Dr. Stangle and his cronies will remain in your custody."

"Thank you, Madam President," he graciously responded.

"I am an American citizen," Dr. Stangle yelled, "and I demand protection under the constitution of the United States. I have a right to trial by a jury of my peers and not a bunch of apes from another planet!"

While he was screaming about his rights, the blue Robot brushed past the two FBI agents and seized the doctor by the scruff of his neck and the seat of his pants. He kicked feverishly and wildly flailed his arms about as the five hundred-pound soldier Robot effortlessly carried him from the room and headed toward the troop carrier. The trembling Cabinet members could only watch in awe, realizing how helpless they were in the presence of the mighty soldier Robots.

Commander Assan merely glanced at the Robots and they read his thoughts and bowed. Then the Robots stepped forward and placed their metallic fingers on the hunching figures of those seated at or near the table. They cringed when they felt a strange sensation prickle the back of their heads, and a moment later the Robots gently rested their heads on the tabletop, while others merely slumped in their chairs. Only the president, Commander Assan, Harpie and Martha Colcek, and the three FBI agents were still awake.

"They're only asleep," Commander Assan assured the startled president. "When they wake, they will not remember a thing that was said or occurred during this meeting. Unfortunately, they will forget some minor things such as where they left their car keys or where they parked the car, but they'll be okay.

"Many of my people were hoping to openly migrate here, and we were willing to share our secrets, minerals, and plants with Earth's brightest scientists. Over time, our freighters could have deposited millions of tons of those rare minerals from Minerva on Earth. They are essential for developing the drugs defined in the photos and documents brought here by Mr. and Mrs. Colcek. Of course, that is not going to happen anytime soon.

"However, after your Armageddon is over, we will begin that task so that a thousand years from now, when Earth's geologists find those minerals in great abundance, they will surmise they are native to Earth. Someday one of Earth's future scientists will uncover the time capsule and decipher the documents and photos and discover that our remedies will cure many of the diseases that will still be afflicting mankind."

The president was stunned in knowing that soon nothing might be left of Earth, but she tried one more approach to win his support. "Commander Assan, as I said before, if you let the civilizations of Earth destroy themselves, the Di who migrated here will perish with us."

"Our sun is dying, and it was their choice to migrate here," he answered, "knowing earth is a troubled planet; it is too late for me or anyone else in the Supreme Confederation to help them. My best advice to you, Madam President, is to continue to strive for peace in any way you can.

"I will remain here for six months, and during that time you must allow the Colceks to finish deciphering the documents and photos they brought from Rau. If you need to contact me for any reason, Trooper Robert Andersen of the Texas State Police knows how to get hold of me. Goodbye, Madam President, and good luck." Then he confiscated the video tapes of the Russian and Chinese dictators as per their agreement.

Without saying another word, the commander and his soldier Robots formed up and marched out of the Cabinet meeting room past the White House security personnel and the president's administrative staff. They seemed to be frozen in time by the mystical power of the Robots, whether they were in the hallways, their offices, or the Cabinet meeting room.

As the *Star Voyager* and *Galactic Guardian* rose from the south lawn of the White House, the sleepers woke and carried on their duties as though their dream state was but a moment in time, although they later remarked how quickly the night had passed, and they became puzzled when they couldn't remember where they parked their cars in the multileveled garage. Others couldn't readily recall their spouse's first name. Both incidents seemed to be a rather common problem at the moment.

CHAPTER
13

On April 17, 2051, the president of the General Assembly of the United Nations again called an emergency meeting at the request of the United States. It seemed the president was gravely concerned about the continuing nuclear power proliferation and the social unrest in the world. The Eternal President of the People's Republic of China and Secretary General of the Communist Party, Zhang Li, and the president of the Russian Federation, Sergei Sukov, declined the invitation to attend.

The President Elect of the General Assembly, the current president, member states, and the Secretary General of the United Nations agreed to open a debate on the subject of immediate nuclear disarmament. Per the UN rules, each speaker was allotted fifteen minutes in which to speak, and as was the custom, the Brazilian ambassador spoke first.

Then Nancy Hamilton, the President of the United States, addressed the 193 members of the General Assembly. "And in conclusion," she said, "three permanent members of the Security Council—the United States of America, France, and the United Kingdom, and the ten current nonmembers—urge the governments of China and the Russian Federation to join us in adapting a unilateral nuclear disarmament resolution in the interest of world peace and to prevent the advent of mutually assured destruction."

While President Hamilton spoke, a group of representatives from China, the Russian Federation, Iran, Syria, Lebanon, North Korea, Yemen, and a host of other countries that had once been a part of the Union of Soviet Socialist Republics, got up and walked out of the General Assembly Hall in protest.

It was a devastating moment for Nancy Hamilton and the world, and no one in the hall seemed to notice the concerned look of the man with the gray pompadour sitting in the back row, nor did they detect the miniature transmitter pinned to his lapel. It was transmitting the proceedings to the *Star Voyager* that was resting on a remote mesa in Cap Rock Canyons State Park, and in turn its communications center was relaying the broadcast to the members of the Supreme Confederation on the planet Rau.

The next day the US ambassador to China, Gene V. Wertz, informed President Hamilton that the Chinese ambassador, Zhou Wei, had a letter from the Chinese president concerning her nuclear disbarment request. The president opened and silently read the letter.

June 1, 2051

> Madam President, now that our axis fighter planes and bombers rule the skies and our navies control the seas, you want to talk of world peace.

But it is not world peace you desire. It is your fear in knowing that the combined strength of our nuclear armed ICBMs far outnumbers those of the United States and its allies. If you truly desire a lasting world peace, then you must order your imperial military to stand down and disband. Then and only then can we can talk of a unilateral nuclear disarmament.

Zhang Li
Eternal President of the
Peoples Republic of China

June 1, 2051, started out as a routine day for the Americans stationed at Peterson Air Force in Colorado Springs, Colorado, when suddenly Staff Sergeant Dan Haliday, a radar operator at NORAD's Cheyenne Mountain complex shouted, "What in the hell is that?"

Airmen from adjacent radar stations hastily replied, "We don't know!"

"On my screen," another radar operator responded, "it's about ten thousand miles out in space, and it's not in orbit; it's stationary and aligned with the North Pole."

He pressed the red-alert button, an indication of unusual or suspicious activity, and moments later General Hammond shouted to the head of security, "Major Dunn, close the outer doors."

The twenty-five-ton outer and inner doors shielding the complex closed again, sealing the occupants inside for the duration of the emergency, whether for days, weeks, months, or perhaps even years.

"Colonel Hasting," the general commanded, "get me the Chief of Staff on the line, pronto!"

At that moment, in the headquarters of the Chinese Liberation Army in Beijing, the colonel in charge of the National Space Administration approached the Chairman of the Military Commission, General Zhao Hong, with an urgent message.

"General," he said rather excitedly, "we have detected several strange objects located about sixteen-thousand kilometers out in space, which is out of range of our satellite weapons. I believe they are secret American or Russian weapons systems."

The general bolted to his feet and shouted, "Get me the executive office of the Eternal President, Zhang Li; tell him it is a national emergency."

Vladimir Nicholai, the Prime Minister of Russia, was stunned, as he listened to the general in charge of the Roscosmos State Corporation for Space Activities.

"There are four of them, sir," he reported. "One is stationed sixteen-thousand kilometers above the north pole; another one the same distance from the south pole, and two more are located in line with the equator, but in different hemispheres. The bizarre thing is that they are stationary and not in orbit."

The Prime Minister immediately contacted the president, Sergei Sukov, and he called the head of the Defense Ministry in Moscow, who advised him, "The position of those satellites places them in a position so that they can hit any country on earth, Mr. President.

"However, our National Security Council doesn't believe the Chinese space program is sophisticated enough to launch satellites that far from Earth and have them remain stationary. Therefore, we have concluded they are an American-made space weapons system— perhaps their dreaded Strategic Defense Initiative first proposed by their former president Ronald Reagan."

"But we monitor every American launch," the president retorted. "How did we miss these four launches?"

"Perhaps they discovered how to disguise a launch, Mr. President," the defense minister said, "and they might have put those four satellites into space at once. Either that or they were launched by extraterrestrials."

They both laughed at the prospect; the levity was what both men needed at the moment.

Texas State Trooper Robert Andersen stood before Commander Assan aboard the *Star Voyager* and said, "The president needs to know what those four space crafts are about, sir."

A Robot read the commander's thoughts and said, "The Supreme Confederation heard President Hamilton's plea before the United Nations and judged her heart to be true. It therefore authorized my limited interference to try to prevent a nuclear holocaust, but not to engage any country if the ruse does not work and Armageddon ensues.

"Those spacecraft surrounding Earth are called star-bursters, Trooper Andersen," the digitized Robot's voice said, "because they were designed to destroy any large asteroids or meteors that endangered Rau. They cannot tract or destroy missiles, but their massive lasers can destroy an entire city with one blast, and while they cannot win the battle for America or its allies, they can help even the score.

"Tell your president that on July 1, I will order the star bursters to sink one aircraft carrier from each of the countries that comprise the United Nations Security Council, since they pose the greatest threat of mutually assured destruction. Simultaneously sinking one ship from each of those countries might convince them that the real threat comes from a source other than Earth, and hopefully those nations will come to terms to fight this unknown adversary. It is heartless, but if it works it will save hundreds of millions of other Earthlings and Di lives."

On July 1, 2051, at 10:30 a.m., the American and Chinese fleets patrolling the South China Sea watched one another on radar and through binoculars. They heard a sudden sonic boom and then a huge red streak resembling lightning struck the American carrier *Gerald R. Ford*; it exploded into hundreds of pieces that quickly disappeared beneath the waves with all hands aboard.

The Chinese fleet admiral looked on in horror from his flagship, the aircraft carrier, *Dalian III*. His command hadn't fired a missile or launched an aircraft, yet he knew the Americans would blame him for starting World War III. He turned toward his vice admiral and started to say something when another sonic boom, followed by an enormous laser, obliterated his flagship. The splintered vessel joined the debris of the American carrier lying on the bottom of the South China Sea.

In other parts of the world, the British carrier *Ark Royal* somehow exploded and disappeared below the murky waters of the North Sea; the French vessel *Charles de Gaulle* mysteriously vanished in the North Atlantic, and remnants of the Russian carrier *Ivanov* lay scattered about the bottom of the Chukchi Sea. Then the stationary satellites mysteriously disappeared.

All five nations on the Security Council of the United Nations were now gearing up for war, and once again President Nancy Hamilton appeared before an emergency session of the United Nations.

"Our investigation proves that all five carriers were struck simultaneously in different parts of the world," she said. "It is obvious the strikes came from those spacecraft stationed around the earth. The people, who fear a world war, are saying it was a freak accident of nature. But that is impossible, since all five carriers were struck at nearly the same time.

"I sincerely believe those laser satellites are controlled by a civilization far superior to those on Earth," the US president said, "and I urge all nations to band together to resist this foreign invader."

However, her words were viewed by many countries as a vain attempt to maintain peace, especially since the world's major powers had so vehemently rejected the existence of UFOs and ETs for decades. Therefore, her belief carried little weight in light of the current emergency, in spite of her sincerity.

Earth was on the verge of a nuclear war, and the billions of people watching the broadcast were stunned by her remarks about extraterrestrials, and this time the Chinese and Russian delegations did not walk out of the General Assembly in protest. Chinese President Zhang Li and Russian President Sergei Sukov remained seated.

The Americans were willing to sacrifice almost five thousand of their sailors and a multibillion-dollar carrier, Zhang Li thought, *in order to cover up their advanced weapons system.* The Secretary General of the United Nations declared a two hour recess for lunch; the meeting would resume at 2:00 p.m.

"Several years ago," President Sukov whispered to the Chinese president, "our Intel uncovered a top secret occurrence that the American government calls the Phantom Effect, and of course it raised our suspicions. The secret was sold to one of our agents by a man who worked as an air traffic controller at Lubbock International Airport. He has since been apprehended and imprisoned by their CIA."

"So the Americans are aware that we know about their secret project known as the Phantom Effect?" Zhang Li asked.

"Yes, I am certain of it," Sergei Sukov answered, "but they only discovered it recently by using a new truth serum called thioscopola, and our Intel says the Phantom Effect explains how the Americans could launch and recover these weapon satellites for years without being detected. Their radar operators in the Cheyenne Mountain Complex jokingly refer to those secret satellite launches and recoveries as Santa's Ghost, because it occurs every Christmas Eve at exactly 11:55 p.m. When we learned of their secret project and saw the blips on our new radar, we determined their launch rockets and the satellites are made of a material similar to their stealth bombers, which are still barely detectable even on the most advanced detection systems, such as the ones in Cheyenne Mountain and the Lubbock airport."

"Why on Christmas Eve?" Zhou Li asked.

"The whole world is distracted on Christmas Eve," Sergei Sukov answered, "and we first thought they retrieved one satellite each Christmas Eve to repair and update it. But our sources say there have been multiple launches and recoveries this year for several days after Christmas Eve. Why? Because we think the Americans know we have the Intel on this top secret project, so it no longer matters when they launch or recover."

"Okay," the Chinese president answered. "But those laser satellites were recovered simultaneously, so they must have a central control point somewhere."

"Yes," Sergei Sukov replied, "but the Pentagon is too obvious a place, as is Area 51 in Nevada or Houston. Remember, in the beginning, only NORAD's radars could detect the Phantom Effect."

"Yes," General Zhao Hong, the Commander in Chief of the People's Liberation Army said as he leaned closer to the Eternal President. "The control point must be NORAD. If we triple out missile hits on the Cheyenne Mountain Complex, we would damage their communications systems enough so they won't be able to relaunch those laser satellites. Thus there would be no retaliatory strikes against us—except by their land-based and sea based ICBMs, and we have more than enough antiballistic armaments to destroy all their incoming missiles, but they do not have enough to destroy all of ours."

"If what you say is true, General Zhao, what was the purpose of the laser strikes on the carriers?" Zhang Li asked.

"Testing, Eternal President," General Zhao Hong replied. "All weapons systems have to be tested before being committed to combat and the Americans were willing to sacrifice one of their carriers and a few belonging to their allies to prove it works. The Americans thought it would keep the existence of the laser satellites a secret by blaming it on extraterrestrials!"

"Are you absolutely certain if we triple our missile strikes on NORAD that it will be impossible for them to relaunch the laser satellites, General?" the Chinese president asked.

"I would stake my life on it," he replied.

"And you, President Sukov?" he asked.

The Chinese Eternal President trusted the general's judgement explicitly, and as he stared at Sergei Sukov, the Russian Federation President nodded and said, "Our Intel agrees with General Zhao's assessment."

Zhang Li thought for a long moment and said, "Very well. Operation Dragon and Bear's Teeth is a go on July Fourth. The Chinese Dragon and the Russian Bear will chew up the American Eagle and spit it out. Our civilization is more than five-thousand years old, and Russia has been ruled by tsars for centuries. And now you, President Sukov, are its eternal president.

"Americans call their young government a democracy, but it has endured a mere two hundred seventy-five years and is in terrible debt and domestic chaos, proving that ordinary people cannot govern themselves. The world needs strong authoritative leaders to control and guide them, and it is our solemn duty to do so."

Two hours before midnight on July 3, 2051, Chinese missiles began rolling out of underground caves on their steel tracks. Russian ICBMs sat at the ready on their launch pads, and aboard their typhoon class nuclear submarines the crews were on full alert.

The launch crew chiefs in Iran, Pakistan, Syria, and several countries of the former Union of Soviet Socialist Republics synced their time with their counterparts; the hour of destiny for mother earth was rapidly approaching. It would either be the hour of victory or mutually assured destruction!

At exactly midnight on July 4, 2051, the 275th anniversary of the birth of the United States of America, fiery streaks lit up the night sky on the Eurasian Continent as more than five thousand missiles raced toward the major cities of the United States, the European Union, Israel, and Canada, certain cities in Central and South America, and several uncooperative countries in Africa.

CHAPTER
14

At 12:01 a.m. the president's red phone rang, but Nancy Hamilton and her husband were wide awake.

"Madam President," Chief of Staff General Gonzalez blurted out, "it's happening. NORAD has detected multiple ICBM missile launches originating in China, Russia, Iran, Pakistan, and Syria; we are certain they're directed at the United States, our European allies, and Israel. You must get into the Presidential Emergency Operations Center and authorize a retaliatory strike!"

Nancy Hamilton knew the American Armed forces had been on "silent alert" for weeks, and she bolted out of bed, and with her husband and three children rushed into the oval office. A Secret Service agent opened the trapdoor beneath the Resolute Desk, and the president entered first and descended six stories belowground to the Presidential Emergency Operations Center. From there the president moved through the tunnel leading to the Deep Underground

Command Center. The realization of what she was about to do awed and frightened her; only she, the president, has the authority to initiate a retaliatory strike!

Her military aide was already in the Secure Room, and she immediately tapped in the esoteric code from the Biscuit card into the computer that identified her as the president, and upon confirmation she and her military aide began reviewing the Retaliatory Strike Options listed in the Black Book, a part of Ops Order 8010. Then she entered the dreaded strike codes to identify targeted cities and military installations in China, Russia, Iran, Pakistan, Syria, and a host of other countries.

The Chairman of the Joint Chiefs of Staff alerted the Secretary of Defense, who confirmed the president's order. He immediately contacted the National Military Command Center, and the overall commander there issued orders to all military units to launch every missile in the American arsenal against their predetermined targets. It was mutually assured destruction, and the time of the first enemy missiles to strike American soil was now fewer than thirty minutes.

Under the aegis of the Air Force Global Strike Command, US missile silos opened, and soon their glowing tails of death went roaring toward the sky as the ICBMs lifted off and homed in on their targets in China and Russia and a dozen other enemy countries. Planes of the manned stealth bomber groups and unmanned drones soon followed.

On the high seas, miniature waterspouts erupted as Trident missiles from the US Navy's Ohio Class submarines broke through the surface, and carrier planes scrambled from the flight decks to attack a yet unseen enemy.

In the Deep Underground Command Center below the West Wing of the White House, President Hamilton gazed in horror at how few government officials and Cabinet members and their families had thus far made it into the shelter on time; they had been warned, but many had chosen to stay at home with their families. Thirty minutes later the lights blinked and then went out, and emergency generators kicked on.

Those who made it into the DUCC prayed when they felt the ground tremors and were thankful they were safe. But they knew that six stories above them the capitol of the Unite States of America no longer existed, and that New York, Los Angeles, Chicago, Houston, Phoenix, Philadelphia, San Antonio, San Diego, and other key American cities would soon be piles of rubble, thanks to several progressive and socialist administrations that had decimated the United States military. No one suspected that those debris mounds would one day be the only monuments and memories left of a once-mighty nation known as the United States of America.

The North American Air Defense Command shook—not once but three times—as each successive missile detonated its nuclear warheads on Cheyenne Mountain. The men and women trapped inside the complex barely heard the fearful sounds of a million tons of granite rock and debris rolling down the mountain slopes.

The lights blinked, but emergency generators kept the radar screens aglow, and moments later a staff sergeant shouted, "General Hammond, the enemy is knocking out most of our ICBMs. And look at this, sir those four laser satellites are back."

"Yeah, I see them, but what are those long streaks of light I see on the radar screen, Staff Sergeant?" General Hammond asked.

The staff sergeant looked back at the screen and then stared up at the general in disbelief. "They're our radar pulses bouncing off the ionized trails of their lasers, sir."

"But they're firing at targets in Eastern Europe and Asia, so they can't be Chinese or Russian, and they sure as hell aren't ours," the general replied. "So who are they?" The staff sergeant stared at the radar screen for a moment and then incredulously looked up at the general and the other air force personnel that were now surrounding his workspace.

"It's the Phantom Effect, sir," the radar operator astonishingly replied, "and now I know why we could never see or find them. The president was telling the truth when she addressed the United Nations. Santa's Ghost wasn't an enemy aircraft planting agents or nuclear bombs in our country. Those blips were visitors from another world!"

In the Chinese and Russian Command Centers, an uproar of cheers was heard upon confirming that their first atomic blast in America occurred in the skies over Washington, DC. The Chinese raised their goblets of rice wine and the Russians their glasses of vodka and toasted their fellow conspirators on the wide screens.

But their gleeful celebration turned to sudden fear when a Chinese radar operator screamed, "General Zhou-the laser satellites are back!"

"General Zhou," the Eternal President shouted, "you and President Sukov assured me the Americans could not relaunch the satellites if we hit NORAD with three nuclear missiles."

"Eternal President," General Zhou replied, "the Americans only launched retaliatory ICBMs and antiballistic missiles; nothing was launched into outer space!"

"We didn't detect any space launches either," President Sukov interjected over the big screen.

"If they are not American satellites," the Eternal President said, "then perhaps President Hamilton—"

The ground shook and the lights blinked, and then there was only darkness.

Aboard the *Star Voyager*, Harpie and Martha Colcek stood next to Commander Assan and stared at the screen in horror.

"The Supreme Confederation would not authorize me to destroy the axis powers," Commander Assan said, "because I would kill too many of the Di and their legatees as well as the Pi. But it is the right thing to do, and now I must return to Rau and face a court martial."

They stood by helplessly and watched the ICBMs from both sides unleash their Multiple Independent Reentry Vehicles. The MIRVs, armed with atomic warheads, sought out predetermined and distant targets, some of which were aimed at the cities in different countries located on multiple continents. There was no such place as Washington, DC, anymore, and with it died the principle that "All men are created equal." The American flag Harpie had folded in with his belongings was the only remaining vestige of what had once been the greatest nation on earth. *We had many rights,* Harpie thought, *perhaps too many.*

Alongside Harpie and Martha stood Trooper Robert Andersen with his wife and two children, and they too could see the mushroom clouds erupting all over America; tears stained their faces. But soon the Chinese cities of Shanghai, Guangzhou, Beijing, Shenzhen, Wuhan, Chengdu, and others were also blown to smithereens. China had shot down most of the American and allied retaliatory missiles before they reached their targets, but it couldn't fend off the mighty laser streaks emanating from the powerful star bursters that were sixteen-thousand meters out in space. The heroics of the thousands of Chinese rebels murdered in Tiananmen Square by the so-called Chinese Liberation Army in Beijing would now be just a faded memory.

In cities around the globe, citizens heard the sonic booms of the death lasers penetrating the atmosphere, and moments later every living and inanimate object was vaporized into a cloud of dust. The Colceks and the Andersens watched Red Square and Moscow vanish into a massive stem of dust and debris that seemed to push a humungous dust cloud tens of thousands of feet into the heavens, and with it went a thousand years of history of the tsars, the communist revolution, World War II, and the Putin regime. Saint Petersburg,

Novosibirsk, Yekaterinburg, and other Russian metropolises also disappeared off the face of the earth as though they had never existed.

Damascus, Syria; Teheran, Iran; Islamabad, Pakistan; and other lesser-known cities were now merely dust. Every continent on Earth was festooned with radiated clouds of death or the horrible vapors and powder left by the laser rampage!

Eskimos in the Canadian northlands gazed at the flashes in the darkened sky and knew it wasn't the aura borealis, and on the savannas of Africa, black men and women watched the early morning sunlight disappear and pondered their fate. Many of the tribes in the remotest areas of the continent that was known to the ancients as Alkebulan—Mother of Mankind—would survive and contribute to the revitalization of Mother Earth, for there were few targeted cities in Africa.

On the Asian continent, shepherds were driving their herds of yaks, horses, and caribou toward greener pastures, when suddenly the steppes shook and the sky darkened, causing the herds to stampede in panic and trample their masters-and sometimes each other-to death in their quest to stay alive.

The mushroom shroud hovering over Mexico City disguised the searing fate of the blood, flesh, and bones of the ten million human beings that forever disintegrated in the atomic cloud. Almost every city in Central America was spared the devastation, since none posed a nuclear counter threat.

Vaqueros, droving ganados on the Argentine pampas, saw their herds stampede, and they halted their caballos and stared in trepidation and wonder at the shimmering dust cloud that was once Buenos Aires.

The erratic behavior of the kangaroos, emus, rheas, kookaburras, the rapidly slithering snakes, and the crocs thrashing wildly about in the water warned the Indigenous people in the Australian outback of an impending doom. Suddenly an emergency alert signal blared from their portable radios and then abruptly ceased; the ground shook. Dark hazes blackened the sky and drifted across this island continent from every direction. Those foreboding clouds merged and completely blotted out the afternoon sun. The native aborigines huddled in fear, not yet knowing Sydney, Melbourne, Perth, Brisbane, and many other Australian cities ceased to exist, or that they were among the very few races on Earth that would survive the initial nuclear holocaust, although the Strontium 89 and 90 would eventually take a toll on their numbers.

Buckingham Palace and Élysée Palace were now only memories, and no cars would ever again drive on the autobahn. The windmills in the Netherlands would never again spin in the wind, and the Holocaust monuments in Poland were forever lost to history. Western Europe was now a nuclear wasteland.

In every country on Earth, fire storms ignited by the atomic blasts burned millions of buildings and houses that had survived the initial strikes. From within the piles of rubble could be heard the voices of those who were trapped therein; but no one heard their cries. Survivors wandered aimlessly about in shock with terrible wounds and horrible radiation burns as they pathetically cried out for succor. But there were no policemen, fireman, EMTs, doctors, nurses, clinics, or hospitals left to help them. There would be a long and painful death for most of them, not only from their wounds but from thirst and hunger.

There were other victims of this Armageddon too. Days later, the survivors who were able to walk migrated to the beaches of the world, where millions of tons of colorful but dead fish, octopi, sharks, whales, and every imaginable type of sea creature were being washed toward the shore by the relentless waves. Several missiles had been blown from the sky and exploded in the depths of the oceans, and the resultant carnage stretched far beyond what the human eye could see. The slaughter became a cornucopia of food for what was left of mankind and the once domesticated cats, dogs, and feral animals.

Vermin that had survived the blasts in their underground tunnels emerged from the sewers in every city around the globe and burrowed into the mounds of rubble to feast on the decaying flesh of the people and animals buried beneath tons of dirt, cement, stone, and steel. Within several months the feasts would cause their worldwide numbers to swell into the hundreds of billions.

"There is nothing left for you on Earth," Commander Assan informed his guests. "Harpie and Martha, you can return to Rau. There are still plenty of years left there for people your age to live out your lives in peace. And Trooper Andersen, you and your family are young enough to spend your lives on another world that we recently discovered. We call it Juneau, and it has a sun and changing seasons and is therefore much like earth. It is still a pristine planet, and many of the Di are migrating there. The land is fertile and free and you can become pioneers, much like those who once settled the American west. In one lightyear we will dock with the nearest major supply station, where you can board a flight to Juneau."

The Colceks and Andersens were the only passengers on board. It was a sad decision, with each Earthling nodding and stripping naked before climbing aboard their glass-enclosed habitats, and a Robot soon hooked up the wires and tubes necessary to keep them alive and asleep for each two-week period until they reached their final destination.

Harpie and Martha Spiller Colcek would happily spend the rest of their lives on Rau on Zenoid Street. One lightyear after they first boarded the *Star Voyager*, Robert Andersen and his family boarded a shuttle at a mass supply station, heading for Juneau and a new destiny. It was a relatively new discovery amongst the more than eight billion earth-like planets in the galaxy of the Milky Way.

Commander Assan would be tried and convicted by court martial for disobeying the orders of the Supreme Confederation by firing the star bursters at the axis cities, and thus participating in the deaths of millions of the Di and Pi during Earth's Armageddon. He chose to be euthanized rather than be banished to the mines on Minerva, and up until the moment of his death he insisted that what he did was the right thing to do.

Months after Earth's holocaust, the sky cleared, and the sun again warmed the air and ground of a planet that was once known as the Garden of Eden. Its Armageddon was due to mankind's greed and selfishness, for the despotic leaders had refused to obey the Master's two cardinal rules: love God and love your neighbor as you love yourself.

Decaying marine creatures, floating on the lakes, rivers, ponds, seas, and littering the world's beaches and the banks of the world's mightiest rivers had bloated and now emitted the most horrific stench. The vermin thrived on the rotting flesh, but the starving human survivors who gorged themselves on the putrid remains soon died of ptomaine poisoning; it was a horrible death, but their remains provided the feral wildlife with another feast.

On the plains, savannahs, and steppes on every continent on Earth, grazing herbivores innocently nibbled at the fragrant herbs, moss, and green grasses that grew there. They breathed in the plutonium and strontium and ingested the cesium-137. The Strontium 89 and 90—the initial fallout of the atomic fission bombs—had been widely disbursed around the globe by the winds and alit on the leaves and stems of flora worldwide. Those radionuclides, plus the element known as Cesium 137, would be radioactive for up to thirty years.

The herbivores ingested the radioactive material, and it was absorbed like calcium into their teeth, bones, bone marrow, and the surrounding soft tissues. Before long, their carcasses covered the earth, reminding the surviving Native Americans of the epic tales their ancestors told of the slaughter of millions of buffalo that once roamed the American plains. But these animals were not shot with hunting rifles; they died of a variety of radiation-induced cancers, as did the humans who ate them. The same was true of the fauna on the Asian steppes.

Long thereafter, a hush fell over the decimated world. The sun still shined each day; clouds appeared in the sky, and the ocean waves once again pounded the barren shores. But no planes crisscrossed the sky; no automobiles traveled the rural roads; the sports stadiums were mere splinters of wood and cement, and there were no marvelous cities with multistory buildings, schools, universities, theaters, restaurants, or churches.

However, some of the larger animal species did survive and multiplied, as they had for eons before mankind arrived on the scene. The herbivores thrived on the new uncontaminated flora now abundant on every landmass on Earth; the carnivores ran down and ferociously killed the herbivores and ate them; the omnivores ate both the plants and the meat eaters. But without the sights, sounds, and laughter of human activity, it seemed like a useless, silent, and empty world.

As for the few humans who survived? On every continent they hid in caves, igloos, and dilapidated remnants of their lost cultures for generations, barely clinging to life, praying to God for mercy—the God they had once written out of their hearts—and out of their schools, their literature, and their governments. They clothed themselves in animal skins, fashioned weapons for protection and hunting, and made crude tools to grow plants and harvest the wild berries and fruits.

When food was very scarce, starving groups of men hunted and murdered the weaker clans and stole their food, raped or kidnapped their women, and resorted to cannibalism to stay alive. It was a new beginning for mankind. But would the human race learn from the lessons of the past?

As this new breed of mankind sat on the rubble of what had once been flourishing cities, they looked up at the twinkling stars and planets and dreamed of what they were and what lay beyond. Every so often they spied pinpoints of light moving between those shining orbs at fantastic rates of speed and wondered what they were.

It was the Di shuttles still moving their people and their culture to the earth-like planet Juneau from a planet once known on Earth as Proxima b in the Constellation Centaurus. But although the shuttles were still functional, the Phantom Effect would never again be seen on the radar screens of NORAD for the complex was buried forever inside Cheyenne Mountain, and spaceships similar to *Star Voyager* and *Space Explorer* wouldn't land on a decimated Earth again for a thousand years.

CHAPTER
15

In the Earth year 3051, an archeologist was walking across an open plain that was covered with a blanket of prairie grass and sod. According to the yellowed map he held, he was walking across a piece of land that was once known as Kansas, a state located in what the ancient world called the United States of America. At least, that was what the professors at the university were able to decipher from the ancient scripts and tomes recovered from a cavern located hundreds of feet beneath a pile of rubble.

The mound was located near a river the ancients called the Potomac, and it held the remains of several hundred people who were entrapped there. There were strange machines there too that had endured the centuries, but no one knew what they were used for or how they worked. The caverns were thought to be some kind of burial site for royalty or government officials, and the archeologists surmised the machines were designed to transport their spirits to a heavenly world somewhere beyond the stars.

There were many such mounds scattered across every continent on Earth, but only a few had subterranean caverns with hundreds of skeletons and the same type of machines as those found beneath the mound near the old Potomac River. All the mounds were buried beneath the earth and sand that had been blown against them by the winds for centuries and were now overgrown with trees and grass. Millions of human bones were discovered beneath the debris, and scientists correctly ascertained they were the result of a catastrophic cataclysm, which they believed was caused by global earthquakes or a large asteroid impacting the earth.

Another odd thing scientists could not understand was the thousands of tons of rare minerals piled near the mounds. Those minerals were not found in any other place on earth. It was as though some strange and powerful force from another world had deposited them there.

Archeologist Johnny Warbold glanced up at the sun and was thankful for such a beautiful day in which to search for the site indicated on his hand-drawn map, but so far, he didn't have any luck. He was six feet tall, with bronzed skin, blue, almond-shaped eyes, and dark curly hair that lent proof to his multiracial heritage. Even though a few children were born with white skin, light-colored eyes, and blond hair, and others had dark skin, black curly hair, and brown eyes, most human beings bore the same genotypes of racial traits he had. All the races on Earth had intermarried or were concubines at one time or another, since the Great Apocalypse had wiped out much of the human race.

His universal language contained phrases and written symbols derived from every ancient tongue once spoken on Mother Earth, so that no matter what country one traveled to in the Supreme Confederation, everyone could understand one another.

There was no Christianity, Islam, Hinduism, Chinese traditionalism, Buddhism, Judaism, Bahai, Shinto, or any other organized religion. The world had begun anew, yet almost everyone realized something or someone more powerful then themselves had created this world and the entire universe. It didn't matter what you believed about a God or creation; that was your own personal business; there were no right or wrong religious beliefs.

Diseases still plagued the world, and there were murders, rapes, Robberies, and other crimes that had to be dealt with, and that was handled by local police departments. There were no provincial armies, and anyone who tried to declare himself a dictator, king, or queen was suppressed by the Supreme Confederation, an international government composed of representatives of every nation on Earth; it was once known as the United Nations. A professional military organization, called a rapid response team that mimicked the old United Nations Peacekeeping Force, quelled hostilities before they got out of hand.

Armageddon was a horrific lesson for mankind, and therefore all international disputes were settled by the Supreme Confederation, and for the first time in the history of mankind, there was peace on Earth that lasted for the better part of a thousand years.

As Johnny Warbold continued walking through the tall prairie grass, his boot struck something hard, and he stooped and parted the foliage to investigate. An object that looked like the tip of a spear was protruding through the ground. It was a manmade object and composed of polished stone, and although he pulled as hard as he could, it wouldn't budge.

Two weeks later a team of student volunteers brushed away the last few remnants of dirt from around what looked like a huge stone monument with a pointed spire. But upon careful examination, they discovered an entranceway with the date July 4, 2051, notched in the lintel above the door, and the volunteers anxiously hammered their way through the decomposing cement.

Once inside, the astonished crew discovered a chamber that resembled a sarcophagus. Strange words were chiseled in the stone walls, and after they pried away a large steel plate attached to one of the partitions, they were flabbergasted to discover it had sealed off another chamber filled with a plethora of books and round flat discs they had never seen before. It also contained thousands of documents and photos encased in a strange clear material.

Johnny Warbold carefully picked up one of the encapsulated documents. He didn't understand all the words, but he believed in the legend and recognized the names Hamilton and Colcek. As he scanned the sheet, he managed to decipher their reference to a planet called Rau in the Constellation Centaurus and a man named Assan, who commanded a spaceship named *Star Voyager*. *It's true*, the archeologist thought, *the legend is true!*

The folklore about the legend had been passed down by generations of mankind in the aftermath of a worldwide apocalypse, as they sat around their campfires in darkened caves or hovels made from the remnants of once great civilizations. When paper remnants were available, they wrote the episode down, but Johnny Warbold was certain the stories had become distorted over time, yet those ancient notes and stories had kept alive the horrible memory of the global Holocaust and Legend of the Phantom Effect, a tale the storytellers said began in the mountains of a land once known as Colorado.

He gazed at the document for a long moment and then clutched it to his breast before looking up at his anxious and puzzled volunteers; he then excitedly exclaimed, "This is it! We've found the fabled time capsule foretold in the Legend of the Phantom Effect!"

The University of Switzerland had survived the Great Apocalypse since it was in a valley sheltered by enormous mountain ranges, and its linguists determined the materials found in the time capsule were written in five ancient languages: English, Chinese, Russian, Spanish, and Arabic.

One book told the story of the Phantom Effect and the journey of the Colceks and their trek to the Constellation Centaurus, and how Proxima Centauri was a red dwarf star and that its exoplanet, Proxima b once known as Rau, was destined to become a black star. They read about Commander Assan and his *Star Voyager*, and how he tried to help a sick and warring Earth by having the Colceks decipher the documents they brought from Rau and hid them away in a protective time capsule.

The documents solved the mystery of the rare mineral deposits too and described how to make the medicines that could wipe out most of the illnesses on Earth. But the most amazing thing they discovered was that the Constitution upon which the Supreme Confederation now rested was not original. That mighty nation once known as the United States of America also had a Constitution, and it too defined the God-given rights of mankind. But it also had a document called the Declaration of Independence that stated, "All men are created equal and have the right to life, liberty, and the pursuit of happiness." The Supreme Confederation was currently debating whether to incorporate those words in its constitution.

Two years later, Johnny Warbold once again stood near the site where he'd discovered the legendary time capsule. The thirty year old was too excited to sleep, for there were millions of fossils and artifacts buried in the soil of these storied plains and the civilizations cloaked beneath its assorted mounds. He and his new bride, Aimee, who was also an archeologist, held hands as they stood beneath the stars and gazed into the heavens, while the rest of their expedition was asleep in their tents. It was a clear and frigid night on the prairie, and Aimee put her hand over her mouth as she yawned. Johnny looked at his watch; it was exactly 11:55.

Aimee seized his shoulder and pointed up in wonder at a speck of light, and they recalled a portion of the legend of the Phantom Effect; the season and the timing were right. The pinpoint of light was rapidly moving between the stars, but then it abruptly dropped as though it were falling from the sky. The light suddenly disappeared, and a few minutes later they stood in alarm and awe when they felt a warm gentle breeze. Moments later they spied a blue-tinged light just a few yards away, and it darkened when a huge figure emerged.

A seven-foot metal monster stopped directly in front of them, and scanned their retinas with its red protruding eyes; but there was nothing to fear. They Warbolds knew it wasn't a guard Robot, because Earth was now a friendly planet.

The Robot extended its metallic hand and a digitized voice said, "Greetings from Commander Jocan of *Star Voyager IV.*"

"How did you know we were here in the middle of nowhere?" Johnny asked.

"We have been landing here each year for centuries," the Robot replied. "We knew that sooner or later someone would discover the time capsule."

When the remainder of expedition members woke the next morning, they found a note on Johnny Warbold's cot:

Dear friends,

Aimee and I are off on an adventure to the planet Juneau, with Commander Jocan aboard *Star Voyager IV.* Juneau is the home of the Di, the people depicted in the documents Harpie and Martha Colcek brought from Proxima b, which is now a black dwarf star.

Juneau is very much like Earth, but many times larger, and is about five lightyears away and is located somewhere amongst the stars in the galaxy of the Milky Way. We will spend one year there just as Harpie and Martha Colcek did on Rau, and when we return we'll bring back the Di's latest advances in science, medicine, and social mores. Please don't worry. We shall return in about eleven years, so until then, keep the Legend of the Phantom Effect alive!

Love,
Johnny and Aimee Warbold

Printed in the United States
By Bookmasters